JULIE KAGAWA

IRON LEGENDS

HARLEQUIN®

entertain, enrich, inspire™

ISBN-13: 978-0-373-21074-9

THE IRON LEGENDS

Copyright © 2012 by Harlequin Books S.A.

The publisher acknowledges the copyright holder
of the individual works as follows:

WINTER'S PASSAGE
Copyright © 2010 by Julie Kagawa

SUMMER'S CROSSING
Copyright © 2011 by Julie Kagawa

IRON'S PROPHECY
Copyright © 2012 by Julie Kagawa

SURVIVAL GUIDE TO THE NEVERNEVER
Copyright © 2011 by Julie Kagawa

Original drawings "I Dare You" (Ash); "You May Have Heard of Me" (Puck);
and "I Am a Cat" (Grimalkin) copyright © 2012 by Julie Kagawa

Recycling programs
for this product may
not exist in your area.

Books by Julie Kagawa
from Harlequin TEEN

The Iron Fey series

(in reading order)

The Iron King
Winter's Passage (ebook)*
The Iron Daughter
The Iron Queen
Summer's Crossing (ebook)*
The Iron Knight
Iron's Prophecy (ebook)*

*Also available in print in *The Iron Legends* anthology

The Iron Fey—Call of the Forgotten series

The Lost Prince

and coming in 2013

The Traitor Son

The Blood of Eden series

The Immortal Rules

CONTENTS

WINTER'S PASSAGE

CHAPTER ONE

KEEPING PROMISES

In the shadows of the cave, I watched the Hunter approach. Silhouetted black against the snow, it stalked closer, eyes a yellow flame in the shadows, breath coiling around it like wraiths. Ice-blue light glinted off wet teeth and a thick shaggy pelt, darker than midnight. Ash stood between the Hunter and me, sword unsheathed, his eyes never leaving the massive creature that had tracked us for days, and now, had finally caught up.

"Meghan Chase." Its voice was a growl, deeper than thunder, more primitive than the wildest forests. The ancient golden eyes were fixed solely on me. "I've finally found you."

My name is Meghan Chase.

If there are three things I've learned in my time among the fey, they are this: don't eat anything you're offered in Faeryland, don't go swimming in quiet little ponds and never, ever, make a bargain with anyone.

Okay, sometimes, you have no choice. Sometimes, you've been backed into a corner and you have to make a deal. Like when your little brother has been kidnapped, and you have to convince a prince of the Unseelie Court to help you rescue him instead of dragging you back to his queen. Or, you're lost, and you have to bribe a smart-mouthed, talking cat to guide you through the forest. Or you need to get through a

certain door, but the gatekeeper won't let you through without a price. The fey love their bargains, and you have to listen to the terms *very* carefully, or you're going to get screwed.
If you do end up in a contract with a faery, remember this:
there's no way you can back out, not without disastrous con-
sequences. And faeries *always* come to collect.

Which is how, forty-eight hours ago, I found myself walking across my front yard in the middle of the night, my house
growing smaller and smaller in the background. I didn't look
back. If I looked back, I might lose my nerve. At the edge
of the woods, a dark prince and a pair of glowing, blue-eyed
steeds waited for me.

Prince Ash, third son of the Winter Court, regarded me
gravely as I approached, his silver eyes reflecting the light of
the moon. Tall and pale, with raven-black hair and the un-
attainable elegance of the fey, he looked both beautiful and
dangerous, and my heart beat faster in anticipation or fear, I
couldn't tell. As I stepped into the shadows of the trees, Ash
held out a pale, long-fingered hand, and I placed my own in
his.

His fingers curled over mine, and he drew me close, hands
resting lightly on my waist. I lay my head against his chest
and closed my eyes, listening to his beating heart, breathing
in the frosty scent of him.

"You have to do this, don't you?" I whispered, my fingers
clutched in the fabric of his white shirt. Ash made a soft noise
that might've been a sigh.

"Yes." His voice, low and deep, was barely above a murmur. I pulled back to look at him, seeing myself reflected in
those silver eyes. When I'd first met him, those eyes were
blank and cold, like the face of a mirror. Ash had been the
enemy, once. He was the youngest son of Mab, queen of Winter and the ancient rival of my father, Oberon, the king of the

Summer Court. That's right. I'm half-fey—a faery princess, no less—and I didn't even know it until recently, when my human brother was kidnapped by faeries and taken into the Nevernever. When I found out, I convinced my best friend, Robbie Goodfell—who turned out to be Oberon's servant, Puck—to take me into Faeryland to get him back. But being a faery princess in the Nevernever proved to be extremely dangerous. For one, the Winter Queen sent Ash to capture me, to use me as leverage against Oberon.

That's when I made the bargain with the Winter prince that would change my life: help me rescue Ethan, and I'll go with you to the Winter Court.

So, here I was. Ethan was home safe. Ash had kept his side of the bargain. It was my turn to uphold my end and travel with him to the court of my father's ancient enemies. There was only one problem.

Summer and Winter were not supposed to fall in love.

I bit my lip and held his gaze, watching his expression. Though I had once viewed it as frozen solid, his demeanor had thawed somewhat during our time in the Nevernever. Now, looking at him, I imagined a glassy lake: still and calm, but only on the surface.

"How long will I have to stay there?" I asked.

He shook his head slowly, and I could feel his reluctance. "I don't know, Meghan. The queen doesn't disclose her plans to me. I didn't dare ask why she wanted you." He reached up and caught a strand of my pale blond hair, running it through his fingers. "I was only supposed to bring you back," he murmured, and his voice dropped even lower. "I swore I would bring you back."

I nodded. Once a faery promises something, he's obligated to carry it through, which is why making a deal is so tricky. Ash couldn't break his vow even if he wanted to.

I understood that, but… "I want to do something before we go," I said, watching for his reaction. Ash raised an eyebrow, but otherwise his expression stayed the same. I took a deep breath. "I want to see Puck."

The Winter prince sighed. "I suppose you would," he muttered, releasing me and stepping back, his expression thoughtful. "And, truth be told, I'm curious myself. I wouldn't want Goodfellow dying before we ever resolved our duel. That would be unfortunate."

I winced. Puck and Ash were ancient enemies, and had already engaged each other in several savage, life-threatening duels before I was even in the picture. Ash had sworn to kill Puck, and Puck took great pleasure in goading the dangerous ice prince whenever he had the chance. It was only because I insisted they cooperate that they had agreed to an extremely shaky truce. One that wouldn't last long, no matter how much I intervened.

One of the horses snorted and pawed the ground, and Ash turned to put a hand on its neck. "All right, we'll check on him," he said without turning around. "But, after that I *have* to take you to Tir Na Nog. No more delays, understand? The queen won't be happy with me for taking this long."

I nodded. "Yes. Thank y— I mean…I appreciate it, Ash."

He smiled faintly and offered a hand again, this time to help me into the saddle. I gingerly picked up the reins and envied Ash, who swung easily aboard the second horse like he'd done it a thousand times.

"All right," he said in a faintly resigned voice, staring up at the moon. "First things first. We have to find a trod to New Orleans."

Trods are faery paths between the real world and the Nevernever, gateways straight into Faeryland. They can be anywhere, any doorway: an old bathroom stall, the gate to a cemetery, a child's closet door. You can go anywhere in the world if you know the right trod, but getting through them is another matter, as sometimes they're guarded by nasty creatures the fey leave behind to discourage unwanted guests.

Nothing guarded the enormous rotting barn that sat in the middle of the swampy bayou, so covered in moss it looked like a shaggy green carpet was draped over the roof. Mushrooms grew from the walls in bulbous clumps, huge spotted things that, if you looked closely enough, sheltered several tiny winged figures beneath them. They blinked at us as we went by, huge multifaceted eyes peering out from under the mushroom caps, and took to the air in a flurry of iridescent wings. I jumped, but Ash and the horses ignored them as we stepped beneath the sagging frame and everything went white.

I blinked and looked around as the world came into focus again.

An eerie gray forest surrounded us, mist creeping over the ground like a living thing, coiling around the horses' legs. The trees were massive, soaring to mind-boggling heights, interlocking branches blocking out the sky. Everything was dark and faded, like all color had been washed out, a forest trapped in perpetual twilight.

"The wyldwood," I muttered, and turned to Ash. "Why are we here? I thought we were going to New Orleans."

"We are." Ash pulled his horse around to look at me. "The trod we want is about a day's ride north. It's the quickest way to New Orleans from here." He blinked and gave me an almost smile. "Or were you planning to hitchhike?"

Before I could reply, my horse suddenly let out a terrifying whinny and reared, slashing the air with its forelegs. I grabbed for the mane, but it slipped through my fingers, and I tumbled backward out of the saddle, hitting the ground behind the horse, snapping bushes underneath. Snorting in terror, the fey steed charged off toward the trees, leaped over a fallen branch and vanished into the mist.

Groaning, I sat up, testing my body for pain. My shoulder throbbed where I'd landed on it, and I was shaking, but nothing seemed broken.

Ash's mount was also throwing a fit, squealing and tossing its head, but the Winter prince was able to keep his seat and bring it back under control. Swinging out of the saddle, he tied the horse's reins to an overhead branch and knelt beside me.

"Are you all right?" His fingers probed my arm, surprisingly gentle. "Anything broken?"

"I don't think so," I muttered, rubbing my bruised shoulder. "That lovely patch of bramble broke my fall." Now that the adrenaline had worn off, dozens of stinging scratches began to make themselves known. Scowling, I glared in the direction my mount had disappeared. "You know, that's the second time I've been thrown off a faery horse. And another time one tried to eat me. I don't think horses like me very much."

"No." Abruptly serious, Ash stood, offering a hand to pull me to my feet. "It wasn't you. Something spooked them." He gazed around slowly, hand dropping to the sword at his waist. Around us, the wyldwood was still and dark, as if the inhabitants were afraid to move.

I looked behind us, where the trunks of two trees had grown into each other, forming an archway between. The space between the trunks, where the trod lay, was cloaked in shadow, and it seemed to me that the shadows were creeping closer. A cold wind hissed through the trunks, rattling branches and tossing leaves, and I shivered.

With a frantic rushing sound a flock of tiny winged fey burst from the trod, swirling around us in panic and spiraling into the mist. I yelped, shielding my face, and Ash's horse screamed again, the sound piercing the ominous quiet. Ash took my hand and pulled me away from the trod, hurrying back to his mount. Lifting me to sit just behind the saddle, he grabbed the reins and climbed up in front.

"Hold on tight," he warned, and a thrill shot through me as I slipped my arms around his waist, feeling the hard muscles through his shirt. Ash dug in his heels with a shout, and the horse shot forward, snapping my head back. I squeezed Ash tightly and buried my face in his back as the faery horse streaked through the wyldwood, leaving the trod far behind.

We stopped infrequently, and when we did, it was only to let me and the horse rest for a few minutes. As evening fell, Ash pulled several food items from the horse's pack and gave them to me; bread and dried meat and cheese, ordinary human food. Apparently, he remembered my last experiment with eating faery food, which hadn't turned out so well. I nibbled the dry bread, gnawed on the jerky and hoped he wouldn't mention the Summerpod incident and the embarrassment that followed.

Ash didn't eat anything. He remained wary and suspicious, and never truly relaxed the entire journey. The horse, too, was jumpy and restless, and it panicked at every shadow, every rustle or falling leaf. Something was following us; I felt it every time we stopped, a dark, shadowy presence drawing ever closer.

As we rode on through the night, the eternal twilight of the wyldwood finally dimmed and a pale yellow moon rose into the sky. Ash and the fey horse both had seemingly unlimited endurance, more so than me, anyway. Riding a horse for hours and hours is not easy, and the stress of being chased by an unknown enemy was taking its toll. I struggled to stay awake, dozing against the prince's back, leaning dangerously off the sides until a jolt or sharp word from Ash snapped me upright.

I was dozing off once more, fighting to keep my eyes open, when Ash suddenly pulled the horse to a stop and dismounted. Blinking, I looked around dazedly, seeing nothing but trees and shadows. "Are we there yet?"

"No." Ash glared at me in exasperation. "But you keep threatening to fall off the horse, and I can't keep reaching back to make sure you're still on." He motioned to the front of the saddle. "We're switching places. Move forward."

I eased into the saddle and Ash swung up behind me, wrapping an arm securely around my waist, making my pulse beat faster in excitement.

"Hold on," he murmured as the horse started forward again. "We're almost to the trod. Once we're in the mortal realm, you can rest. We should be safe there."

"What's following us?" I whispered, making the horse's ears twitch back. Ash didn't reply for several moments.

"I don't know," he muttered, sounding reluctant to admit it. "Whatever it is, it's persistent. We've been keeping a pretty steady pace and haven't lost it yet."

"*Why* is it following us? What does it want?"

"Doesn't matter." Ash's grip around my waist tightened. "If it wants you, it'll have to get past me first."

My stomach prickled, and my heart did a weird little flop. In that moment, I felt safe. My prince wouldn't let anything happen to me. Settling back against him, I closed my eyes and let myself drift.

I must have dozed off, for the next thing I knew Ash was shaking me gently. "Meghan, wake up," he murmured, his cool breath fanning my neck. "We're here."

Yawning, I looked at the small glade ahead of us. Without the cover of the trees, I could see the sky, dotted with stars.

The glade was clear, except for one massive gnarled oak in the very center. Roots snaked out over the ground, huge thick things that prevented anything bigger than a fern to flourish. The trunk was wide and twisted, like three or four trees had been squashed together into one. But even with the oak's size and dominating presence, I could see that it was dying. Its branches drooped, or had snapped off and were scattered about the base of the tree. Most of its broad, veined leaves were dead and brittle; the rest were a sickly yellow-brown. The glade, too, looked withered and sick, as if the tree was leeching life from the forest around it.

"It wasn't like this before," Ash murmured behind me. I gazed at the dying tree and felt an incomprehensible sadness, as if I were seeing an old friend about to die. Shaking it off, I looked around for a doorway or gate, but the tree was the only thing here.

"Will it still work?" I wondered as he urged the horse into the clearing, toward the ancient tree. "The trod, I mean. Will it open?"

"We'll see." Ash dismounted and led the horse up to the trunk. When it stopped, I slid out of the saddle and joined him.

"So, how does the trod work?" I asked, peering at the trunk for a door of some kind. Doors in trees were not unusual in the Nevernever. In fact, during my first time to Faeryland, I'd spent the night in a wood sprite's tree, somehow shrinking down to the size of a bug to fit through his door. "I don't see a gate. How do you get it to open?"

"Easy," Ash replied. "We just ask."

Ignoring my scowl, he faced the trunk and put a hand on the rough bark. "This is Ash," he said clearly, "third son of the Unseelie Court, requesting passage to the mortal realm and the clearing of the Elder."

"Please," I added.

For a moment, nothing happened. Then, with a loud groaning and creaking, one of the massive roots snaked out of the ground, shedding dirt and twigs. Rising into the air, it formed an archway between itself and the ground, and the space between shimmered with magic.

"There's your trod," Ash murmured, as my heart beat faster in my chest. Puck was through that gateway. If he was still alive.

Clutching Ash's hand, almost pulling him along in my impatience, I ducked through the arch.

I tripped over a root on the other side and stumbled forward, barely catching myself. Straightening, I gazed around the moonlit grove of New Orleans City Park, recognizing the huge mossy oaks from our last visit. The air was humid, warm and peaceful. Crickets buzzed, leaves rustled and moonlight shimmered off the nearby lake. Nothing had changed. It had been this peaceful the last time we were here, though my world had been falling apart.

Ash touched my arm and nodded at a tree, where a willowy girl with moss-green skin watched us from the shadow of an oak, her dark eyes wide and startled.

"Meghan Chase?" The dryad swayed toward us, moving like a wind-blown branch. "What are you doing here?" I blinked at the fear in her voice. "You must not stay!" she hissed as she drew close. "It is not safe. There is something dangerous following you."

"We know," Ash said beside me, calm and unflustered as always. The dryad blinked and shifted her gaze to him. "But we came through the Elder gate, so hopefully she won't let whatever is hunting us into this world."

Elder gate? I glanced behind me, and my stomach twisted so hard I felt nauseous.

It was the Elder Dryad's tree, the great oak that once stood tall and proud, looming over the others. Now, like its twin in the clearing, it was dying. Its branches were bare of leaves, the shaggy moss that covered it brown and dead.

A lump rose to my throat. I remembered the Elder Dryad from our first visit here: an old, grandmotherly fey with a soft voice and kind eyes who had given the very heart of her tree to make sure I could rescue my brother. And kill the faery who'd kidnapped him. The Elder had known she would die if she helped me. But she gave us the weapon we needed to take down the enemy fey and get Ethan back.

The dryad girl stepped beside me, gazing at the dying oak. "She lives still," she murmured, her voice like the whisper of leaves. "Dying, yes. Too weak to leave her tree, she sleeps now, dreaming of her youth. But not gone, not yet. It will take a long time for her to fade completely."

"I'm so sorry," I whispered.

"No, Meghan Chase." The dryad shook her head with a faint rustling sound, and a shiny beetle crawled across her face to burrow into her hair. "She knew. She knew all along what was going to happen. The wind tells us these things. Just as it tells us you are in terrible danger now." She suddenly fixed me with piercing black eyes. "You should not be here," she said firmly. "It is very close. Why have you come?"

My skin prickled, but I shook off the feeling of trepidation and held her gaze. "I'm here for Puck. I need to see him."

The dryad's expression softened. "Ah. Yes, of course. I will take you to him, but I fear you will be disappointed."

"It doesn't matter." I felt cold, even in the warm summer night. "I just want to see him."

The dryad nodded and shuffled back, swaying in the breeze. "This way."

CHAPTER TWO

THE HEART OF THE OAK

Puck, or the infamous Robin Goodfellow, as he was known in *A Midsummer Night's Dream,* had another name, once. A human name, belonging to a lanky, red-haired boy, who had been the neighbor of a shy farm girl in the Louisiana bayou. Robbie Goodfell, as he called himself back then, had been my classmate, confidant and best friend. Always looking out for me, like an older brother. Goofy, sarcastic and somewhat over-protective, Robbie was…different. When he wasn't around, people barely remembered him, who he was, what he looked like. It was like he simply faded from their memories, despite the fact that whenever anything went wrong in school—mice in desks, superglue on chairs, an alligator in the bathrooms one day—Robbie was somehow involved. No one ever suspected him, but I always knew.

Still, it came as a shock when I discovered who he really was: King Oberon's servant, charged with keeping an eye on me in the mortal world. To keep me safe from those who would harm a half-human daughter of Oberon. But also, to keep me blind to the world of Faery, ignorant and unaware of my true nature, and all the danger that came with it.

When Ethan was kidnapped and taken into the Nevernever, Robbie's plans to keep me blind and ignorant unraveled. De-fying Oberon's direct orders, he agreed to help me rescue my brother, but his loyalty came at a huge cost. During a battle with an Iron faery, a brand-new species of fey born from technology and progress, he was shot and very nearly killed. Ash and I brought him here, to City Park, and the dryads took him into one of their trees to sleep and heal from his wounds. Suspended in stasis, the dryads kept him alive, but they didn't know when he would wake up. If he woke up at all. We had to leave him behind when we left to rescue Ethan, and the guilt of that decision had haunted me ever since.

I pressed my palm against the mossy trunk, wondering if I could feel his heartbeat within the tree, a vibration, a sigh. Something, *anything*, that told me he was still there. But I felt nothing except sap, moss and the rough edges of the bark. Puck, if he still lived, was far from my reach.

"Are you sure he's in there?" I asked the dryad, not taking my eyes from the trunk. I didn't know what to expect: his head to pop out of the wood and grin at me, perhaps? But I felt that if I took my eyes away for a second, I would miss something.

The dryad girl nodded. "Yes. He lives still. Nothing has changed. Robin Goodfellow sleeps his dreamless slumber, waiting for the day he will rejoin the world."

"When will that be?" I asked, running my fingers down the trunk.

"We do not know. Perhaps days. Perhaps centuries. Perhaps he does not want to wake up." The dryad placed her hand on the trunk and closed her eyes. "He is resting comfortably, in no pain. There is nothing you can do for him but wait, and be patient."

Unsatisfied with her answer, I pressed my palm against the tree and closed my eyes. Summer glamour swirled around me, the magic of my father, Oberon, and the Summer court, the glamour of heat and earth and living things. I prodded the tree gently, feeling the sun-warmed leaves and the life running through their emerald veins. I felt thousands of tiny insects swarming over and burrowing into the trunk, the rapid heartbeat of birds, dreaming in the branches.

I pressed deeper, past the surface, past the softer, still-growing wood, deep into the heart of the tree.

And there he was. I couldn't physically see him, of course, but I could sense him, feel his presence in front of me, a bright spot of life against the heartwood. I felt the wood cradling his thin, lanky frame, protecting it, and heard the faintest *thump-thump* of a beating heart. Puck hovered limply, his chin on his chest and his eyes closed. He seemed much smaller in sleep, fragile and ghostlike, as if a breath could blow him away.

I drifted closer, reaching out to touch him, brushing insubstantial fingers over his cheek, pushing back unruly red bangs. He didn't stir. If I didn't hear his heartbeat, vibrating faintly through the tree, I would've thought he was already dead.

"I'm so sorry, Puck," I whispered, or maybe I just thought it, deep inside the giant oak. *"I wish you were here with me now. I'm scared, and I don't know what's going to happen. I really need you to come back."*

If he heard me, he didn't show it. There was no flicker of eyelids, no twitch of his head responding to my voice. Puck remained limp and motionless, his heartbeat calm and steady, echoing through the wood. My best friend was far from me, beyond my reach, and I couldn't bring him back.

Depressed, feeling strangely sick, I pulled out of the tree, returning to my own body. As the sounds of the world returned, I found myself fighting back tears. So close. So close to Puck, and still so far away.

Ash's expression was grave as I met his eyes; he knew what I'd done, and could guess the outcome.

"He's still alive," he told me. "That's all you can hope for." I sniffed, turning away, and Ash sighed. "Don't worry too much about him, Meghan. Robin Goodfellow has always been extraordinarily difficult to kill." His voice hovered between irritation and amusement, as if he spoke from experience. "I can almost guarantee Goodfellow will pop up one day when you least expect it, just be patient."

"Patience," said an amused voice somewhere over my head, "has never been the girl's strong suit."

Startled, I looked up, into the branches of the oak. A pair of familiar golden eyes peered down at me, attached to nothing else, and my heart leaped.

"Grimalkin?"

The eyes blinked slowly, and the body of a large gray cat appeared, crouched on one of the lower branches. It *was* Grimalkin, the faery cat I met on my last journey to Faery. Grim had helped me out a few times in the past…but his help always came with a price. The cat loved collecting favors and did nothing for free, but I was still happy to see him, even if I still owed him a debt or two from our last adventure.

"What are you doing here, Grim?" I asked as the feline yawned and stretched, arching his fluffy tail over his back. True to form, Grimalkin finished stretching, sat down and gave his fur several licks before deigning to reply.

"I had business with the Elder Dryad," he replied in a bored voice. "I needed to know if she'd heard anything about the whereabouts of a certain individual." Grim scratched behind an ear, examined his back toes and gave them a lick. "Then I heard that you were on your way here, so I thought I would wait, to see if it was true. You have always proved most entertaining."

"But…the Elder Dryad is asleep," I said, frowning. "They told me she's too weak to even come out of her tree."

"What is your point, human?"

"Never mind." I shook my head. Grimalkin was exasperating and secretive, and I learned long ago he wouldn't share anything until he was ready. "It's still good to see you, Grim. Wish we could stay and talk awhile, but we're in sort of a hurry right now."

"Mmm, yes. Your ill-contrived deal with the Winter prince." Grimalkin's eyes shifted to Ash and back to me, blinking slowly. "Hasty and reckless, just like a human." He sniffed, staring straight at Ash, now. "But…I would have thought that you knew better, Prince."

Before I could ask what he meant by *that,* I felt a hand on my arm and turned to meet Ash's solemn gaze. "We should go," he murmured, and though his voice was firm, his expression was apologetic. "If something is chasing us, we should try to make it to Tir Na Nog as soon as we can. It won't be able to follow us, then. And I can protect you better in my own territory than the wyldwood or the mortal realm."

"One moment." Grimalkin yawned and sidled down from the tree, landing noiselessly on the roots. "If you are leaving now, I believe I will come with you. At least part of the way."

"Really?" I stared at him, surprised. "You're going to Tir Na Nog? Why?"

"I told you before. I am looking for someone."

"Who?"

"You ask a wearying amount of questions, human." Grimalkin hopped down from the roots and trotted off, tail in the air. Several yards away, he glanced back over his shoulder, twitching an ear. "Well? Are you coming or not? If you say there is something after you, it would make sense not to be here when it comes to call, yes?"

Ash and I shared a bemused look and trailed after him.

The Elder Gate loomed before us, tall and imposing even though the tree was dying. As we approached, the entire trunk suddenly shifted with a groan. A face pushed its way out of the bark, old and wrinkled, part of the tree come to life. The Elder Dryad opened her eyes, squinting as though it was difficult to focus, and her gaze fastened on me.

"Noooooooo," she breathed, barely a whisper in the darkness. "You must not go back this way. *He* waits for you on the other side. He will…" Her voice trailed off, and her face sank back into the wood, vanishing from sight. "Run," was the last thing I heard.

I shivered all the way down to my toes. Ash immediately took my hand and drew me away, striding in the opposite direction, his body tense like a coiled wire. Grimalkin slipped after us, a gray ghost in the shadows, the fur on his tail standing on end. It would've been funny if I didn't feel eyes on the back of my neck, old, savage and patient, watching us flee into the night.

Ash paused beneath the limbs of another oak, put his fingers to his lips and let out a piercing whistle. Moments later, the fey horse trotted out of the shadows, snorting and tossing its head, skidding to a stop before us.

"Where are we going now?" I asked, as Ash helped me into the saddle.

"We can't use the Elder Gate to get back," the prince replied, swinging up behind me. "We'll have to find another way into the Nevernever. And quickly." He gathered the reins in one hand and snaked an arm around my waist. "I know of another trod that will take us close to Tir Na Nog, but it's in a part of the city that's…dangerous for Summer fey."

"You are speaking of the Dungeon, are you not?" Grimalkin said, appearing suddenly in my lap, curled up like he belonged. I blinked in surprise. "Are you sure you want to take the girl there?"

"Not much choice, now." Tightening his grip on my waist, Ash kicked the horse forward, and we galloped into the streets of New Orleans.

I'd forgotten what it was like to be a half faery in the real world, or at least in the company of a powerful, full-blooded fey. The horse trotted down brightly lit streets, weaving through cars and alleyways and people, and no one saw us. No one even glanced our way. Regular humans couldn't see the faery world, though it was all around them. Like the two goblins sifting through a spilled Dumpster in an alley, gnawing on bones and other things I didn't want to dwell on. Or the dragonfly-winged sylph perched atop a telephone pole, watching the streets with the intensity of an eagle observing her territory. We nearly ran into a group of dwarves leaving one of the many pubs on Bourbon Street. The short, bearded men shouted drunken curses as the horse swerved, barely missing them, and galloped away down the sidewalk.

We were deep in the French Quarter when Ash stopped in front of a wall of stone buildings, old black shutters and doors lining the sidewalk. A sign swinging above a thick black door read: Ye Olde Original Dungeon, and there was red paint spattered against the frame in what was supposed to be blood, I guessed. At least, I hoped it was paint. Ash pushed open the door, revealing a very long, narrow alleyway, and turned to me.

"This is Unseelie territory," he murmured close to my ear. "There's a rough crowd that frequents this place. Don't talk to anyone, and stay close to me."

I nodded and peered down the closed-in space, which was barely wide enough to walk through. "What about the horse?"

Ash removed the horse's pack and pulled off its bridle,

tossing it into the shadows. "It'll find its own way home," he murmured, swinging the pack over one shoulder. "Let's go."

We slipped down the narrow corridor, Ash in front, Grim trailing behind. The alley ended in a small courtyard, where a scraggly waterfall trickled into a moat at the front of the building. We crossed the footbridge, passed a bored-looking human bouncer who paid us no attention and entered a dark, red-tinged room.

From the shadows along the wall rose something huge and green, crimson eyes glaring out of the monstrous, toothy face of a female troll. I squeaked and took a step back.

"I smell me a Summer whelp," she growled, blocking our way. Up close, she stood nearly eight feet, with swamp-green skin and long, taloned fingers. Beady red eyes glared at me from her impressive height. "You're either really brave or really stupid, whelp. Lost a bet with a phouka or something? No Summer fey allowed in here, so get lost."

"She's with me," Ash said, stepping up to block the troll's line of sight. "And you're going to step aside now. We need to use the hidden trod."

"Prince Ash." The troll took a step back but didn't move aside completely. Facing a prince of the Unseelie Court, she turned almost sniveling. "Your Highness, of course I would let you in, but…" She glanced over Ash's shoulder at me. "The boss says absolutely no Summer blood in here unless we're going to drink it."

"We're just passing through," Ash replied, still in that same calm, cool voice. "We'll be gone before anyone notices us."

"Your Highness, I can't," the troll protested, sounding more and more unsure. She glanced back over her shoulder, lowering her voice. "I could lose my job if I let her through."

Very casually, Ash dropped his hand to the hilt of his sword.

"You could lose your head if you don't."

The troll's nostril's flared. She glanced at me again, then back at the Winter prince, claws flexing at her side. Ash didn't move, though the air around him grew colder, until the troll's breath hung in the air before her face.

Sensing her dire predicament, the huge faery finally backed off. "Of course, Your Highness," she muttered, and pointed at me with a curved black claw. "But if she gets stuffed into a bottle and served as the next drink special, don't say I didn't warn you."

"I'll keep that in mind," said Ash, and led me into the Dungeon.

The Dungeon, for all its eerie decor, turned out to be nothing more than a bar and nightclub, though it definitely catered to the more macabre crowd. The walls were brick, the lights dim and red, casting everything in crimson, and snarling monster heads hung on the walls over the bar. Music pounded the ceiling from an overhead room, AC/DC screaming out the lyrics to "Back in Black."

There were human patrons at the bar and sitting throughout the room with drinks in hand, but I saw only the inhuman ones. Goblins and satyrs, phouka and redcaps, a lone ogre in the corner, drinking a whole pitcher of a dark purple liquid. Unseen and invisible, the Unseelie fey milled through the throng of humans, spitting in their drinks, tripping the drunker ones, stealing items from purses and wallets.

I shivered and drew back, but Ash took my hand firmly. "Stay close," he murmured again. "This isn't as bad as upstairs, but we'll still have to be careful."

"What's upstairs?"

"Skulls, cages and the dance floor. Not something you want to see, trust me."

Ash kept a tight hold on my hand as we navigated around tables and bar patrons, moving toward the back of the room.

Grimalkin had disappeared—normal for him—so it was just us receiving the cold, hungry glares from every corner of the room. A redcap—a short, evil faery with sharklike teeth and a cap dipped in his victim's blood—reached for me as we passed his table, snagging my shirt. I tried to dodge, but the space was tight and narrow, and the clawed fingers latched onto my sleeve.

Ash turned. There was a flash of blue light, and a half second later the redcap froze, a glowing blue sword at his throat.

"Don't. Try. Anything." Ash's voice was colder than the chill coming off his blade. The redcap's Adam's apple bobbed, and he very slowly pulled back his claws. The rest of the Unseelie fey had frozen as well and were staring at us with glowing, hostile eyes.

"Meghan, go." Ash kept his threatening gaze on the rest of the crowd, daring anyone to get up. No one moved. I slipped past him and the redcap, who was keeping very still in his seat, and moved toward the back of the room.

"This way, human." Grimalkin appeared at the edge of a hallway, his eyes coming into focus before the rest of his body. Behind him, the narrow corridor was tight, dim and full of smoke. Strangely enough, bookshelves lined the walls, floor to ceiling—the type you'd find in a library or old mansion, not a shadowy bar in the French Quarter.

"Okay, why is there a library in the back of a goth bar?" I asked, peering around at the books. "Spell books for the black arts? Recipes for human hors d'oeuvres?"

Grimalkin snorted.

"Watch and learn, human."

At that moment, the bookshelf at the very end of the hallway swung open, and two college-age girls walked out, laughing and giggling. I blinked and moved aside as they passed, reeking of smoke and alcohol, and stumbled back toward the main bar. Looking back, I caught a glimpse of the room behind the panel as it swung closed—a toilet, a sink and a mirror—and stared wide-eyed at Grimalkin.

"The *bathroom?*"

Grimalkin yawned. "What humans will not do to keep themselves entertained," he mused with half-lidded eyes. "It is even more amusing when they are drunk and cannot find the door. But I suggest we get moving. That redcap motley has taken quite an interest in you."

I looked back to see that the redcap had been joined by three of his friends, and all four faeries were staring at us and muttering among themselves. Ash joined us in the hall, his icy blade still unsheathed, tendrils of mist writhing off it to mingle with the smoke.

"Hurry," he growled at us, pushing me toward the end of the hall. "I don't like the attention we're getting. Cat, have you opened the trod?"

"Give me a moment, Prince." Grimalkin sighed, and sauntered toward the panel that had so recently opened.

"Wait, aren't you their prince?" I wondered. "They're Unseelie, too, right? Can't you just order them to leave us alone?"

Ash gave a low, humorless chuckle. "I'm *a* prince," he replied, still keeping an eye on the redcaps, who in turn were keeping an eye on us. "But I'm not the only one. My brothers are looking for you, as well. Rowan has eyes and ears everywhere, I'm sure. He's much more ruthless than I am. Those redcaps could work for him, or they could be spies for Mab herself. Either way, they're going to inform *someone* of our passing the moment we leave this place. I can guarantee it."

"Sounds like a great family," I muttered.

Ash snorted. "You have no idea."

"Done," said Grimalkin from the end of the hallway. "Let us go."

"After you," Ash said, motioning me forward. "I'll make sure nothing follows us."

I slid the panel open, half expecting to see the tiny bathroom with the stained sink and toilet and scrawled-on walls. Instead, a cold breeze blew into the hallway, smelling of frost and bark and crushed leaves, and the gray, misty forest of the Nevernever stretched away through the door.

Grimalkin slipped through first, becoming nearly invisible in the fog. I followed, stepping through the doorway that became a split tree trunk on the other side. Ash ducked through and shut the door firmly behind us, where it faded into nothingness as soon as he let it go, leaving the mortal world behind.

It was colder in this part of the wyldwood. Frost coated the ground and the branches of the trees, and the mist clung to my skin with clammy fingers. I couldn't see more than a few yards in any direction. Everything was overly quiet and still, as if the forest itself was holding its breath.

"Tir Na Nog is close," Ash said, his voice muffled by the clinging fog. His breath did not puff or hang in the air like mine did. Trembling, I rubbed my arms to get warm. "We should move quickly. I want to get to Winter as fast as possible."

I was tired. My legs were cramped, both from riding and walking, my head hurt and the cold was sapping the last of my willpower. And I knew from personal experience that it would only get colder the closer we got to Tir Na Nog.

Thankfully, Grimalkin noticed my reluctance. "The human is about to fall over from exhaustion," he stated bluntly, twitching his tail. "She will only slow us down if we push her much farther. Perhaps we should look for a place to rest."

"Soon," Ash said, and turned to me. "Just a little farther, Meghan. Can you do that? We'll stop as soon as we cross the border into Tir Na Nog."

I nodded wearily. Ash took my hand, and with Grimalkin leading the way, we walked into the curling mist.

Minutes later, the howl rang out behind us.

CHAPTER THREE

THE LIVING COLD

Ash stopped, every muscle in his body coiling tight, as the echo of that eerie cry faded into the mist.

"Impossible," he murmured, his voice frighteningly calm. "It's on our trail again. How? How could it find us so quickly?"

Grimalkin suddenly let out a long, low growl, which shocked me and caused goose bumps to crawl up my arms. The cat had never done that before. "It is the Hunter," Grimalkin said, as his fur began to rise along his back and shoulders. "The Eldest Hunter, the First." He glanced at us, teeth bared, looking feral and wild. "You must flee, quickly! If he has your trail he will be coming fast. Run, now!"

We ran.

The woods flashed by us, dark and indistinct, shadowy shapes in the mist. I didn't know if we were running in circles or straight into the Hunter's jaws. Grimalkin had disappeared. Direction was lost in the coiling mist. I only hoped that Ash knew where he was going as we fled through the eerie whiteness.

The howl came again, closer this time, more excited. I dared a backward glance, but could see nothing beyond the swirling fog and shadows. But I could *feel* whatever it was, getting closer. It could see us now, fleeing before it, the back of my neck a tempting target. I stifled my panic and kept running, clinging to Ash's hand as we wove through the forest.

The trees fell away, the fog cleared a bit and suddenly a great chasm opened before us, wide and gaping like the maw of a giant beast. Ash jerked me to a stop three feet from the edge, and a shower of pebbles went clattering down the jagged sides, vanishing into the river of mist far below. The crack in the earth ran along the edge of the wyldwood for as far as I could see in either direction, separating us from the safety on the other side.

Beyond the chasm, a snow-covered landscape stretched away before us, icy and pristine. Trees were frozen, covered in ice, every twig outlined in sparkling crystal. The ground beneath looked like a blanket of clouds, white and fluffy. Snowdrifts glittered in the sun like millions of tiny diamonds. Tir Na Nog, the land of Winter, home to Mab and the Unseelie Court.

"This way." Ash tugged my hand and pulled me along the chasm, where the mist from the wyldwood rolled off the edge and down the cliff sides like a slow-moving waterfall. "If we can get to the bridge, I can stop him."

Panting, I followed the edge of the gorge and gasped in relief. About a hundred yards away, an arched bridge, made completely of ice, sparkled enticingly in the sun.

Something snapped in the woods at our right, something huge and fast. The Hunter was silent now, no howls or deep throaty bays; it was moving in for the kill.

We reached the bridge, and Ash pushed me forward onto the icy surface. There were no guards or handrails, just a narrow arch over a terrifying drop. Stomach clenching, I started across, trying not to look down. Because the bridge was ice, it was perfectly clear; I felt I was walking out over nothing, seeing the dizzying fall right beneath my feet.

My foot slipped, and my heart slammed against my ribs, pounding wildly as I flailed. Right behind me, Ash grabbed my arm tightly, and somehow we made it to the other side.

As soon as we were off, the Winter prince drew his sword. Sunlight flashed along the blade as he raised it and brought it slashing down on the narrow bridge. The bridge cracked, icy shards glittering as they spiraled into the air, and he raised the sword for another blow.

Across the chasm, something dark and monstrous broke out of the trees, fog swirling around it. Through the mist and shadows, I couldn't see it clearly, but it was huge, black and terrifying, with burning, yellow-green eyes. When it saw what Ash was doing, it roared, making the air tremble, then bounded for the bridge.

Ash brought his sword down again, then once more, and with a deafening crack, the ice bridge shattered. Our end slid away and dropped into oblivion, taking with it the entire arch, which clashed and screeched its way down the side of the cliff. The shadow on the other side slid to a halt, green eyes blazing with fury as it stalked up and down the edge for a moment, panting. Then, with a snarl that showed a flash of huge white teeth, it turned and slipped back into the misty wyldwood, vanishing from sight.

I shuddered with relief and sank down into the snow, gasping, feeling as if my lungs and legs and whole body were on fire. But as the adrenaline wore off, I realized how frigidly cold it was on this side of the chasm. The icy wind cut through my bones and stabbed into me like a knife.

Ash knelt beside me and gently pulled me close, wrapping me in his arms. I leaned into him, felt his heart racing and shivered against his chest. He was silent, resting his forehead against mine, saying nothing. Just there.

"Come on," he murmured after a few moments. "Let's find a place to rest."

"What about the Hunter?"

He rose, pulling me to my feet. "The Ice Maw runs for miles in either direction," he said, nodding at the chasm behind us, "until it meets the Wyrmtooth Mountains in the north and the Broken Glass Sea in the south. The Hunter won't find a way across for a long time. Besides," he added, narrowing his eyes, "this is *my* realm. I doubt he'll attack us here."

"Do not be too sure of that, Prince," said Grimalkin, popping into view on what was left of the shattered bridge. "The Hunter is older than you—much older. He does not care whose realm he is in when tracking his prey. If he is after you, you will see him again."

I sneezed, causing the cat to pin his ears. Ash took my elbow and drew me away from the chasm, positioning himself so that he blocked the wind howling up from the gap. "We'll worry about that if he ever gets across," the prince stated calmly as I hugged myself to conserve heat. "But night is coming, and so is the cold. We have to get Meghan inside."

"Before she turns into an icicle? I suppose." Grimalkin hopped off the shattered post, landing lightly in the snow. "The only shelter I know of is old Liaden's place in the frozen wood. Surely you are not taking the girl there?" He blinked under Ash's steady gaze. "You are. Well, this will be interesting. Follow me, then." He trotted away, making light paw prints in the snow, a fuzzy cloud gliding over the whiteness.

"Who's Liaden?" I asked Ash.

An icy gale howled up from the chasm before he could answer, slicing into me and tossing drifts of snow into the air. "Later," Ash said brusquely, giving me a slight push. "Follow Grimalkin. Go."

We trailed the paw prints into the woods. Icicles hung

from frozen trees, some longer than my arms and as sharp as a spear. Every so often one would snap off and plummet to the ground with the tinkle of breaking glass. The cold here was a living thing, clawing at my exposed skin, stabbing my lungs when I breathed. I was soon shivering violently, teeth chattering, thinking longingly of sweaters and hot baths and burrowing under a thick feather quilt until spring.

The woods grew darker, the trees closer together, and the temperature dropped even more. By now I was losing feeling in my fingers and toes, the cold making me sluggish. I felt as if icy hands were grabbing my feet, dragging me down, urging me to curl up in a ball and hibernate until it was warm again.

A flash of color in the trees caught my eye. On the branch above me, a small bird perched on a twig, bright red against the snow. Its eyes were closed, and it was fluffed out against the cold, looking like a feathery red ball. And it was completely encased in ice, covered head-to-toe in crystallized water, so clear that I could see every detail through the shell.

The sight should have chilled me, but I was so cold all I felt was the spreading numbness. My legs belonged to someone else, and I couldn't even feel my feet anymore. I tripped over a branch and fell, sprawling in a snowbank, ice crystals stinging my eyes.

I was suddenly very sleepy. My eyelids felt heavy, and all I wanted to do was lay my head down and sleep, like a bear through the winter. It was an appealing thought. I wasn't cold anymore, just completely numb, and darkness beckoned temptingly.

"Meghan!"

Ash's voice cut through the layers of apathy, as the Winter prince knelt in the snow. "Meghan, get up," he said, his voice urgent. "You can't lie here. You'll freeze over and die if you don't move. Get up."

I tried, but it seemed a Herculean effort to even raise my head when all I wanted to do was sleep. I muttered something about how tired I was, but the words froze in the back of my throat, and I only grunted.

"The cold has her." Grimalkin's voice seemed to come from far away. "She is already icing over. If you do not get her up now, she will die."

My eyelids were slipping shut, even though I tried keeping them open. If they closed, they would freeze and stay shut forever. I tried using my fingers to pry them open by force, but a layer of ice now covered my hands and I couldn't feel them anymore.

Give in, the cold whispered in my ear. *Give in, sleep. You'll never feel pain again.*

My eyelids flickered, and Ash made a noise that was almost a growl. "Dammit, Meghan," he snarled, grabbing both my arms. "I am not going to lose you this close to home. Get *up!*"

He rose, pulling me to my feet and, before I could even register what was going on, pressed his lips to mine.

The numbness shattered. Surprise flooded in, as my heart leaped and my stomach twisted itself into a knot. I laced my arms around his neck and kissed him back, feeling his arms around me, crushing us together, breathing in the sharp, frosty scent of him.

When we finally pulled back, I was breathing hard, and his heart raced under my fingers. I was also shivering again, and this time I welcomed the cold. Ash sighed and touched his forehead to mine.

"Let's get you out of the cold."

Grimalkin had vanished again, perhaps annoyed with our display of passion, but his delicate paw prints cut plainly through the snow. We followed them until the trail finally ended at a small, dilapidated cabin beneath two rotting trees.

I wouldn't think anyone lived there, but smoke curled from the chimney and a dim orange light glowed through the windows, so someone must've been home.

I was eager to get inside, out of the biting chill, but Ash took my hand, forcing me to look at him.

"You're in Unseelie territory now, remember that," he warned. "Whatever you see in that room, don't stare, and don't make any comments about her baby. Understand?"

I nodded, willing to agree to anything if I could just be warm again. Ash released me, stepped onto the creaking, snow-covered porch and knocked firmly on the door.

A woman opened it, peering out with tired, bloodshot eyes. A gray robe and cowl draped her body like old curtains, and her face, though fairly young, was lined and weary.

"Prince Ash?" she said, her voice breathy and frail. "This is a surprise. What can I do for you, Your Highness?"

"We wish to spend the night here," Ash stated quietly. "Myself and my companion. We won't bother you, and we intend to be gone by morning. Will you let us in?"

The woman blinked. "Of course," she murmured, opening the door wide. "Please, come inside. Make yourselves comfortable, poor children. I'm Dame Liaden."

That's when I saw her baby, cradled lovingly in her other arm, and bit my lip to stifle a gasp. The wrinkled, ghastly creature in a stained white blanket was the most hideous child I'd ever seen. Its deformed head was too large for its body, its tiny limbs were shriveled and dead, and its skin had an unhealthy blue tinge, like it had been drowned or left out in the cold. The child kicked weakly and let out a feeble, unearthly cry.

It was like watching a train wreck. I couldn't tear my eyes away…until Ash nudged me sharply in the ribs. "Nice to meet you," I said automatically, and followed him over the threshold into the room. Inside, a fire crackled in the hearth, and the warmth seeped into my frozen limbs, making me sigh in relief.

There was no crib anywhere in the cabin, and the woman didn't put her infant down once, moving about the room clutching her baby as if she feared something would snatch it away.

"The girl can take the bed under the window," Liaden said, wrapping the baby in another ratty, once-white blanket. "I fear I must go out now, but please make yourselves at home. There is tea and milk in the cupboards, and extra blankets in the closet. But midnight draws close, and we must depart. Farewell."

Holding her infant close to her chest, she opened the door, letting in a blast of painfully cold air, and slipped out into the night. The door clicked behind her, and we were alone.

"Where is she going?" I asked, moving closer to the fireplace. My fingers were finally getting some feeling back, and were all tingly now. Ash didn't look at me.

"You don't want to know."

"Ash…"

He sighed. "She's going to wash her baby in the blood of a human infant to make her own child whole and healthy again. If only for a little while."

I recoiled. "That's horrible!"

"You asked."

I shuddered and rubbed my upper arms, looking out the cabin's grimy window. Moonlight sparkled through the glass, and the land beyond was frozen solid. This was Unseelie territory, like Ash had said. I was far from home and family and the safety of a normal life.

Closing my eyes, I started to shake. What would happen to me once I reached the Winter Court? Would Mab throw me in a dungeon, or maybe feed me to her goblins? What would a centuries-old faery queen do to the daughter of her ancient rival? Whatever it was, I couldn't imagine it would be good for me. Fear twisted my gut.

I felt Ash move behind me, so close that I could feel his breath on the back of my neck. He didn't touch me, but his presence, quiet and strong, calmed me somewhat. Though the logical part of my mind told me he might be the one I should fear the most.

"So, how will this work?" I asked casually, trying to keep the accusation from my voice. It crept out, anyway. "Am I a prisoner of the Winter Court? A guest? Will Mab toss me in a cell, or is she planning something much more interesting?"

He hesitated, and I could hear the reluctance in his voice when he finally spoke. "I don't know what she intends to do," he said softly. "Mab doesn't share her plans with me, or anyone."

"It's going to be dangerous for me there, isn't it? I'm Oberon's daughter. Everyone will hate me." I remembered the red-cap's hungry gaze and rubbed my arms. "Or want to eat me."

His hands lightly grasped my shoulders, making my skin tingle and my heart flutter in my chest. "I will protect you," he murmured, and his voice went even lower, as if talking to himself. "Somehow."

Grimalkin appeared abruptly, leaping onto a stool by the fire, making me jump and Ash withdraw his hands. I mourned the loss of his touch. "Get some rest," the Winter prince said, moving away. "If nothing else happens, we should reach the Winter Court by tomorrow night."

Gingerly, I lay down on the bed beneath the window, trying not to imagine the last thing that used the mattress. Ash claimed a chair by the fire, turning it so he faced the door, and drew his sword into his lap. Surprisingly, the bed was warm and comfortable, and I drifted off to the outline of Ash's profile keeping watch by the fire.

I must've woken sometime in the night, or perhaps I dreamed, for I remember opening my eyes to see Ash and Grimalkin standing before the hearth, talking quietly. Their voices were too low to hear, but the look on Ash's face was scary in its bleakness. He raked a hand through his hair and said something to Grimalkin, who nodded slowly and replied. I blinked, or maybe drifted off again, because when I opened my eyes again Grimalkin was gone. Ash stood with his hands braced on the mantel and his shoulders hunched, staring into the flames, and didn't move for a long time.

CHAPTER FOUR

THE HUNTER

"Get up."

The cold voice was the first thing I heard the next morning, cutting through layers of sleep and grogginess, bringing me fully awake. Ash loomed over me, his posture stiff, regarding me with empty silver eyes.

"We're leaving," he said in a flat voice, and tossed something on the bed, where it landed in a cloud of dust. A thick, hooded cloak, gray and dusty, as if all color had been leeched out of it. "Found that in the closet," Ash continued, turning away. "It should keep you from freezing. But we need to go, now. The sooner we reach the Winter Court the better."

"Where's Grim?" I asked, struggling upright, reeling from his sudden change in mood. Ash opened the door, letting in a blast of frigid air.

"Gone. Left early this morning." He waited, still holding the door, as I swirled the cloak around my shoulders. When I drew up the hood, the prince nodded briskly. "Let's go."

"Is something coming?" I asked, jogging after him through the snow, my breath puffing in the air. Everything was covered in a new layer of ice. "Is the Hunter getting close again?"

"No." He didn't look at me. "Not that I can tell."

I swallowed. "Did I...do something wrong?"

He hesitated this time, then sighed. "No," he said in a softer voice. "You did nothing wrong."

"Then why are you being like this? Ash? Hey!" I lunged forward and grabbed his sleeve, bringing us both to a halt.

"Let go." Ash's voice held the subtle hint of warning. I shook off my fear and stubbornly planted my feet.

"Or what? You'll kill me? Haven't you already made that threat?"

"Don't tempt me." But his voice had lost its coldness—now it just sounded tired. He sighed, raking his free hand through his hair. "It's not important. Just…something Grimalkin said. Something I already knew."

"What?"

He turned. "Meghan…"

In the distance, a howl echoed over the trees.

I jerked, and Ash straightened, his gaze sharpening. "The Hunter," he muttered. "Again. How could it catch up so quickly?"

The howl came again, and I shivered, drawing closer to Ash. "What *is* it?"

The prince's eyes narrowed. "I don't know. But this stops now. Come on!"

Ash kept a tight hold on my hand as we sprinted through the snow. I thought of the bridge and the impossible chasm that Hunter had, somehow, cleared, and hoped this plan would work out better. It didn't seem likely that we would outrun whatever tireless beast was behind us.

The forest thinned, and jagged cliffs rose up on either side of us, sparkling in the sun. Huge blue-and-green crystals jutted out from the sides, sending fractured prisms of light over the snow. Ash led me through a narrow canyon, sheer cliff walls pressing in on either side until it opened up in a snowy clearing surrounded by mountains.

The howl rang out again, echoing eerily through the gully we had just come through. Whatever it was, it was closing fast.

"This way." Ash tugged on my hand and pulled me toward the far side of the clearing. Between two pine trees, a dark blot in the cliff face marked the entrance to a cave, icicles dangling from the opening like teeth.

"Go," Ash said, pushing me forward. "Get inside, hurry."

I scrambled through the opening, being careful not to stab myself on the icicles, and straightened, looking around. The cave was huge, a vast, ice-covered cavern, sunlight slanting in through the holes in the roof far, far above us. The ceiling sparkled, every square inch covered with sharp, gleaming icicles, some longer than I was tall. A breeze howled through the cave, and the icicles tinkled like wind chimes, filling the cavern with song.

"Ash," I said as the Winter prince came through the opening, shaking snow from his hair. "What—"

"Shh." Ash put a finger against my lips, shaking his head in warning. He pointed to the skeletons scattered about the cave, half-buried in snow. The bones of some large animal lay sprawled on the ground nearby, a fallen icicle jutting through its ribs. I winced and nodded my understanding.

And then something black and monstrous exploded through the cave mouth, snapping at my face.

Ash jerked me backward, his hand snaking around my mouth to stifle my shriek, as the snap of teeth echoed inches from my head. If Ash's hand hadn't been pressed hard against my lips, I would've screamed again as two burning, yellow-green eyes peered at me from the face in the door.

It was a wolf, a huge black wolf the size of a grizzly bear, only longer and leaner and a thousand times more frightening. This wasn't the majestic creature you saw on the nature channels, loping through the snowy wilderness with its pack. This was the rabid beast in every horror movie about wolves: dark shaggy fur, slavering muzzle, glowing, pupil-less eyes. Its lips were curled back to reveal shiny fangs longer then my hand, and ribbons of drool dripped from its jaws, crystallizing in the snow. Only its head fit through the opening, but it turned its muzzle in my direction, and I swore it grinned at me.

"Meghan Chase. I finally found you."

Ash pulled me back farther, toward the far end of the cave, as the enormous wolf thrashed and wriggled in the doorway, somehow, impossibly, sliding through. My heart thudded as the creature rose to its full height inside the cave. He seemed to fill the chamber. Ash shoved me behind him, pressing me against the wall beneath a rocky overhang, and drew his sword. The wolf chuckled, the deep tone making my skin crawl, and bared his teeth in a savage grin.

"Think you're going to hurt me with that little thing?" His guttural voice echoed through the cavern, and icicles clinked above him, swaying dangerously. "Do you know who I am, boy?" He lowered his head, peeling his lips back. "I am *Wolf.* I am older than you, older than Mab, older than the most ancient faery to walk this realm. I was in stories long before the humans knew my name, and even then they feared me." He took one step forward, his huge paw sinking into the snow. "I am the wolf at the door, the creature that stalked the girl in the red hood to Grandma's house. I am the wolf who becomes a man, and the man who is a beast inside. My stories outnumber all the tales ever told, and you cannot kill me."

"I know who you are." Ash's voice shook slightly, which chilled me even more. That Ash, fearless, unshakable Ash, was afraid of this thing filled me with dread. "But you're here for the Summer princess, and I have my own vow to bring her back to my court. So I can't let you take her." He brandished his sword, the faery glamour of Winter swirling around him. "You'll have to go through me first."

The Wolf smiled. "As you wish."

He lunged with a roar, jaws gaping wide, tongue lolling between dripping fangs. Insanely fast, he covered the area in a single bound and leaped at us, a dark blur in the air. I shrank back as the Wolf charged but Ash whirled, glamour snapping around him, and slammed his sword hilt into the wall.

A deafening crack echoed throughout the cavern, like a gunshot. The ceiling trembled, icicles clicking wildly and then, like a million china plates being smashed at once, collapsed in a deadly gleaming rain. The Wolf paused for an instant, looking up...and was buried under a ton of pointed crystal shards.

I turned away, covering my eyes as a single high-pitched yelp rose over the clatter of smashing ice. The snow cleared, the cacophony died away and there was silence.

I started to peek through my fingers, but Ash grabbed my hand, blocking my view. "Don't look," he warned softly, and I saw a spatter of red behind him, seeping through the snow, making my stomach curl. "Let's get out of here."

Deliberately not looking at the dark mass in the center of the room, we fled the cave, scrambling through the hole back into the clearing. Snow was falling, light wispy flakes that danced on the breeze. I took a shaky breath, and the cold burned my lungs, reminding me I was still alive. I glanced at Ash, who was staring back at the cave mouth.

"The Wolf," he murmured, almost to himself. "The Big Bad Wolf. Few ever live to tell of seeing him." He shook his head in wonder, glancing back at me. "I wonder why he was after you? Who sent him, that he would track us this far?"

"Mab?" I guessed. Ash snorted and his lips curled in a smirk.

"Mab wants you alive," he said, walking away from the

cave mouth, back toward the gully. I pulled my hood up and hurried after him, jogging through the snow. "You're no use to her dead. She was very specific about that. Besides, she wouldn't put me at risk like that." He paused, frowning slightly. "I think."

He sounded terribly unsure. I felt a pang of sympathy, that Ash didn't know if his queen, his own mother, would send the Wolf after us, not caring if it hurt him. I closed the last few paces and reached out to touch his arm.

The Wolf's giant, bloody head lunged between us with a roar, knocking me back, sending me sprawling. Lightning quick, Ash drew his sword, a second too late. The monster's jaws clamped shut on his arm, and the Wolf hurled him away. I screamed.

"I told you, you can't kill me!" the Wolf snarled, stalking toward Ash, who had rolled to his feet with his sword in front of him. The thick, shaggy pelt was covered in blood. It dripped in a steady rain to the ground, raising faint puffs of steam where it struck the snow. Icicles stuck out of his body like a hundred jagged spears. Despite that, he moved smoothly, easily, as if he felt no pain.

"Foolish boy," the Wolf growled, circling Ash, leaving a crimson trail behind him. "You will not win this. I am immortal."

"Meghan, run," Ash ordered, his eyes never leaving the Wolf. His own blood dripped from his sword arm to stain the ground. "The Winter Court isn't far from here. You'll be protected—tell whomever you meet that Ash sent you. Run, now."

"I'm not leaving!"

"Go!"

The Wolf shook himself, sending blood, foam and icicles flying. "I will deal with you momentarily, Princess," he growled, lowering himself into a crouch. Muscles bunched under his shaggy pelt, and the icicles gleamed as they stuck out of his thigh and bony ribs. "Are you ready, boy? Here I come!"

He leaped. Ash brought up his sword. And I charged the Wolf.

The Wolf hit Ash with the full weight of his body behind him, driving them both into the snow, ignoring the sword that slashed into him. His massive paws slammed into Ash's chest and arms, pinning the sword beneath them. They hit the ground with the Wolf on top, those huge jaws gaping wide to bite off Ash's head.

I slammed into the Wolf with every bit of strength I had, aiming for one of those gleaming ice spears, driving my shoulder into it. The sharp edge sliced into me, cutting my skin through the cloak, but I felt the spear jam farther into the Wolf's ribs. The huge creature let out a startled, painful yelp and swung around, pinning me with a blazing yellow glare.

"Foolish girl! What are you doing? I'm trying to help you!"

Shocked, I stared at him, panting. Still pinned beneath the Wolf, Ash tried to get up, but two giant paws held him down. "What are you talking about?" I demanded. "Let Ash up, if you say you're helping me."

The beast shook his head. "I was sent to rescue you and kill this one," he replied, shifting his weight to better lean on Ash, who gritted his teeth in pain. "You are a prisoner no more, Princess. Just let me finish him off and you can return to the Summer Court."

"No!" I lunged forward as the Wolf turned back, opening his jaws. "Don't kill him! I'm not a prisoner. We made a deal, a contract—I would go to the Winter Court in return for his help. He's not keeping me here by force. I *chose* this."

The Wolf blinked slowly. "You made a contract," he repeated.

"Yes."

"A contract with this one."

"Yes!"

"Then...your father was mistaken."

"*Oberon?*" I stared at him, aghast. "Oberon ordered you to do this?"

The Wolf snorted. "No one orders me," he growled, baring his fangs. "The Summer Lord thought you had been captured. He asked me to find you, kill your captor and free you to return to the Summer Court. He thought the hunt might be difficult, so deep within Winter's territory, and I could not pass up the challenge." The Wolf paused, scrutinizing me with intense yellow eyes, a flicker of irritation crossing his face. "However, if you have made a deal with the Winter prince, that changes things. The agreement with Oberon was to rescue you from your captor, and you do not have a captor. Therefore..." He snarled in annoyance and reluctantly stepped back, freeing Ash from beneath his paws. "I must honor the contract and let you go."

He glared at us as he moved aside, the Hunter so close to his prey only to have it ripped from his jaws. I stepped between him and Ash, just in case the Wolf changed his mind, and helped the prince to his feet. Ash's sword arm bled freely, and the other was wrapped around his ribs, as if the Wolf's weight had crushed them. Sheathing his blade, he faced our pursuer and gave a slight bow.

The Wolf nodded. "You're very lucky," he told Ash. "Today." Backing off, he shook himself once more and glared at us with grudging respect. "It was a good chase. Pray we do not meet again, for you will not even see me coming."

Throwing back his head, the Wolf howled, wild and chilling, making the hairs on my neck stand up. Bounding into the trees, his huge dark form vanished instantly, swallowed up by snow and shadows, and we were alone.

I looked at Ash in concern. "Are you all right? Can you walk?"

He took a step and winced, sinking to one knee. "Give me a moment."

"Come on." I slipped an arm under his shoulder and carefully eased him upright. The clearing looked like a war zone: trampled snow, crushed vegetation and blood everywhere. It could attract Unseelie predators and, though I was sure none were as scary as the Big Bad Wolf, Ash was in no shape to fight them off. "We're going back to the cave."

He didn't argue, and together we limped across the clearing to the ice cave, ducking inside. The floor was a mess of shattered icicles, making passage difficult and treacherous, but we found a clear space near the back of the room. Ash sank down against the wall, and I tore a strip off the hem of my cloak.

He was silent as I wrapped the makeshift bandage around his arm, but I could feel his eyes on me as I tied it off. Releasing his arm, I looked up to meet his silvery gaze. Ash blinked slowly, giving me that look that meant he was trying to figure me out.

"Why didn't you run?" he asked softly. "If you didn't stop the Wolf, you wouldn't have to come back to Tir Na Nog. You would have been free."

I scowled at him.

"I agreed to that contract, same as you," I muttered, tying off the bandage with a jerk, but Ash didn't even grunt. Angry now, I glared up at him, meeting his eyes. "What, you think just because I'm human I would back out? I knew what I was getting into, and I am going to uphold my end of the bargain, no matter what happens. And if you think I would leave you to that monster just so I wouldn't have to meet Mab, then you don't know me at all."

"It's *because* you're human," Ash continued in that same quiet voice, holding my gaze, "that you missed a tactical opportunity. A Winter fey in your position wouldn't have saved me. They wouldn't let their emotions get in the way. If you're going to survive in the Unseelie Court, you have to start thinking like them."

"Well, I'm *not* like them." I rose and took a step back, trying to ignore the feelings of hurt and betrayal, the stupid angry tears pressing at the corners of my eyes. "I'm not a Winter faery—I'm human, with human feelings and emotions. And if you want me to apologize for that, you can forget it. I can't just shut off my feelings like you can. Though the next time you're about to get eaten or killed, I guess I won't bother saving your life."

I whirled to stalk away in a huff, but Ash rose with blinding speed and gripped my upper arms. I stiffened, locking my knees and keeping my back straight, but struggling with him would have been useless. Even wounded and bleeding as he was, he was much stronger than me.

"I'm not ungrateful," he murmured against my ear, making my stomach flutter despite itself. "I just want you to understand. The Winter Court preys on the weak. It's their nature. They will try to tear you apart, physically and emotionally, and I won't always be there to protect you."

I shivered, anger melting away as my own doubts and fears came rushing back. Ash sighed, and I felt his forehead touch the back of my hair, his breath fanning my neck. "I don't want to do this," he admitted in a low, anguished voice. "I don't want to see what they'll try to do to you. A Summer faery in the Winter Court doesn't stand much of a chance. But I vowed that I would bring you back, and I'm bound to that promise."

He raised his head, squeezing my shoulders in an almost painful grip as his voice dropped a few octaves, turning grim and cold. "So, you have to be stronger than they are. You can't let down your guard, no matter what. They will lead you on, with games and pretty words, and they will take pleasure in your misery. Don't let them get to you. And don't trust anyone." He paused, and his voice went even lower. "Not even me."

"I'll always trust you," I whispered without thinking, and his hands tightened, turning me to face him almost savagely.

"No," he said, narrowing his eyes. "You won't. I'm your enemy, Meghan. Never forget that. If Mab tells me to kill you in front of the entire court, it's my duty to obey. If she orders Rowan or Sage to carve you up slowly, making sure you suffer every second of it, I'm expected to stand there and let them do it. Do you understand? My feelings for you don't matter in the Winter Court. Summer and Winter will always be on opposite sides, and nothing will change that."

I knew I should be afraid of him. He was an Unseelie prince after all, and had basically admitted he would kill me if Mab ordered him to. But he also admitted to having feelings for me—feelings that didn't matter, true, but it still made my stomach squirm when I heard it. And maybe I was being naive, but I couldn't believe Ash would willingly hurt me, even in the Winter Court. Not with the way he was looking at me now, his silver eyes conflicted and angry.

He stared at me a moment longer, then sighed. "You didn't hear a word I said, did you?" he murmured, closing his eyes.

"I'm not afraid," I told him, which was a lie; I was terrified of Mab and the Unseelie Court that waited at the end of this journey. But if Ash was there, I would be all right.

"You are infuriatingly stubborn," Ash muttered, raking a hand through his hair. "I don't know how I'm going to protect you when you have no concept of self-preservation."

I stepped close to him, placing a hand on his chest, feeling his heart beat under his shirt. "I trust you," I said, rising up so our faces were inches apart, trailing my fingers down his stomach. "I know you'll find a way."

His breath hitched, and he regarded me hungrily. "You're playing with fire, you know that?"

"That's weird, considering you're an ice prin—" I didn't get any further, as Ash leaned in and kissed me. I looped my arms around his neck as his snaked around my waist, and for a few moments, the cold couldn't touch me.

We spent the night in the cave, both to give Ash a chance to heal from his wounds and to give us one more night of rest before entering Tir Na Nog. It didn't take long for Ash to recover. The fey heal insanely fast, especially if they are within their own territories, and by the time darkness fell his bite wounds were almost gone. As the temperature dropped, he started a fire, solely for my benefit, and we sat around the flames sharing the last of the food, lost in our own thoughts.

Outside, the snow continued to fall, piling outside the entrance and in the center of the room through the holes in the ceiling. It sparkled in the icy moonlight, like flakes of diamonds drifting from the sky, tempting me to stand in the center of the light and catch them on my tongue.

Ash was silent through most of the evening. He'd broken the kiss earlier, pulling away with a guilty, agonized look, and mumbled something about making camp. Since then, he'd given me short, one-word answers whenever I tried talking to him, and avoided eye contact whenever possible.

He sat across from me now, chin on his hands, brooding into the fire. Part of me wanted to walk up to him and hug him from behind, and part of me wanted to hurl a snowball at his perfect face to get some kind of reaction.

I opted for a less suicidal route. "Hey," I said, poking at the flames with a stick, making them cough sparks. "Earth to Ash. What are you thinking about?"

He didn't move, and for a second I thought he would reply with his favorite one-word answer of the night: *nothing.* But after a moment he sighed and his eyes flickered, very briefly, to mine.

"Home," he said quietly. "I'm thinking of home. Of the court."

"Do you miss it?"

Another pause, and he shook his head slowly. "No."

"But it's your home."

"It's the place I was born. That's all." He sighed and gazed into the fire. "I don't go back often, and I rarely stay at court for any length of time."

I thought of Mom, and Ethan, and our tiny little farm-house out in the bayou, and a lump rose to my throat. "That must be lonely," I murmured. "Don't you get homesick once in a while?"

Ash regarded me across the flames, understanding and sympathy dawning in his gaze. "My family," he said in a solemn voice, "is not like yours."

He rose gracefully, abruptly, as if the subject had become tiring. "Get some sleep," he said, and the chill was back in his voice. "Tomorrow we reach the Winter Court. Queen Mab will be anxious to meet you."

My gut twisted. I curled up inside my cloak, as close to the fire as I dared, and let my mind go blank. I was certain that Ash's last words would prevent me from getting any sleep, but I was more exhausted than I realized and soon drifted into oblivion.

That night, for the first time, I dreamed of the Iron King. The scene was eerily familiar. I stood atop a great iron tower, a hot wind stinging my face, smelling of ozone and chemicals. Before me, a huge metal throne rose into the mottled yellow sky, black iron spikes raking the clouds. Behind me, Ash's cold, pale body was sprawled against the edge of a fountain, blood oozing slowly into the water.

Machina the Iron King stood at the top of his metal throne, long silver hair whipping in the wind. His back was to me, the numerous iron cables extending from his shoulders and spine surrounding him like glittering wings.

I took a step forward, squinting up at the silhouette on the throne. "Machina!" I called, my voice sounding weak and small in the wind. "Where's my brother?"

The Iron King raised his head slightly, but didn't turn around. "Your brother?"

"Yes, my brother. Ethan. You stole him and brought him here." I kept walking, ignoring the wind that tore at my hair and clothes. Thunder boomed overhead, and the mottled yellow clouds turned black and crimson. "You wanted to lure me here," I continued, reaching the base of the throne. "You wanted me to become your queen in exchange for Ethan. Well, here I am. Now let my brother go."

Machina turned. Only it wasn't the Iron King's sharp, intelligent face that stared down at me.

It was my own.

I jerked awake, my heart hammering against my ribs, cold sweat trickling down my back. The fire had gone out, and the ice cave lay dark and empty, though the sky showing through the holes was already light. Snow lay in huge glimmering piles where it had drifted in through the roof, and several new icicles were already forming on the ceiling, growing back like teeth. Ash was nowhere to be seen.

Still trembling from the nightmare, I rolled away from

the dead campfire and stood, shaking snow clumps from my hair. Pulling my cloak tighter around myself, I went searching for Ash.

I didn't have to look far. He stood outside in the clearing, snow flurries drifting around him, his sword glowing blue against the white. From the sweeping footprints in the snow, I knew he'd been practicing sword drills, but now he stood motionless, his back to me, gazing toward the entrance of the gully.

I pulled up my hood and walked out, tromping through the deep snow until I stood beside him. He acknowledged me with a flick of his eyes, but otherwise didn't move, his gaze riveted to the edge of the canyon.

"They're coming," he murmured.

A group of horses appeared then, seeming to materialize out of the falling snow, pure white and blue-eyed, trotting a few inches above the ground. Atop them sat Winter knights in icy blue-and-black armor, their gazes cold beneath their snarling wolf helms.

Ash stepped forward, very subtly moving in front of me as the knights swept up, horses snorting small geysers from flared nostrils. "Prince Ash," one knight said formally, bowing in the saddle. "Her majesty the queen has been informed of your return and has sent us to escort you and the half-breed back to the palace."

I bristled at the term *half-breed* but Ash didn't seem terribly fazed by their arrival.

"I don't need an escort," he said in a bored voice. "Return to the palace and tell Queen Mab I will arrive shortly. I'm fairly capable of handling the half-breed by myself."

I cringed at his tone. He was back to being Prince Ash, third son of the Unseelie Court, dangerous, cold and heartless. The knights didn't seem at all surprised, which somehow made me even more apprehensive. This cold, hostile prince was the Ash they were used to.

"I'm afraid the queen insists, Your Highness," the first one replied, unapologetic. "By order of Queen Mab, you and the half-breed will come with us to the Winter Court. She is rather impatient for your arrival."

Ash sighed.

"Very well," he muttered, not even looking at me as he swung into an empty saddle. Before I could protest, another knight reached down and pulled me up in front of him. "Let's get this over with."

We rode for several silent hours. The knights did not speak to me, Ash or each other, and the horse's hooves made no sound as they galloped over the snow. Ash didn't even look in my direction; his face remained blank and cold throughout the ride.

Completely ignored, I was left to my own thoughts, which were dark and growing more disturbing the farther we went. I missed home. I was terrified of meeting Queen Mab. And Ash had turned into someone cold and unfamiliar. I replayed our last kiss in my mind, clinging to it like a life vest in a raging sea. Had I imagined his feelings for me, misread his intentions? What if everything he'd said was just a ploy, a scheme to get me to Tir Na Nog and the queen?

No, I couldn't believe that. The emotion on his face that night was real. I had to believe that he cared, I had to believe in him, or I would go crazy.

Night was falling and a huge frozen moon was peeking over the tops of the trees when we came to a vast, icy lake. Jagged ice floes crinkled against one another near the shoreline, and fog writhed along the surface of the water. A long wooden dock stretched out toward the middle of the lake, vanishing into the hanging mist.

As I wondered how close we were to the Winter Court, the knights abruptly steered their horses onto the rickety dock and rode down single file, the dark waters of the lake lapping the posts beneath us. I squinted and peered through the fog, wondering if the Winter Court was on an island in the center.

The mist cleared away for just a moment, and I saw the edge of the dock, dropping away into dark, murky lake water. The horses broke into a trot, then a full gallop, snorting eagerly, as the end of the dock rushed at us with terrifying speed.

I closed my eyes and the horses leaped.

We hit the water with a loud splash and sank quickly into the icy depths. The horse didn't even try to resurface, and the knight's grip was firm, so I couldn't kick away. I held my breath and fought down panic as we dropped deeper and deeper into the frigid waters.

Then, suddenly, we resurfaced, bursting out with the same noisy splash, sending water flying. Gasping, I rubbed my eyes and looked around, confused and disoriented. I didn't recall the horse swimming back up. Where were we, anyway?

My gaze focused, my breath caught and I forgot about everything else.

A massive underground city loomed before me, lit up with millions of tiny lights, gleaming yellow, blue and green like a blanket of stars. From where we floated in the black waters of the lake, I could see large stone buildings, streets winding upward in a spiral pattern and ice covering everything. The cavern above soared into darkness, farther than I could see, and the twinkling lights made the entire city glow with hazy etherealness.

At the top of a hill, casting its shadow over everything, an enormous, ice-covered palace stood proudly against the black. I shivered, and the knight behind me spoke for the first time.

"Welcome to Tir Na Nog."

I glanced at Ash and finally caught his gaze. For a moment, the Unseelie prince looked torn, balanced between emotion and duty, his eyes begging forgiveness. But a half second later he turned away, and his face shut into that blank mask once more.

We rode through the snow-laced streets toward the palace, and the denizens of the Unseelie Court watched us pass with glowing, inhuman eyes. We stopped at the palace doors, where a pair of monstrous ogres glared menacingly, drool dripping from their tusks, but let us through without a word.

Even within the palace, the rooms and hallways were coated with frost and translucent, crystal ice in various colors; it was possibly colder inside than it was outside. More Unseelie roamed the corridors: goblins, hags, redcaps, all watching me with hungry, evil grins. But since I was flanked by a group of stone-faced knights and one lethally calm Winter prince, none dared do more than leer at me.

The knights escorted us to a pair of soaring double doors carved with the images of frozen trees. If you looked closely, you could almost see faces peering at you through the branches, but if you blinked or looked away they would be gone. A chill wafted out from between the cracks, colder than I thought possible, even in this palace of ice. It brushed across my skin and tiny needles of cold stabbed into me. I shivered and stepped back.

The knights, I realized, were now standing at attention along the corridor, gazing straight ahead, paying us no attention. As I rubbed my stinging arm, Ash stepped close, not touching me, but close enough to make my heart beat faster. With his back to the knights, he put a hand on the door and paused, as if gathering his resolve.

"This is the throne room," he murmured in a low voice. "Queen Mab is on the other side. Are you ready?"

I wasn't, really, but nodded, anyway. "Let's do this," I whispered, and Ash pushed open the door.

A blast of that same cold, stinging air hit my face as we went through, nearly taking my breath away. The room beyond was painfully cold; ice columns held up the ceiling, and the floor was slick and frozen. In the center of the room, surrounded by pale, aloof Winter gentry and pet goblins, the queen of the Unseelie Court waited for us.

Queen Mab sat atop her throne of ice, regal, beautiful and terrifying. Her skin was paler than snow, her blue-black hair coiled elegantly atop her head, held in place with icy needles. She wore a cloak of white fur and held a crystal goblet in one delicate, long-fingered hand. Her eyes, black and as depthless as space, rose slowly, capturing me in a piercing stare. Above the furred ruff, bloodred lips curled into a slow smile.

"Meghan Chase," Queen Mab purred. "Welcome to the Winter Court. Please, make yourself comfortable. I'm afraid you could be here a long, long time."

"I Dare You"

SUMMER'S CROSSING

CHAPTER ONE

AND AS I AM AN HONEST PUCK

Names.

What's in a name, really? I mean, besides a bunch of letters or sounds strung together to make a word. Does a rose by any other name really smell as sweet? Would the most famous love story in the world be as poignant if it was called *Romeo and Gertrude?* Why is what we call ourselves so important?

Heh, sorry, I don't usually get philosophical. I've just been wondering lately. Names are, of course, very important to my kind. Me, I have so many, I can't even remember them all. None of them are my True Name, of course. No one has ever spoken my real name out loud, not once, despite all the titles and nicknames and myths I've collected for myself over the years. No one has ever come close to getting it right.

Curious, are you? Wanna know my True Name? Okay, listen up, I've never told anyone before. My True Name is…

Hahahaha! You really thought I would tell you? Really? Oh, I kill me. But, like I said, names are important to us. For one thing, they tie us to this world; they ground us in reality somewhat. If you know your True Name—not everyone in our world finds it—you're more "real" than if you don't know who you are. And for a race that has a tendency to fade away if we're forgotten, that's kind of a big deal.

My name, one of many, is Robin Goodfellow.

You may have heard of me.

Once upon a time, I had two close friends. Shocking, I know, given my natural charm, but there are those who just don't appreciate my brilliance. We weren't supposed to be friends, the three of us, or even friendly with each other. I was part of the Seelie Court, and they...weren't. But I'd never been one for following the rules, and who knew Queen Mab's youngest son could be such a rebel, as well? And Ariella... I'd known Ash a long time before Ariella came into the picture, but I never begrudged her presence. She was the buffer between us; the one who could calm Ash when he slipped too far toward his ruthless Unseelie nature, or advised caution when one of my plans seemed a little...impulsive. Once upon a time, we were inseparable.

Once upon a time, I did something stupid. And lost them both in the process.

Which brings us to...now. Today. Where, once more, it was me and my former best friend, getting ready to head off on another adventure. Just like old times.

Except, he still hadn't forgiven me for what had happened all those years ago. And he hadn't really invited me along, either. I sort of...invited myself.

But if I made a habit of waiting for an invitation, I'd never get to go anywhere.

"So," I said brightly, falling into step behind the brooding prince. "Grimalkin. We're going to find him, right?"

"Yes."

"Any idea where he is?"

"No."

"Any idea where to start looking?"

"No."

"You do realize that doesn't constitute much of a plan, right ice-boy?"

He turned to glare at me, which I considered a small triumph. Ash usually ignored my goading. Anytime I could poke through his icy indifference was a victory. Of course, when poking the Winter prince, one had to proceed with caution. There was a fine line between irritation and having icicles hurled at your face.

He glared at me a moment longer, then sighed, raking a hand through his hair—a sure sign that he was frustrated. "Do you have any suggestions, Goodfellow?" he muttered, sounding reluctant to even ask. And for just a moment, I saw how lost he was, how uncertain of the future and what lay ahead. Anyone else wouldn't have seen it, but I knew Ash. I could always catch those tiny flashes of emotion, no matter how well he hid them. It almost made me feel sorry for him.

Almost.

I grinned disarmingly. "What? Are you actually asking for my opinion, ice-boy?" I taunted, and that doubt vanished, replaced by annoyance. "Well," I went on, leaning back against a tree trunk, "since you asked, we might want to check if anyone around here owes him a favor."

"That narrows things down," Ash said sarcastically. I rolled my eyes, but he did have a point. If we started naming everyone that might owe our feline friend a favor, the list would fill several books.

"Well, then." I crossed my arms. "If you have a better suggestion, Prince, I'd love to hear it."

Before he could answer, a ripple of glamour shivered through the air. Glitter and streamers of light swirled around us, and a chorus of tiny voices sang out a single note. I winced, knowing there was only one person who thought a normal entrance, like walking through a door, wasn't good enough for her; she had to announce her presence with sparkle and glitter and St. Peter's choir.

"Darlings!"

Sometimes, it sucks being right all the time.

"Leanansidhe," Ash grumbled, sounding about as thrilled as I felt as the Queen of the Exiles stepped out of the glitter and light and smiled down at us. She looked like she was going to a party where the theme was Most Sparkly Evening Gown, or maybe Quickest Way to Blind Someone. She paused a moment, striking a dramatic pose for her sadly unimpressed audience, before waving her hand and dispersing with the fireworks.

"Lea," I echoed, smirking at her. "This is a shock. To what do we owe the pleasure of your company, away from the Between and all?"

"Puck, darling." Leanansidhe gave me a smile that was about as welcoming as a viper eyeing a mouse. "Why am I not surprised to see you here? It seems I just got rid of you, pet, and here you are again."

"That's me." I raised my chin. "The bad penny that always pops up. But you didn't answer my question. What do you want, Lea?"

"From you? Nothing, darling." Leanansidhe turned to Ash, and he stiffened. "Ash, darling," she purred. "You *are* a trouper, aren't you, pet? I was certain, after you made your knightly oath, that you and the girl would go all Romeo and Juliet on me. But you survived the final battle, after all. Bravo, pet, bravo."

I snorted. "So what am I, chopped liver?"

Leanansidhe shot me an annoyed glance. "No, darling." She sighed. "But the Winter prince and I have unfinished business, or didn't he tell you?" She smiled and looked at Ash again. "He owes me a favor—a rather large favor—for helping him out, and I have come to collect."

A bargain with the Exile Queen? For a second, I wasn't sure I'd heard right. "Ice-boy." I shook my head, exasperated. "Really? You made a deal with *her?* Are you crazy? You, of all people, should know better."

"It was for Meghan." Ash's voice was low, defensive. "I needed her help." He looked at Leanansidhe, quietly pleading. "Can this not wait?" he asked in a calm voice, and the question surprised me. Ash rarely made deals, but when he did, he was religious about upholding them. It was a point of personal honor, I guessed, to keep his bargains without fail, without complaint, even if he'd managed to get the bad end of one. This was the very first time I'd heard him ask for more time, the first I'd heard him plead for anything.

But he'd find no sympathy with the Exile Queen. I could've told him that. "No, darling," Leanansidhe said briskly. "I'm afraid it cannot. I know you and Goodfellow are about to go tromping off after Grimalkin, and that, I fear, might take a long time. A very long time. Time I do not have. I am calling in this debt *now,* and you will help me *now.* Besides, darling—" Leanansidhe sniffed, making a dramatic gesture with a gloved hand "—after you are done with this, I might be able to help. Finding Grimalkin if he does not wish to be found is a near impossible task. I could, at least, point you in the right direction."

Ash sighed, looking impatient, but there was nothing he could do. Even I couldn't wiggle my way out of a contract, though if I had to strike a deal, I always left myself *some* kind of loophole. You'd get screwed eight ways from Sunday, otherwise. In the courts, the nobles all loved this game, each one trying to pull a fast one on the other, though most of them knew better than to make a deal with me anymore. Especially after the fiasco with Titania and the donkey ears. Being a legend does have its advantages sometimes.

Ash knew his way around the fey courts, too; he'd grown up having to watch his back. I was surprised he'd allowed himself to strike a bargain with Leanansidhe; he should've known it would come back to bite him.

As if he sensed what I was thinking, Ash glared at me, proud and defiant, daring me to say something. He did know, I realized. Mr. Cold, Dark and Broody might be a lot of things, but he wasn't stupid. He knew Faery always came to collect, he knew the dangers of bargaining with a dangerous, exiled faery queen. But he'd done it anyway, because of her. Because of the girl we were both crazy for, who was now far away, beyond our reach.

Meghan.

"Fine." Ash faced the Exile Queen again. "Let's get this over with. What do you need, Leanansidhe?"

Leanansidhe preened. "Just a small request, darling." She smiled. "A teensy favor, hardly worth mentioning. You'll be done in no time."

Which was Faery speak for "huge, ginormous, dangerous ordeal." I frowned, but Leanansidhe continued without looking in my direction.

"I'm afraid I've lost something," she continued with a heartfelt sigh. "Something I prize most dearly. Something that cannot be replaced. I would like you to get it back."

"Lost?" I broke in. "Lost how? Lost like you dropped it down the sink, or lost like it walked out the door and ran off into the woods?"

Leanansidhe pursed her lips and shot me a glance. "Puck, darling, I don't mean to sound rude, but why are you still here? I made a bargain with the Winter prince, and it does not involve you in any way. Shouldn't you be off annoying Oberon or his basilisk of a wife?"

"Ouch." I mock grimaced. "Well, it's nice to feel so wanted." The Exile Queen narrowed her eyes, looking a bit more dangerous, and I grinned back. "Sorry to burst your bubble, Lea, but I was here first. If ice-boy wants me to leave, he can say so. Otherwise, I'm not going anywhere."

I wasn't anyway, and they both knew it, but Leanansidhe looked at Ash. When he didn't say anything, she huffed. "You both are impossible," she stated, throwing up her hands. "Oh, very well. Stay or go, darling, it makes no difference to me. In fact…" She stopped then, midgesture, regarding me with a faint smile that made me nervous. "Now that I think of it, this might be for the best. Yes, of course. This will work out nicely."

Ash and I exchanged a glance. "Why do I get the feeling I'm not going to like what's coming next?" I muttered. He shook his head, and I sighed. "Okay, enough dancing around. For the ten-million-dollar question—what exactly did you lose, Lea?"

"A violin," Leanansidhe exclaimed, as if that were obvious. "It is most upsetting, and I have been a broken wreck because of it." She sniffed, clutching at her heart. "My favorite violin, stolen right out from under me."

"A violin?" I echoed, making a face. "Really? You're calling in a favor for that? What, you don't want to wait until you've lost a pipe organ or something?"

Ash regarded her solemnly. "You want us to find the thief," he said, and it wasn't really a question.

"Well, not really, darling." Leanansidhe scratched the side of her face. "I have a good idea who the thief is, and where they took my precious violin. I simply need you to go there and bring it back."

"If you know who the thief is, and where they took the violin, why do you need us?"

Leanansidhe smiled at me. It was a very evil smile, I thought. "Because, my darling Puck," she crooned, "my precious violin was stolen by Titania, your Summer Queen. I need you and the Winter prince to go into the Seelie Court and steal it back."

Oh, fabulous.

"Well," I said cheerfully, "is that all? Steal something back from the Queen of the Seelie Court? I was just thinking we needed to go on a suicide mission, right ice-boy?"

Ash ignored me, typical of him. "*Queen Titania* has your violin?" he asked, incredulous. "Are you certain it was her?"

"Quite certain, darling." Leanansidhe pulled a cigarette flute out of the air, puffing indignantly. "In fact, this was right after you went back into the Nevernever. The jealous shrew made quite sure I knew who was responsible. She *still* believes I stole her wretched golden mirror, all those years ago, and has never forgiven me for it." Lea paused then, and looked right at me. "I do not know how she has come to think that, pet, do you?"

I blinked innocently. "Why are you looking at me, Lea?" I asked, batting my eyelashes. "Is this the face of such a dastardly villain?" Leanansidhe sighed.

"Anyway," she continued, turning back to Ash, "that is the situation. And as I cannot go into the courts any longer, I need someone who can. That's where you two come in."

"I cannot just walk into Arcadia," Ash said. "I will be trespassing, and by law the Summer King may have me executed if we are discovered. You know this."

"I know, darling," Lea placated. "But I suspect you'll be able to come up with something. Especially if you have Master

Goodfellow with you." She smiled and puffed a smoke rabbit at me. "Unless, of course, he is not up to the challenge. Unless he's *afraid* of his terrible Summer Queen."

"Oh, please. Don't think I don't know what you're doing," I told her, raising an eyebrow. "I'm not dumb enough to fall for that, Lea. Who do you think you're talking to, anyway?"

"I would think this is right up your alley, darling," the Exile Queen returned. "Sneak the Winter prince into Arcadia, right under Titania's nose? Steal something from the bitch queen's room, only to hand it over to her rival? It has 'Robin Goodfellow' written all over it."

Yeah, it did, didn't it? This sounded exactly like one of my pranks, and truthfully, under other circumstances, I'd be more than eager. Titania wasn't fond of me, and the feeling was mutual. Any chance I got to annoy, irritate or piss off the Summer Queen, I'd jump at the opportunity. It wasn't that I *hated* her, she was my queen after all, but she really needed to lighten up. Besides, I'd heard about what she did to Meghan the first time they met, and that needed a little payback. No one turns *my* Summer princess into a deer and gets away with it, even if it is the Seelie Queen. Even if Meghan would never know that I'd defended her.

Right now, however, I understood Ash's impatience. The vow he made to Meghan, his promise to return to her, didn't really have an expiration date, but I figured it would be a long, arduous adventure without all these annoying side quests. We needed to be searching for a certain obnoxious furball, not pranking the Seelie Queen, no matter how entertaining that sounded.

Except, Lea really wasn't giving us a choice.

"So, if you two could get right on that—" she smiled, waving her cigarette flute at us "—I'd be ever so grateful. When you have the violin, just meet me back here, darlings. I'll have my spies monitor your progress. But now, you must excuse me. I'm afraid I left Razor Dan in charge of security while I was gone, and I must return quickly before he or his motley eats someone. Good luck, pets! Don't get yourselves turned into a rosebush!"

Another swirl of glitter and lights, and the Exile Queen was gone.

Ash sighed. "Don't say anything, Goodfellow."

"What? Me?" I grinned at him. "Say something? I'm not the type who would point out that, for once, this absurd situation isn't *my* fault. Of course, *I* know better than to make deals with crazy Exile Queens with goddess complexes. And if I did, I would *expect* them to call in the favor at the worst possible time. But I'm certainly not one to rub it in. That would just be wrong."

Ash pinched the bridge of his nose. "I'm beginning to regret inviting you."

"You wound me deeply, Prince." I laced my hands behind my head, enjoying myself. "Especially since you're gonna need my help to get into Summer. Don't think Oberon and Titania won't notice a Winter prince strolling right into the heart of Arcadia. You'd stick out like an ogre in a china shop."

He scowled, whether from the seemingly impossible task of sneaking into Arcadia or because I just compared him to an ogre, I didn't know. "I assume you have a plan?" he muttered, crossing his arms.

I shot him an evil grin and was rewarded by his brief look of trepidation. "Please. Did you forget who you're talking to, ice-boy? Just leave everything to me."

CHAPTER TWO

FOR OBERON IS PASSING FELL AND WRATH

It was twilight when we crossed the barrier from the mortal realm into the wyldwood. Then again, it was always twilight beneath the wyldwood's huge canopy. Sunlight couldn't penetrate the thick branches of the trees rising hundreds of yards into the air. Unlike the vivid brightness of Summer and the frigid harshness of Winter, the wyldwood was eternally dark, tangled and dangerous. It was constantly changing, so you never knew what you'd run into next.

I loved it. Even though I was Summer, this felt more like home than anywhere else.

"Here we are," I said, stepping beneath a pair of cypresses twisted together to form an arch between the trunks. Around us, the murk of the wyldwood closed in, though a few lone will-o'-the-wisps bobbed through the leaves, looking for lost travelers. Thick black briars crawled between trunks, creeping along the ground as they strangled the life from all other vegetation. "Arcadia isn't far. I would've used the trod that takes us through the quartz caverns, but I'm afraid a lindworm has taken up residence since the last time I was there."

Ash looked around, always alert, and raised an eyebrow. "You do realize you've brought us right into the middle of hedge wolf territory."

Inwardly I winced. I was hoping he wouldn't notice that

small fact. "Well, we'll just have to sneak through nice and quiet."

"Hedge wolves don't have ears," Ash continued. "They hunt by sensing the vibrations in the ground. And in the air. They're probably listening to us right now."

"Do you want to reach the Summer Court or not, princeling?" I challenged, crossing my arms. "This is the quickest way."

A rustle in a bramble patch drew our attention, and we caught a glint of a baleful green eye as something huge and bristly drew away into the shadows.

"And…there it goes to alert the rest of the pack." Ash glared at me. "Why do things always happen when I'm around you?"

"Just lucky, I suppose," I said cheerfully, as we hurried away before the rest of the pack could arrive.

It didn't go as well as I planned. Hedge wolves were ambush predators, though certainly not the nastiest monsters we'd ever faced. But they were tricky bastards, and had the bad habit of looking exactly like an innocent briar patch until you were right up on them and then *boom,* you had this big, wolf-shaped bush lunging at your face. We dodged, ducked and slashed our way past the first dozen or so, avoiding the spiky bushes of death that leaped at us with no warning, or lunged out from the briars. Unfortunately hedge wolves also had the audacity to learn from past mistakes, and they started using strategy and group tactics against us.

We stepped into a clearing just as one of the bristly creatures slid into the brambles ahead of us. As we eased forward, tense and wary, four bushes around us sprang to life and charged. Ash and I spun, going back-to-back instinctively as the spiky creatures lunged from all sides. Ash's sword lashed out, slicing one from the air as I stabbed upward with my dagger, caught a hedge wolf under the jaw and hurled it into its friend. The last wolf met a sudden end on Ash's blade, but then without warning, *another* pair of brambles unfurled and lunged, catching us by surprise this time. I felt the spiky body of a huge wolf slam into me, knocking me flat, as the second wolf chomped down on the prince's sword arm.

I felt a flash of cold behind me and winced. Ice-boy's temper had finally snapped. From the corner of my eye, I saw the prince step forward, pushing his arm farther into the wolf's jaws. There was another flash, and the hedge wolf stiffened as icicles burst out of its muzzle, punching through its jaws like giant needles. Ash grabbed the wolf's muzzle with his free hand and yanked it down with a loud crack, snapping its jaw like a frozen twig. The wolf yelped, curled in on itself and stopped moving.

I scowled at the wolf above me, holding those nasty teeth away from my face. "Ugh, my friend, you really need a breath mint," I told him, sending a pulse of glamour into the brambly monster above me. "Let's see what we can do about that doggie breath."

Vines grew from the wolf's thorny head, slithering over its face. They wrapped around its jaws like a muzzle, clamping them shut, and the wolf's eyes got huge and round. Whimpering pathetically, it leaped away, clawing at its face, and ran off, disappearing into the woods.

Dusting myself off, I climbed to my feet. "Well, that was... interesting," I ventured, deliberately ignoring Ash's glare. His sleeve was tattered, and blood smeared his forearm up to his elbow. "I don't remember hedge wolves ever doing that before."

"If I didn't need you to get into Summer..."

"Oh, but you do," I reminded him, grinning. "Let's not forget that, huh, ice-boy?" His expression darkened even more, but he turned away.

"Come on," Ash said, his voice even colder than normal. "We don't have time for your idiocy now."

"That's what I like about you Winter fey...you're all such scintillating wits, such clever purveyors of words, such wise and frolicsome—"

I ducked as a pinecone zipped by my head with enough force to have done more than muss my hair. A chuckle escaped me. "Always good to know you care, ice-boy." With a quick laugh I sprinted ahead, hoping to get out of range of any colder—and sharper—missiles that might be coming my way.

After the fiasco with the wolves, we separated for a bit, with the frosty prince vanishing into the surrounding woods to clean and bind his arm while I made camp. We couldn't wait for a later time. It was never a good idea to tromp through the wyldwood bleeding; you'd attract everything—and I mean *everything*—in the area. Besides, night was falling, and if we ventured any farther, we'd cross into the Fen Marches. Barghests and bog wraiths roamed those swamps at night, looking for victims, and though I wouldn't mind the challenge of crossing the swamps without being eaten or drowned, we had a mission to complete.

So, I found a grotto surrounded by glowing blue-and-orange fungi and carpeted in moss, cleared out a space and made a fire. Spearing a couple wild mushrooms I'd found earlier, I held the stick over the flames, leaning back contentedly. Ash hadn't returned, but knowing ice-boy he'd probably go hunting once he was done with his arm. I wasn't worried; he'd find this place when he was ready.

I snorted, rolling my eyes. Unless the stubborn idiot decided to strike out on his own again. Hopefully he'd learned his lesson the last time he'd tried something like that.

A weight settled in my gut. I hadn't meant to think of that night, but now that I had, there was no use trying to forget. I gazed into the fire, letting my eyes unfocus, and the memories came creeping back.

It was an evening much like this one, in a place surrounded by glowing flowers, except it was Winter's territory and not the wyldwood. They hadn't seen me, hadn't known I was awake, but I had watched Ash and Meghan that night; listened as he told her he was leaving, alone, to retrieve the Scepter of the Seasons. I'd listened as he told her to go home, back to the mortal world, to forget him. I'd watched both their faces, Meghan's streaked with tears as she tried to be brave; Ash's torment carefully sealed away. I'd said nothing, done nothing, as he'd broken her heart, turned away and walked out of her life.

And...I'd been glad.

I scrubbed a hand over my face, disgusted with myself. I'd been *glad,* because Ash had crushed my princess's heart, because he was gone, and perhaps I could finally get her to look at me. I had been too patient, biding my time, waiting for the day the princess would open her eyes and see her faithful Puck as something more than a goofy friend. I would be more than her guardian and champion and the jester who made her laugh. I would be her everything, if I could.

With a sigh, I yanked the mushrooms from the fire and bit into them aggressively. After Ash had left, I'd tried to mend my princess's shattered heart, the one the stone-cold ice-prince had broken so efficiently. And for one blissful moment, I'd thought I had a chance. The memory of Meghan's kiss was seared into my brain, and I would never forget that day, one of the happiest moments of my life. But, against all odds, Meghan and Ash had found their way back to each other, defying every court of Faery to be together, and I was left behind. In the end, I'd lost her.

So why the hell am I still here?

"Goodfellow."

I jerked up. The deep voice wasn't Ash's; it was far too low and powerful to belong to the frosty ice-prince. I knew it instantly; it was a voice that could command entire forests and woodlands, a voice that I had obeyed long before I ever met the mercurial prince of Winter.

Oberon stared at me over the fire, his eyes glowing amber in the shadows, the expression on his narrow face making the very ground quake in fear.

"Hello, Robin," Oberon murmured, unsmiling. "I fear we must have a little talk."

Aw, crap.

I stood warily, careless grin firmly in place, lacing my hands behind my head. Anyone else would've bowed or knelt or curtsied or at least nodded respectfully, but I'd known the Seelie King for such a long time, such formalities between us were completely useless. If I made any show of respect, Oberon would *know* something was up. As well as I knew him, the Summer King knew *me* just as well.

"Why, Oberon." I nodded, still smiling. "What are you doing here?" I eyed his armor and the great bow across his back. "Out for a little hunt? All by yourself? And you didn't invite me along? I'm hurt."

"Dispense with the foolishness, Robin." The Seelie King waved a hand, and thunder rumbled in the distance. Between us, the campfire flared like it wanted to jump out of the pit, and the plants surrounding us went nuts, writhing and twisting and dancing like they were ecstatic to see him. Such was the immense power of the Summer King. "We both know why I am here, I think. Where is the Unseelie prince?"

"Prince?" I frowned, though my heart started racing under my shirt. How had Oberon learned about Ash so quickly? We weren't even in Arcadia yet. "Why would you think I know anything about the Unseelie prince?" I asked, adopting my best innocent expression. "We're supposed to be enemies. In case you haven't heard, he made this teensy little oath to kill me someday."

None of that was a lie. Live as long as I have, and you become an expert at "dancing around the truth," as some put it. Unfortunately Oberon was no spring chicken, either.

"Robin." He gave me a patient look. "I know. I know what you are planning to do. Do you think I have no inkling of what goes on in my own court? Titania is completely enamored of her new plaything. I know she stole it from Leanansidhe—she makes no secret of where she got it. I was wondering how Leanansidhe would react. Then I hear word of you and the Winter prince entering the wyldwood, heading for Arcadia. Do not think me a fool, Goodfellow. I know you plan to take Leanansidhe's toy back to her."

"However," he went on, before I could think of a new plan, one that would get me out of this without being turned into a bird or a rat for who knew how long, "you may relax, Robin. I am not here to stop you."

I didn't relax. In fact, this just made me more wary. I crossed my arms, raising an eyebrow. "Oh?"

"My lady wife has become quite distracted of late," the Seelie lord continued. "She dotes on her new toy and pays no attention to her court, her subjects or her king. I dislike it."

Aha. And the truth came out. Oberon had always been the jealous type. Anything that took Titania's interest off him was cause for huge arguments between the two Seelie rulers. The last time something like this had happened, Titania had refused to give up a little Indian changeling, and Oberon had ordered me to put a love potion in her eyes so she would forget all about it.

We all know how *that* turned out.

I sighed, knowing where this was going. "Let me guess," I said. "You're going to be 'conveniently absent' from the Summer Court for a while. During which time, Titania's newest toy will mysteriously disappear, and you will have no knowledge of where it could have gotten to."

"I am going hunting with my knights and hounds," the Erlking replied with great dignity. "I care not what Titania does while I am away. However…" He stepped closer, filling the small grotto with his presence. His tall shadow loomed over me as he met my gaze. "I want you to think on something as well, Robin. Remember these words, when you go into Arcadia with your plan, whatever it is."

Oberon leaned in, his voice low and dark, whispering to me over the fire. "If your companion was suddenly…gone," he murmured, and a cold hand grabbed my stomach. "If the Winter prince were no longer here, how long do you think it would be before Meghan Chase came to you?"

I felt the breath whoosh out of me. I stared at Oberon, aghast. He gazed back calmly, unmovable as an oak. "What… are you…?" I couldn't even finish the thought. "Why would you think…?"

"I know you love her," Oberon went on, undeterred. "My daughter. I know your feelings for Meghan Chase, Robin. And I am here to tell you that I approve. I would rather see the two of you together, than her with the son of my ancient enemy."

"Don't ask for much, do you?" My voice came out harsh and raspy, and I turned away from him. All pretense of not knowing Ash had fled, along with most of my composure.

Oberon's gaze followed me as I took a few steps forward, grabbing the boughs of a small pine as I stared into the night. The
fire crackled and popped behind me, and the heat of Oberon's
gaze burned between my shoulders like the hottest flame.

"What do you want me to do?" I muttered, gazing out into
the night. "Stick a knife in his back when he's not looking? Is
that what you're ordering me to do now?" My gut clenched at
the thought. "You don't think Meghan will have something
to say about that? I'd never be able to hide that from her."

"You need not do anything," Oberon continued quietly.
"Only expose the prince when you are in the Summer Court.
Titania will do the rest. His blood will not be on your hands—
you would only be doing what a true servant of the Summer
Court would do. When the prince is gone, Meghan Chase
will come to you for comfort. And all will be as it should."

I couldn't answer. I could almost feel Meghan against me,
shaking with sobs as she mourned her Winter prince. I could
feel my arms around her as I whispered that it would be okay,
that she still had me, and I would never leave. And then I
wanted to kick myself in the head for thinking that.

Oberon watched silently. "Robin Goodfellow," he murmured. "Despite our past differences, I consider you my most
trusted servant. We are old, older than the Winter prince. We
have known each other a long time. But sometimes, I wonder if you realize you are still part of the Summer Court. It is
your home. You do not need anything else."

I clenched my fingers, feeling the branch splinter under my
touch. If Oberon saw, he wasn't concerned.

"My daughter is truly one of us now," he went on. "Immortal. A queen of the fey. You have all the time in the world
to make her fall in love with you. It would not be hard—the
two of you are already very close. I know you would find a
way to be with her, even in the Iron Realm. Once you put

your mind to something, Robin, there is no stopping it. But you must be rid of the Winter prince before she can see you."

I didn't answer. I felt the Seelie King draw back, preparing to go. "The choice is yours, of course," he said as the fire died down and the plants around us stopped their crazy writhing. "My hunt will take me far from Arcadia, far from the whispers of mischief plaguing the Summer Court. Do what you will, Robin, but remember, if you love my daughter, this could be your only chance to be with her in the end. Otherwise, you will lose Meghan Chase to the very one who has sworn to kill you."

A warm wind hissed through the grotto, stirring the fire and the leaves. When it faded, the space was empty, save for me. The Erlking was gone.

CHAPTER THREE

MY MISTRESS WITH A MONSTER IS IN LOVE

Ash returned a few minutes later, sweeping into the grotto without preamble, carrying a brace of rabbit, which showed he had indeed been hunting. He tossed one at my feet, and without a word we began cleaning them, working in silence as the night closed in around us.

Kill Ash? Betray him to the Summer Court? What was Oberon thinking? As if I could do anything like that, even if it was technically Titania who would strike the fatal blow. And she would, too. Ash might be a prince, but Titania was a queen. You did not screw around with the queens of Faery; at least, you didn't go toe-to-toe with them, especially in their own court. Even I knew that. And with Oberon conveniently absent, Titania wouldn't spare the Winter prince. She would utterly destroy him.

I couldn't do that to ice-boy. Even after all the years of bad blood and fighting between us, even though he probably *would* try to kill me someday, and actually go through with it, I couldn't leave him to the mercy of Titania.

But…if I didn't, Meghan would never love me. My princess, the girl I'd do anything for, would never see me, never look at me the way she did Ash.

What made him so special? What did he have that I did not?

"You're awfully quiet."

I blinked and looked up from skinning the hare. Ash knelt a few feet from the fire, bent over his task, his hunting knife working with smooth efficiency. "Wh-what?" I blurted, a little too quickly. *Oh, that was brilliant, Goodfellow. Fix it, now.* "Me?" I continued, feigning shock. "Why, ice-boy, whatever do you mean? Could it be that you're actually concerned?"

He didn't look up as he continued. "You're hiding something," Ash said calmly. "If I can hear myself think through your chatter, that means something is up. Or about to go very, very wrong. Anything you want to tell me, Goodfellow?"

Damn, when had ice-boy become able to read me? That was something I was going to have to work on. "Yes," I answered, forcing a grin. "I think turning you into a squirrel is the easiest way to sneak you into Arcadia. What do you think? Or, if you prefer, I could probably turn you into a mouse. Or a bird. Or a rabbit!" I looked at the skinned carcass in my hands. "Though that might go badly if Titania has her hounds anywhere about…"

"Never mind." Ash sighed, shaking his head. "I'm sorry I said anything."

"Ooh, I know!" I snapped my fingers. "A chameleon! That way you can perch on my collar and blend right in. It's brilliant! And you'd make a very handsome chameleon, don't you think, ice-boy?"

Ash rolled his eyes and bent lower over his task, tuning me out. I kept talking at him, useless, idle words that neither of us took seriously. It was a shield, a barrier for my real thoughts, which I couldn't shut away no matter how hard I tried.

Why are you here?

For Meghan. That was the obvious answer. I was here for Meghan. Because I loved my princess and I wanted her to be happy. Even if her happiness meant she was with someone else. Even if that someone else was my arch rival. I wanted her to be happy.

Don't you think you *could make her happy?*

I could. If she had picked me, I would've given her everything. I was the one who could make her laugh, who showed her the wonders of Summer magic, who had taken a bullet for her without question. (Which, by the way, hurt like a mother.) I was the one who protected her from her cruel human classmates, who walked her to and from the bus every day, who remembered her birthday when everyone else, even her own family, forgot. *Princess, why couldn't you have chosen me? Wasn't I good enough? Or is this my fault for waiting? For not making a move sooner?*

Damn. I'd thought I was over this. I'd thought I was fine in the friend zone, but I couldn't get Oberon's words out of my head. The Erlking, though he could be a manipulative, heartless bastard sometimes, was right. As long as Ash was around, Meghan would never see me as anything more than a friend.

So, you have to ask yourself, Goodfellow, who is more important? The woman you love and would do anything for, or the rival who has vowed to kill you one day?

I watched Ash, brooding into the fire, his back to me as he poked at the flames. My once-friend turned enemy. What would the ruthless Unseelie prince do, were he in my position?

Abruptly I stood, making Ash glance back warily. "Going somewhere, Goodfellow?"

"Just for a walk, princeling. But I'm touched that you care." I smirked at him, and he turned away, back to the fire. I made a face at his shoulder blades. "You know, I'm getting a little tired of talking to a stone wall," I continued, walking to the edge of the grotto. "I think having a conversation with a dead fish would be more rewarding than yapping at you."

"It's never stopped you before."

"See? That's what I'm talking about." I rolled my eyes. "But you'll have to excuse me for needing some time alone, Prince. I have to figure out how I'm actually going to smuggle your icy carcass into the Summer Court."

He looked up sharply. "I thought you had this planned out."

"Oh, *now* we're interested in a conversation, are we?" I chuckled and laced my hands behind my head. "Don't worry, ice-boy, I'll figure something out. I always do."

He watched me, silently. I stared back, still smirking, daring him to say something, to argue. Finally he sighed and turned back to the fire.

"It's your court," I heard him mutter. "You know it better than I."

Yeah, it is, I thought as I drew back and left him, walking into the forest. *It is my court; I'm part of Summer, and you're supposed to be my enemy, Ash. Do you ever think about that? How you're walking into enemy territory with someone who is supposed to be loyal to the Seelie Court?*

I hadn't been entirely straightforward. I already knew how I was going to sneak his royal iciness into Arcadia, right under the nose of Titania and the Summer Guard, without anyone knowing he was there. It would be challenging; Ash was a Winter prince through and through. You couldn't just slap a fake mustache on him and hope for the best, not with his glamour aura. Fortunately I'd been doing this a long time. If anyone could get a Winter gentry into the Summer Court unseen, it would be yours truly.

No, I just needed time alone. Time to think. Time to plan. Time to figure out what I really wanted to do.

"No."

I rolled my eyes. "Ice-boy, come on. At least I'm not turning you into a lemur. This is the only way to get into the Summer Court without everyone knowing you're...you."

"There has to be another way."

"There isn't." I crossed my arms and glared. We had reached the border of Arcadia, and stood at the edge of the wyldwood, gazing across the river to the Erlking's lands on the other side. A wooden bridge, blooming with wildflowers, spanned the gulf, and two Summer Knights guarded the far side. Ash and I stood in a cluster of pine trees, watching them across the river, the churning rapids masking our hissed conversation.

"It's a *disguise,* Ash," I said again. "An illusion. We have to mask your Winter glamour with my Summer glamour, and we have to change your appearance so that people don't freak out the second you walk into the court. Really, it's the only way. How did you think this was going to go?"

Ash sighed, tilting his head back. "You're enjoying this far too much."

"Well." I shrugged, biting down a grin. "I can't say anything there." He glared ice-daggers at me, and I raised my hands. "Do you want to get into Arcadia, or not?"

"Fine." He made a frustrated, helpless gesture. "Do it. Let's get this over with."

"Thought you'd never say so." I pulled him farther back into the trees, calling my magic as I did.

"Hold still," I told him as he crossed his arms and tried to look bored and annoyed. "This won't take long, but I have to weave Summer glamour into the illusion so that it's strong enough to hide your Winter aura. If you were a redcap or an ice-gnome, it wouldn't take very much, but you're *you,* so this is going to be considerably more challenging." I felt my Summer magic settle over him, felt it recoil from the icy chill of the Winter glamour surrounding him like a suit of armor, and frowned. "Ice-boy, stop fighting me. If you want to get this stupid favor over and done with, this is the only way. You have to let me help you." He snorted, and the protective cloak of Winter glamour vanished.

I drew more Summer magic to me and sent it toward the prince, weaving the illusion over and around him. His magic resisted me—say what you want about the Winter prince, at his core, Ash was incredibly strong. He knew who he was, and someone of lesser skill couldn't have turned him into something he was not, even if it was just an illusion.

But I'm not your average trickster, either.

Ash's outline shimmered and started to change. He didn't grow, or shrink, but his hair lengthened, falling down his back, and went from jet-black to the color of wheat. His pale skin turned golden-brown, as if he'd spent a lifetime in the sun, and his cold silver eyes flashed before turning a bright, glittering blue.

His clothes changed as well, the long black coat vanishing into mist, replaced with armor of gold and green, the proud head of a huge stag adorning the breastplate. A fancy gold cloak settled around him, the edges trimmed with leaves, something Ash wouldn't be caught dead in. When it was done, no trace of the Winter prince stood in the spot beneath the pines. A Summer sidhe waited in the shadows, only his scowl bearing the faintest resemblance to the youngest son of Queen Mab.

I put a hand to my mouth in mock delight. "Oh, ice-boy, it's…it's…so you!"

"I'm going to kill you for this," Ash growled, then winced at how his voice sounded, high and clear. I bit my cheek to keep from howling with laughter. If he drew his sword, it would shatter the illusion, and then we'd have to go through all this again.

"Yeah, well, do it later, ice-boy. Remember, you can't use any Winter glamour in there at all, or the spell will unravel.

That includes drawing your sword and throwing icicles at me, so let's not start any fights with any Summer gentry while we're here, okay? We just want to get in, grab the violin and get out again."

Ash nodded. I stepped back and tossed the same illusion over myself, making a pair of almost identical Summer Knights. Glancing at my fellow guard, I grinned. "Ready?"

He sighed again, raking his fingers through his now unfamiliar hair. "Lead the way."

The two knights guarding the bridge nodded politely as we crossed, but other than that didn't even glance at us. I caught one of them hiding a smirk as we passed, but that was understandable, given the circumstances. I didn't think ice-boy had seen it, but I was wrong.

"Who are we supposed to be?" Ash asked as we continued into the lands of the Erlking. Past the bridge, the heat of the summer sun blazed down on us, warming my skin and making me sigh with pleasure. Of all the things in the Seelie Court, I missed the sun the most. The wyldwood was too dark and Tir Na Nog was too cold; only in Arcadia did the sun shine full and bright, and the sweetest apples grow on the trees over the thorn fence, always ripe for the picking. If you could get past the two cranky giants who owned the orchard, that is.

"Oh," I said, grinning. "Right. Names. Well, you're Sir Torin, and I'm Sir Fagan, and we're two hedge knights who travel all over the Nevernever on quests of glory for our king and court. You know, we right wrongs and slay dragons and search for mythological treasures, stuff like that."

"So, they're well respected."

"Well..." I scratched the back of my head. "Not exactly."

Ash stared at me. "What do you mean, not exactly?"

"Ever read *Don Quixote?*" I asked. And Ash closed his eyes, indicating that, yes, he had read it. I snickered. "They're very eager," I continued, trying not to laugh at the look on his face, "and they do have very noble intentions, I will give them that. But those two couldn't find their way out of a broom closet without a map. It's sheer dumb luck that they haven't gotten themselves killed or eaten by now. They keep begging Oberon to send them on noble, important quests to prove their worth, and Oberon ends up giving them some ridiculous mission just to get them out of his hair."

"And, of course, these are the identities you stole for us."

"It's perfect, don't you think?" I flung my arms out grandly. "Sir Torin and Sir Fagan are almost never at court, the other knights usually avoid them and we have a reason to go see Queen Titania, to announce the completion of our most recent quest."

"And if the real Torin and Fagan happen to be there?"

"Well." I shrugged, annoyed with his logic. "Then we'll improvise."

I could tell Ash didn't like it; he was always the plan-for-anything type, and usually found my play-it-by-ear tactics annoying and disturbing. But he didn't say anything more, and it wasn't long before we came to the huge mound of grassy earth that marked the entrance into Oberon's court. Thick brambles surrounded the rise, though they parted easily before us, letting us through, and we walked toward the side of the hill without breaking stride.

"Anything else I should know about?" Ash muttered as we approached the mound side by side. "Any small detail you conveniently overlooked that might come up while we're here?"

"Um…" I shot him a sideways glance. "Just one more small thing." He raised an eyebrow, and I chewed my lip. Oh, he was not going to like this. "Torin and the queen are rumored to be…um…involved."

"What?"

But then we were through the side of the hill and stepping into a courtyard teeming with Summer fey—the heart of Arcadia.

Music played, one of my favorite tunes about sun and shadows and growing things, and lying at the bottom of a cool stream while the fish whispered to you. Trees lining the edge of the courtyard sighed softly, moving their branches to the song, and the thousands of flowers blooming everywhere swayed gently in rhythm. Dryads, satyrs, gnomes and other Summer fey milled about the open space, sitting on benches, talking or dancing together in the grass. Yep, I was definitely home.

I could feel Ash's glare on the back of my head, and knew he was ready to kill me, but the fey closest to the edge of the courtyard spotted us and leaped to their feet.

"Be nice, ice-boy," I said through clenched teeth, plastering a grin on my face as the crowd came forward. "They're coming, so smile and don't stab your partner. It's showtime."

"Sir Fagan!" a female satyr exclaimed, skipping up to us. Her hooves clopped daintily over the cobblestones. "Sir Torin! You've returned, and you're alive. Welcome back!"

"How were your travels, Sir Fagan?" asked a nymph, giving me a sly smile. "Did you manage to get the Treasure of the Moonbeast this time? Did you slay the dreaded Worm of the Fellswamp? Tell us of your adventures."

"Yes, yes," echoed a brownie. "What happened?"

"Yes, tell us!"

"Tell us your story!"

I raised a hand. "Enough, fair people, enough! There will be time enough for stories and songs and tales of daring-do, but that time is not now." They quieted down, looking disappointed, and I gave a tired sigh. "Sir Torin and I have traveled far and wide, and we are weary. We have many tales to tell, yes, but first we must speak to our lord."

"Lord Oberon has left court for a time," the satyr explained, watching me with big hazel eyes. Her gaze abruptly flickered to "Torin" beside me, and she grinned. "But Queen Titania is here, and I'm sure she would be pleased to receive you. Would you like me to find a messenger to announce your return?"

"That would be much appreciated, fair lady," Ash said at my shoulder, startling me. The satyr beamed and skipped off, and we made our way toward the gate separating the court-yard from Oberon's inner sanctum. Summer fey smiled at us and nodded or hid grins and whispers behind their hands. We ignored them. So far, so good. Step one, getting into the Summer Court, had gone off without a hitch. Now all we had to do was find Leanansidhe's violin and get out of Arcadia without blowing our cover. And, knowing the Summer Queen and her obsessive tendencies, it would probably be somewhere in her private chambers. That was going to make things...challenging.

I glanced at Ash. I could think of *one* way to get into the queen's bedroom, but he would probably flip out if I suggested that, so I kept my mouth shut.

"What?" Ash sighed. I blinked.

"Huh?"

"You're giving me that look," he continued as we stopped several yards from the gates, which were guarded by two mas-sive trolls in red and brass uniforms. "That look that says you have a plan and I'm not going to like it. At all."

"Well...yes, I do have an idea..."

"And?"

"And...you're not going to like it. At all."

He sighed again, rubbing his eyes. "I think I already have

an inkling of what you're going to say," he muttered, looking pained. I shrugged.

"It *would* be the easiest way to see if she's keeping the violin in her chambers. You could even offer to serenade her."

"If Titania discovers me, I'll be dead before I have a chance to draw my sword."

And wouldn't that be a tragedy? "Ice-boy," I said, grinning, "please. As if I would let that happen. Your disguise is foolproof. Just don't use Winter glamour, and you'll be fine."

Ash ran his fingers through his hair and leaned closer. "Puck," he said in a harsh voice. "I…I can't do it. This isn't a game anymore. You're asking me to seduce the queen of the Summer Court. This is high treason and besides…" He looked away, his face tightening. "I'm still Meghan's knight. My vow…"

"Do you want to get the violin back, or not?" He actually looked stricken, and I felt a little sorry for the guy. "Look, iceboy," I whispered, "I don't expect you to take her to bed, or even kiss her. Just the thought of that…*ugh!*" I shuddered and pushed the thought away, drawing my dagger in a smooth, furtive motion. "Oh, great, now that image is stuck in my head forever. Just…flirt a little. Be charming. Tell her about your 'adventures.' Then if she gets too touchy-feely, excuse yourself and get out. I'll take care of the rest."

"I don't like it."

"I didn't think you would. Hold still." Swiftly I brought the dagger up, cutting a strand of his long hair before he could react. It dropped into my palm, and I curled my fist around it. "Perfect. Much obliged, ice-boy."

Ash reared back, eyes flashing, fingers going to his sword. I shot him a warning glare, and he remembered himself, dropping his hand from the hilt.

"What are you doing, Goodfellow?" he snarled.

"Keep it down, Prince." I studied the strand between my fingers, watching it change from pale blond to jet-black, and smirked. "It's all part of the plan, don't worry."

With a loud creak, the gates swung open and a satyr in a herald's uniform padded through, beckoning to us urgently. "Well, here we go, ice-boy. Try to keep it together in front of the queen."

CHAPTER FOUR

ILL MET BY MOONLIGHT, PROUD TITANIA

We walked through the gate into the flowering tunnel of thorns on the other side. I breathed in deeply and sighed, loving the potent, fragrant smells of the forest. Beside me, Ash did not look as enamored. His posture was stiff, tense. I guess I couldn't blame the guy, walking into the heart of enemy territory, surrounded by Summer fey, unable to use his magic or his weapon. I might've felt bad for him, if the whole thing wasn't so darn amusing.

The tunnel ended in a curtain of vines. Dark shapes and a haunting, eerie tune filled the air on the other side. The melody pulled at my stomach, a sad, sweet sound, before I shook it off. Looking at Ash, and the pale determination on his face, I gave him a savage grin.

"No turning back now, ice-boy," I muttered, and swept through the curtain into the room beyond.

Oberon and Titania's throne room was a massive clearing with cathedral-size trees creating a vaulted ceiling overhead. Thick moss carpeted the floor, and briars hemmed in the edges of the clearing. A waterfall trickled into a crystal pool, where will-o'-the-wisps and piskie lights danced, bobbing through the clearing like drunken stars. Summer gentry, in their ridiculously fancy outfits, sat or stood around a pair of thrones in the middle of the clearing, one empty, but the other quite occupied.

Oberon wasn't here, of course, but Queen Titania sat on her throne with the smug, lazy grace of a cat overseeing a flock of mice.

Everyone says the Summer Queen is stunning, beautiful, absolutely captivating. Yeah, I guess she is, but so is a volcanic eruption, and probably less volatile. Working in the Seelie Court is certainly interesting at times, to say the least. The Summer rulers have caused floods and wildfires in the mortal world with their arguments, and Titania once threatened to sink an entire village into the mud because of a misunderstanding over a missing hairpin. Fortunately Oberon can usually calm her rages and temper tantrums...when he decides to involve himself, that is. Many times, he turns a blind eye to his wife's activities—until they affect him, of course.

None of the nobles in the clearing seemed to notice us as we came in, their attention riveted to Titania, or something at the foot of her throne. Ash took in the room in one smooth, practiced glance, and his eyes suddenly widened. I followed his gaze, and my heart sank.

The music we'd heard in the tunnel, the slow, lilting melody that was haunting and dark and beautiful, wasn't played by any of Titania's harp girls or servants or faery musicians. The melody had been strange at first, because it was of a kind not normally heard in the faery courts. It wasn't a harp, or a flute or any of the strange magical instruments found only in our world.

It was a violin. Being played by a mortal girl no older than eight, her small body tight as she sawed and ripped at the strings. She wore a simple black dress, and her long, mahogany hair was the same color as the instrument in her arms. Her eyes were closed as she played for her inhuman audience, her thin body swaying back and forth, ignorant of the queen's dainty white hand resting atop her skull.

And I knew. Leanansidhe's prized possession, and Titania's newest plaything, wasn't the instrument in the girl's tiny, skillful fingers.

It was the girl herself. This was our "violin."

Well, things just got a lot more complicated.

The song came to an end, and the girl's eyes opened, dark and serious and a tad bemused, as if she wasn't quite sure if this was a dream or not. The gentry tittered, clapping their hands and breathing small sighs of admiration, while Queen Titania gave a small, pleased smile.

"That was beautiful, Vi," she purred, combing the girl's hair with her fingers. The small human blinked and gazed up at the faery queen with solemn eyes.

"The ending was flat," she said regretfully. Her voice was reedy and breathless, as if the violin had taken all the volume from her. "And it was rushed in the beginning." She sniffed and bit her bottom lip. "I'm sorry, I wanted to play it better."

"Oh, my dear, it was perfect." Titania smoothed the hair back from the girl's face. "Wasn't it?" she added, looking fiercely at the nobles, who tittered and nodded and made appropriate noises of agreement. Beside me, Ash muttered something inaudible and shot me a sideways glance.

"A child," he muttered. "Leanansidhe's 'toy' is a child. How are we going to get her out, Goodfellow?"

"I'm thinking."

"Think faster."

"Now," the queen continued, tugging at the girl's dress, straightening it, "would you like something to eat, my darling? Then, if you want, you can play for us again after you've eaten."

Vi sniffled. "Can I have cake?"

"Of course, my dear." The queen smiled indulgently. "Would you like that?"

The girl nodded eagerly. Titania bent down and kissed her cheek. "Then I will have Cook bring you the sweetest cakes she can find."

The child beamed. Titania snapped her fingers, and a brownie appeared at her arm. "You heard her," she told it. "Tell Cook we want her best and sweetest cakes, as quickly as possible."

"The little strawberry ones," Vi added, smiling up at the queen. Titania nodded at the brownie, who bowed and scampered off, fleeing into the hedge. The queen chuckled and patted the girl's head like she would a favorite small dog.

"Isn't she darling?" she mused, and the nobles were quick to agree. "Such talent, and at such a young age. I don't know how Leanansidhe could stand to give her up."

She laughed, and the gentry laughed with her. The girl sat there with her hands in her lap, gazing vacantly at the faeries surrounding her. As the chuckles died down, the queen finally spotted us at the edge of the clearing, and her blue eyes lit up with delight.

"Oh, but my dears, we are being very rude." The queen sat up, raising a slender hand to us. "We have esteemed visitors, returned from yet another impossible quest. Sir Fagan, Sir Torin, please step forward."

I saw Ash draw in a quiet breath, steeling himself, and bit down my anticipation. "Here we go," I whispered, throwing out my chest. "Just follow my lead."

Chin up, chest puffed out, I raised my head and swaggered toward the waiting queen.

Titania laced her fingers together and watched us approach, a small smile on her perfect lips. But her gaze wasn't fastened on me, but the "Summer knight" at my side. Ash, much to his credit, was playing his part, keeping his head up and a faint, proud smile on his face, his gaze only for the queen. *Good,* I thought as we reached the foot of the throne and bowed. *Keep looking at ice-boy. Pay no attention to the buffoon next to him. Pay no attention to the man behind the curtain.*

"Sir Fagan." Titania spared me a cursory glance. "Sir Torin." She smiled widely at Ash. "Welcome back. I apologize for my husband—he is away from court at the moment and I am not sure when he will return."

"We are sorry to have missed Lord Oberon," Ash said, his voice confident and clear, and slightly pompous. He took the queen's outstretched hand and brought it to his lips. "But to be in your presence, my lady—that is worth all the blessings of our good king."

I resisted the urge to stare at him, biting down a grin. *Well, look at you, ice-boy. Playing the part, after all. I forgot you know how to do this, too, if pushed hard enough.*

"Oh, Sir Torin." Titania blushed, somehow managing to look embarrassed and self-conscious even as she preened. "You are such a flatterer. And we are so glad that you have returned. You must have stories to tell, my dear Sirs. The court is most anxious to hear your newest adventures." She clasped her hands together. "I simply insist you join us in the Grand Dining Hall tonight. Let us toast your noble quests, recognize your great deeds and you can hear my newest acquisition play for you." She stroked the girl's hair again, but Ash didn't even glance at the human.

"That would please us greatly, your majesty."

"It is decided, then." Titania nodded regally, dismissing us. "We will meet again tonight. I am most anxious to hear what you have been up to in the time you've been gone."

We bowed, and Ash reached down a second time and

brought the back of the queen's hand to his lips. "Until tonight, my lady," he murmured, and we left the queen's court, feeling her eyes on us until we ducked back into the tunnel.

I held in my laughter until we were well away from the throne room, before turning on Ash with a gleeful cackle. "What was *that,* ice-boy? Since when did you get to be such a charmer? I didn't think you had it in you."

His face flamed. "I did what I had to do," he said, crossing his arms and looking away. "We got close to the queen and saw what Leanansidhe sent us for. Now the question is, how do we get her away from Titania? How do we get her out of the Summer Court?"

"Worry not, ice-boy. I already have a plan." I flashed him my best impish smile, rubbing my hands together. "One brilliant Goodfellow prank, coming right up."

The Grand Dining Hall wasn't really a hall, more of a marble courtyard underneath the stars, surrounded on all sides by a giant hedge maze. In the very center, surrounded by hedgy unicorns and lions, the Summer Queen held her most extravagant parties at a long white-and-gold table, very reminiscent of a certain Mad Hatter's tea party. To be invited to one of these affairs, you had to be a personal favorite of the queen, or the next one on her figurative chopping block. Needless to say, Oberon never attended.

The labyrinth was easy for "Sir Torin" and I to navigate, despite a couple statues that tried pointing us in the wrong direction, and all too soon we reached the table in the center of the maze. It was surrounded by Seelie gentry in their fanciest clothes, gowns of feathers and rose petals, cloaks of baby's breath and spiderwebs. And at the head of the table, her golden hair braided with flowers and sparkling moonstones, the Summer Queen smiled and waved us over.

Vi, the mortal child, sat in a chair on the queen's right, solemnly plowing her way through an impressive fountain of pink-and-blue cake. Her violin sat on a pillow, held by a waiting satyr behind the girl's chair. She didn't look up as we approached, but the queen gave us a welcoming smile.

"Now," Titania purred after introductions were made and the rest of the gentry were settled, "let us hear of your latest adventures, knights. Sir Torin, would you like to regale the court with your mighty quests and deeds?"

Beside me, Torin lowered his head. "Ah, my lady, nothing would make me happier." He nodded to me with a small frown. "However, I believe Sir Fagan has won the right to sing of our adventures this evening. We made a bet on who would have the honor, and I lost. If it pleases you, I will leave the storytelling to him."

Titania pouted a bit then brightened. "Very well, then, Sir Torin. I insist you keep me company for the evening. It is the least you can do." She gestured to the empty spot on her left. "Do sit, Sir Torin. Relax for a while. Let my servants attend you for a change."

"My lady, it is not proper—"

"I will decide what is proper in my court or not, Sir." Titania's voice was like a velvet coating over steel. "As you can see, my husband is not here, so I have the need to be protected from the riffraff at court. What better protection than having a famed knight errant at my side?" She gestured to the seat, more firmly this time. "Sit, Sir Torin. That is an order from your queen."

Sir Torin sat. Vi stared at him over the table, frosting covering her mouth, but Titania didn't even glance at the child. Her attention seemed to have completely shifted to the knight sitting at her elbow. Torin met the queen's gaze and gave a hesitant, furtive smile.

"Well, Sir Fagan," Titania said without looking at me, "it seems we are to listen to you sing of your adventures tonight. I do hope it will prove entertaining."

Oh, you have no idea. "Certainly, my queen." I grinned. Spinning away from the happy couple, I marched to the center of the courtyard, pulling out a lute as I did. Sir Fagan—the real Sir Fagan, that is—could do a fair job of strumming a tune, but tonight would be his most memorable performance yet.

My fingers flew over the lute strings, and I sang about two knights, sent by their king to retrieve the Treasure of the Moonbeast, only neither of them knew what it was. After weeks of searching and getting no answers, it was decided that the Treasure of the Moonbeast must be on the moon itself, and they needed the great pearl at the bottom of the Mermaid Queen's ocean, rumored to be able to draw the moon down from the sky if taken from water. Both knights nearly drowned, fighting off waves of sirens and mermen as they fled back to dry land, but they did manage to steal the pearl. However, when they held it up to see if it would really capture the moon as the legends stated, the pearl slipped from their fingers, rolled off a cliff and fell back into the ocean from whence it came.

The Summer gentry roared with that tale, laughing and clapping, calling for more. I glanced at the head of the table and saw Torin and the queen, deep in conversation, paying little attention to me. Titania was leaning close to the knight, speaking in whispers, and Torin was nodding solemnly. Perfect.

"This next song," I announced, as my audience fell silent, "is a tale about lost love, and how we must never take for granted what we have right now."

This time, the song was soft and slow, full of yearning, about a knight who loved a noblewoman but feared expressing his love because of their difference in rank. It was a sad tune, and I made it as heart-wrenching as I could, weaving a bit of glamour into the notes for a bigger impact. I noticed two gentry who listened, enraptured, then stood and wandered away into the maze together.

I kept my gaze on Torin and the queen as I sang. They didn't look up, but Titania's head moved closer and closer to the knight, until only a few inches separated them. Sir Torin didn't shy away once, capturing her hand as it reached up to his face, pressing it to his lips.

Abruptly the queen stood. Beckoning to a servant, she whispered something to him, pointing to Vi as she did. The satyr bowed his head and returned to the girl, taking away the cake and motioning her to follow. As the human and the satyr left the party, I grinned to myself.

Stage one, complete. Guess Vi isn't going to be entertaining us this evening, after all. Now, my Summer Queen. You've sent away your little pet; are you going to take the bait?

Titania stretched luxuriously, then stepped up and lightly touched Torin's shoulder, bending down to whisper in his ear. Yes, she was. Trailing her fingers down his arm, the queen stepped away, gave him a sultry look and sauntered off into the hedge maze.

Torin waited a few heartbeats, then looked up at me. I nodded.

Casually the knight rose, glancing warily around. No one was paying attention to him, their focus riveted on me, or each other. Several nobles were dancing now, in groups of twos and threes, their expressions dreamy and dazed. No one saw the Summer knight step away from the table and wander into the hedge maze after the queen. I kept the song going for several stanzas after he disappeared, then finally brought it to a close.

And that's stage two. I gazed around at my handiwork. *Yep, you still have it, Goodfellow. Amazing what one teensy love song can do to weaker minds. Too bad we don't have more time; it's been a while since I've made anyone dance for three days straight.*

Now, on to the last stage.

I bowed to my audience. "Everyone!" I called as Summer gentry looked around in dazed confusion. "You've been a fabulous audience! But I'm afraid I really must dash! When the screaming starts, try not to stampede all at once. You all have a wonderful rest of the evening!"

They blinked at me, not really hearing a word I'd said, still caught up in their swirling emotions. I bowed once more and hurried, unchallenged, into the maze.

I knew where Torin and the queen would be. I'd been through this maze countless times, usually to crash the queen's party or spy on the queen's guests. Sometimes it was at Oberon's request, sometimes it was for my own amusement. But I knew where I would find the wayward couple: at the hidden spring in the northeast corner of the maze, where Titania took all her "prospects."

I heard their voices as I approached, slipping past the countless lions, hounds and unicorn topiaries lining the paths. Peeking around a mermaid fountain, I spotted the queen and the Summer knight near the edge of the pool. Titania was very close to Torin and had a slender hand on the knight's chest, leaning close.

"My lady," the knight was saying. "I...I cannot do this... anymore. What of your husband? Lord Oberon—"

"Lord Oberon," Titania murmured, putting a finger against his mouth, "is not here. And what Oberon does not know—" she leaned in closer, her lips parting "—will not hurt him."

I took a deep breath. *Well, here we go.*

"You are so right, Queen Titania!" Dropping my disguise, I stepped out from behind the fountain. "What Oberon doesn't know will not hurt him. Why, I tell myself that almost every single day. It's so nice to know we have so much in common."

Titania jumped, stepping back from Torin, her eyes going wide as she saw me. "Robin Goodfellow!" she spat, curling her lips into a grimace of hate. For just a moment, she hesitated, then rose up to her full height, glaring down her nose at me. "How *dare* you! How dare you come here uninvited, especially when my husband is away from court! Or…did he put you up to this?" She gave me a look of black contempt. "You've always been his little spy, his good little watchdog, always there for the tasks he finds too distasteful to do himself. Pathetic. You both are pathetic!" Lightning flickered overhead, streaking down to smash into a bush, setting it aflame. I resisted the urge to wince. In the flickering shadows, the Summer Queen's eyes blazed blue-white. "Perhaps the great Robin Goodfellow will meet with an unfortunate accident," the queen mused, the wind snapping at her hair as she raised a pale hand. "Something that will silence him completely for a few centuries."

"Now, now." I waggled a finger, giving her a fearsome smile. "I would think you'd want to reward me, my good queen. After all, I just stopped you from making a highly embarrassing mistake. You've been duped, my lady. Taken advantage of. You have an enemy right under your nose, and you didn't even realize it."

Torin glared stonily. I ignored him and faced Titania, who was watching me with wary, but curious, distrust. "What trickery are you playing at, Goodfellow?" she asked.

"Believe what you will," I continued, staring her down. "Call me what you want, hate me if you will, but I'm still a faithful servant of the Summer Court. This is my home, and I would do anything to protect it. And when it comes to my attention that we've been invaded by an enemy, I can't sit by and do nothing, even if it means warning *you*."

"What are you—" The queen straightened abruptly. "Lean-ansidhe," she hissed, narrowing her eyes. "She sent someone. Someone to steal my human pet. Where—"

"Right under your nose, my queen. Just like I told you." And before either of them could react, I spun on Torin and stripped away glamour, shredding his Summer disguise and revealing the form of the Winter prince to the Summer Queen. "*There's* your enemy, Queen Titania. Do with him what you will."

CHAPTER FIVE

IF WE SHADOWS HAVE OFFENDED

Betrayal.

That was the first look Ash turned on me, his silver eyes wide with shock and disbelief. I grinned at him, crossing my arms, as Titania's outraged shriek rose above the howl of the wind. Before Ash could do anything, she swept her arm down, and a streak of lightning slammed into the prince's chest, hurling him away. He smashed into the mermaid statue and crumpled at the base, dazed.

"Ouch." I winced. "That looked painful. Hit him again, just to make sure he stays down."

Titania spun on me. "You!" she raged, her eyes seriously scary now. I blinked at her innocently and took a step back. "I do not know how you did this, or why, but this is one of your pranks, I know it! What foul mischief do you have up your sleeve this time?"

"Me?" I grinned and laced my hands behind my head. "You give me too much credit, Queen Titania."

"I am not a fool, Robin Goodfellow." Titania loomed over me, lightning flashing threateningly overhead. "The Winter prince is cunning and strong, but he could not have acted alone. You snuck the prince into Arcadia—you are the only one whose glamour is strong enough to hide him from me. Before I make the son of Mab beg for mercy, I want to know why you did this! You were *friends* once, long ago. Why this sudden change of heart?"

I stuck my hands deep in my pockets, looked the Seelie Queen right in the eye and muttered, "Because. He fell in love with *my* princess."

Silence for a few heartbeats. At the base of the fountain, Ash stirred, but the Queen's attention was solely on me.

"Ah." Titania actually smiled, the scary look in her eyes fading slightly. "And now, it makes sense. Robin Goodfellow, you *do* have a bit of a nasty streak in you, after all. Oberon's little dog has some bite." The queen tittered, giving me an appraising look. "I'm almost proud of you."

"I didn't do it for you," I replied. "I did it for Meghan. And I did it for me. And if you want to make ice-boy pay for your humiliation, you'd better do something about him real soon. He's on his feet already."

Titania spun. Ash stood beside the fountain, glaring at me as he backed away, his sword drawn. The Summer Queen sent another bolt of lightning at him, but Ash ducked behind the fountain and the bolt smashed several fish into marble fragments. The queen hissed in fury, and I gave Ash a lazy smile.

"Better run, ice-boy!"

The Winter prince was already going. Diving away, he rolled behind a lion shrub as another bolt came slashing down, barely missing him. Leaping to his feet, he tore off into the maze.

"Stop him!" The Summer Queen raised her arms, glamour whirling and snapping about. "Stop him!" she called again, as the hedge lions, hounds, unicorns and other topiaries stirred, then leaped off their bases with howls and roars. "Go!" shrieked the queen, flinging out a hand. "Find the Winter prince. Hunt him down and tear him to pieces!"

The bushes roared and scattered into the maze. I heard

yelps and screams coming from the center of the courtyard as the nobles' party was rudely interrupted. Titania waited a moment, and then turned on me.

"I will find him!" she snarled, eyes flashing electric blue in the darkness. "He will pay for this humiliation! Goodfellow, call the guards, the knights, the servants. Alert the rest of Arcadia. The Winter prince will not leave this court alive!"

I bowed. "Certainly, my queen," I drawled. "And may I suggest squads of at least four to six knights if you're going to have them looking for ice-boy? Unless you want to find frozen shish kebabs littering the halls all the way to the wyldwood. Ash is pretty handy with that sword."

Titania's eyes glowed as she raised her hand. With a flash of lightning, the smell of burned earth and smoke rose up from the ground, and the Summer Queen was gone.

I took a deep breath and clenched my fists to stop the shaking. *Final stage, complete. That was easier than I thought. Now… if only the other part went off without a hitch…*

"Nice performance, Goodfellow," said a voice at my back.

I turned wearily as Ash stepped out of the shadows of the maze, still wearing his disguise as a Summer knight. He carried a sleeping child, held tightly to his chest. Vi snored softly, smears of blue frosting around her mouth. With the amount of sleeping powder she'd gorged on tonight, she would probably be out for several hours. All that flirting with the huge troll cook in the kitchen, just to sneak the powder into the frosting mix, hadn't gone to waste at least.

"Oh, good, you found her." I tried to grin at him, but I was feeling oddly tired at the moment. "Yeah, it *was* quite the performance, wasn't it? Good enough to fool a faery queen and the entire Summer Court. This will probably go down in history." Ash didn't smile, and I sighed. "So, how much of that did you hear?"

"Enough."

"That so?" I gave him a half weary, half challenging look. "And do you have anything to say about that, ice-boy?"

"No." He shook his head solemnly. "You said what you had to. You did what was required to get the job done."

"Oh? That's awfully generous of you, Prince."

"None of it was a lie, Goodfellow." Ash gave me a hard stare. "Nothing you said or did was against your nature. That's why Titania believed you so quickly. I would have believed it, too."

I sighed. "Good to know where I stand," I muttered, and scrubbed a hand over my eyes. "Well, come on, then, ice-boy. Let's get out of here before Titania catches your doppelganger and finds nothing is holding him together but twigs, string and a bit of your hair. With all the commotion going on, it should be easy to sneak out nice and quiet."

Not entirely. Thanks to my little Ash clone, the Summer Court was in chaos, scrambling over each other looking for him, but our escape wasn't entirely without problems. We ran into a lion topiary that needed to be cut down, and ice-boy's disguise finally shattered when he drew his sword to battle the creature. Of course, right after that, we ran into a squad of Summer knights and played a rousing game of catch-me-if-you-can before we finally escaped into the hedge. With the knights hot on our heels, I led us down a twisting tunnel of bramble that got smaller and smaller until it abruptly came to an end.

Ash muttered a curse and looked around as the sound of booted feet crashed toward us through the branches.

"Did you take a wrong turn, Goodfellow?" he growled.

"Relax, ice-boy. I know what I'm doing." Fishing under an old log, I pulled out a simple green cloth, ripped and torn with use. Shaking it open, I hung it on a pair of thorns then peeled it back to reveal a narrow hole in the brambles. Ash ducked through carrying Vi, and I followed, tearing the cloth away as I did. The wall of thorns vanished, and the sounds of pursuit cut out as suddenly as if you flicked off the TV. As darkness closed in, I sighed in relief.

"Where are we?" Ash whispered close by.

I snapped my fingers, and a cheerful fire leaped up in a stone fireplace, illuminating a small log cabin with wooden floors and pillars made of live trees. A thatch roof covered the ceiling, and small animals peered at us from the corners, more curious than afraid.

"Welcome," I said, grinning at Ash, "to my humble abode."

Ash gazed around the tiny cabin in wary amazement. "This is *your* house, Goodfellow?"

"One of several." I shooed a fox out of an armchair and sank down into it with a sigh. "I like to have a little place I can retreat to, to escape the craziness of the court, to relax without anyone knowing where I am."

"To hide out when Oberon is ready to kill you."

"Ouch, ice-boy. Be nice in my home, will you? Don't make me regret bringing you here." I leaned back in the chair and propped my feet on a nearby footstool, crossing my legs. "Don't worry, this place is in the mortal world—no one from court can sense where we are anymore."

Ash looked relieved. "So, we're out," he murmured, glancing back at the wall where, a few seconds ago, we had supposedly come straight through the wood. "We found the 'violin' and got out of the Summer Court." He looked at the sleeping girl in his arms and sighed. "So, I guess the only question is, what do we do now?"

I pointed to a bed in the corner. He approached and laid the mortal atop the covers, surprisingly gentle for a Winter prince. I didn't remember him being so careful before he met

Meghan. Vi stirred a little and muttered "Mommy" in her sleep, but didn't wake up.

"Leanansidhe will be waiting for us," I said as the fox jumped into my lap and curled up again, wrapping its bushy tail around its nose. I absently stroked its short red fur. "She's probably on her way right now."

"Yeah." Ash sighed, crossing his arms as he watched the girl. "How do you want to do this, Goodfellow?"

I thought a few moments, then swung my feet off the stool and rose, dumping the fox to the floor again. It gave an annoyed bark and trotted out the door. "Don't worry, ice-boy," I said cheerfully, and walked upstairs to grab something. "I have one last little trick up my sleeve."

CHAPTER SIX

AND ROBIN SHALL RESTORE AMENDS

"Darlings!"

Standing in the long grass in front of the cabin, Leanansidhe beamed at us as we stepped outside, the girl still fast asleep in the prince's arms. "You found her, darlings! I knew you would. I had complete faith in your abilities. Oh—" she sighed, bringing a hand to her chest "—I wish I could see the look on Titania's face when she discovers her little toy is missing."

Ash stepped forward. "Our deal is finished," he said firmly. "We found what was stolen and brought it back to you. I've upheld my end of the bargain. I owe you nothing else."

"Of course, darling." Leanansidhe smiled at him. "You've done a marvelous job. So, if you would just set her down there, dove, my servants will take her off your hands."

Ash didn't release the girl. I felt him hesitate, then take a furtive breath. "Now," he continued in a quiet voice, "what will it take for you to let her go?"

"What?" Leanansidhe blinked, staring at the Winter prince, who faced her calmly. "*What* did you say, pet? I'm not quite sure I heard you correctly."

I quickly stepped up beside him.

"She's a kid, Lea." The Exile Queen spun on me, bristling

like an enraged cougar. "You can't keep her like this. She has a family, somewhere. She needs to go home."

"*I* am her home, pet." Leanansidhe swelled indignantly, her copper-gold hair whipping madly around her. "And the girl belongs to me! Ash, darling." She glanced at the Winter prince. "I cannot believe this. Your own queen does far worse to the humans in her court. And you—I know what *you* have done to mortals over the years, you and Goodfellow both! How dare you judge me? Have you gone soft, darlings? Have you forgotten that we are fey?"

Jeez, pissing off two volatile faery queens in one day. We must hold some kind of record. I stepped up before Lea could turn Ash into a harpsichord.

"Not at all," I said quickly, smiling in the face of the enraged Exile Queen. "Calm down, Lea. It's not like we're going to take the kid and run. We're prepared to offer a trade."

Leanansidhe calmed somewhat. "A trade, darling?" she mused, feigning disinterest, though I knew she was curious. She couldn't help it; it was part of our nature. "And what, may I ask, could you possibly offer for the girl's freedom? The price will be high, my pet, just so you know. The girl is one of my favorites, after all. I'm afraid that your offer will have to be quite—"

I reached into my shirt and held up a mirror, letting it flash in the sun. A small, golden hand mirror, with jeweled flowers around the rim and silver vines curled around the handle. It sang as I brought it out, a sweet, piercing note that made all the nearby birds start chirping and drew a curious pair of deer out of the forest.

Leanansidhe's eyes went wide. "That...that is..." She blinked at me, astonished, then threw back her head and laughed. "Oh, Robin, you naughty, brilliant boy. You *did* take it, after all. How in the world did you manage?"

"That," I said, "is a very long story. One that should be told another time." I tossed the mirror in the air and caught it again, holding it out to Leanansidhe. "So, Lea, do we have a trade, or not?"

"Take the girl back to her family, pet." Leanansidhe plucked the mirror from my hand with obvious delight. "I found her in some tiny little town in the Ozarks. She can probably tell you where she lives…I haven't had her for very long. In any case, I believe our business here is concluded."

"One more thing, if you would." Ash stepped forward before the Exile Queen could depart. "Grimalkin. We need to find him. You said you knew where he was."

"No, pet." Leanansidhe admired herself in the mirror's surface, pleased as a full cat. "I said I could perhaps point you in the right direction."

"And what direction would that be?"

Leanansidhe tore her gaze away from the mirror, smiling at us. "Well, darlings," she said, waving an airy hand, "there is a trio of witches who live somewhere in the Wraithwood. I would start there. It is as good a place as any. Now, my pets, I really must dash. I have a violin to replace. Good luck finding Grimalkin. If you do manage to catch up to the devious creature, be a dear and tell him I said hello. *Ciao,* darlings!"

A swirl of glitter and light, and we were alone.

Ash sighed. "The Wraithwood," he said, shifting the girl into a more comfortable position. She mumbled and snored in his arms. "That's…unfortunate. I was hoping we'd never have to go back."

I grinned at him. "What, you mean because of the ogre tribe we pissed off, or the giant dead god we accidentally woke up?"

"*You* accidentally woke up."

"Details." I waved my hand. "So, are we going to get this adventure started, or what?"

Ash shook his head, but I saw the shadow of a smirk on his face. "You know I'm probably going to kill you soon, right?" he muttered as we headed off into the trees.

"Old news, ice-boy." I chuckled, falling into step beside him. "And you know I wouldn't miss it for the world."

"You May
Have Heard of Me"

IRON'S PROPHECY

CHAPTER ONE

Darkness surrounded me.

I stood in the center of a familiar room, the walls and shelves covered with the macabre and strange. Snakes floating in jars, teeth scattered among feathers and bones and pestles. A skeleton in a top hat grinning at me from the corner. Frightening, but I wasn't afraid. I knew this place. I just couldn't remember from where.

An old wooden rocking chair creaked softly at the edge of the light. It was facing away from me, and I could see a body slumped in the seat, withered arms dangling over the sides. I took a step closer and smelled the decay, the stench of grave dust and rags and ancient newspapers, crumbling in the attic. Walking around to face the chair, I gazed down at the shriveled corpse of an old woman, her nails curved into long, steely talons, her head slumped on her sunken chest.

Then she raised her head, and her eyes burned with black fire as she opened her mouth and breathed the words that stopped my heart in fear.

And I awoke.

My name is Meghan Chase.

And I've been working way too hard, lately.

I lifted my head from my desk, blinking at my computer

and the nonsensical words scrolled across the screen. A quick glance at the clock proclaimed it 6:32 a.m. Had I pulled another all-nighter? I yawned, shaking cobwebs from my mind, as memory returned. No, I'd come here only an hour ago, to check the status of the new railroad system that was going up around the Iron Realm. It was a pet project of mine; the Iron Realm, despite being the smallest and newest realm in the Nevernever, was still large and sprawling. It needed a way for its citizens to travel safely and quickly, particularly if they were coming to Mag Tuiredh to see their new queen. The railroad was the perfect solution, though it would be a while before it was finished.

I rubbed my eyes, the remnants of a dream fading from my mind. Something with a skeleton and a creepy old corpse… I couldn't remember. Maybe I needed to slow down, take a break or a vacation, if the Iron Queen was allowed such things. It wasn't such an impossible idea now. The Iron Court, despite all the fear and hatred it still faced from the other courts, was doing well. There were a few hiccups, particularly involving the Winter Court, as Tir Na Nog's boundaries rested very close to Iron, but as a whole things were going far more smoothly and peacefully than I could've hoped for.

Which reminded me. Today marked the first day of Winter. The Winter Court Elysium was this afternoon in Tir Na Nog. I groaned at the thought.

At my feet, Beau, my German shepherd, raised his head and thumped his tail hopefully, and I smiled down at him.

"Hey, boy. You need to go out?"

The big dog panted and surged to his feet, wagging his tail. I ruffled his fur and stood, then winced as the floor swayed and a cloud of nausea bloomed in my stomach. Frowning, I put my hand on the desk to steady myself, clenching my jaw until the spell passed. Beau nudged my hand and whined.

I patted his neck, and the sick feeling faded and everything was normal again. "I'm okay, boy," I assured the dog, who gazed up at me with worried brown eyes. "Working too hard, I guess. Come on, I bet Razor is waiting for his daily game of catch-me-if-you-can."

We slipped into the hallway of the palace, where I was instantly trailed by several gremlins, tiny Iron fey that lived for trouble and chaos. They laughed and skittered around me, climbing walls and hanging from the ceiling, taunting poor Beau, until we reached the doors that led to the gardens surrounding the palace. As soon as I opened the doors, the gremlins shot through, buzzing challenges, and Beau took off after them, barking like mad. I rolled my eyes and shut the door as quiet returned to the Iron palace, if only temporarily. I couldn't help but smile as I headed back to my chambers, nodding at the Iron knights who bowed as I passed. This was my life now, crazy and weird and strange and magical, and I wouldn't have it any other way.

As soon as I wandered back into the bedroom, my gaze strayed to the large bed along the wall and the lump beneath the covers. Pale light streamed through the half-open curtains, settling around the still-sleeping form of a Winter sidhe. Or a former Winter sidhe. Pausing in the door frame, I took advantage of the serene moment just to watch him, a tiny flutter going through my stomach. Sometimes, it was still hard to believe that he was here, that this wasn't a dream or a mirage or a figment of my imagination. That he was mine forever: my husband, my knight.

My faery with a soul.

He lay on his stomach, arms beneath the pillow, breathing peacefully, his dark hair falling over his eyes. The covers had slipped off his lean, muscular shoulders, and the early-morning rays caressed his pale skin. Normally, I didn't get to watch him sleep; he was usually up before me, in the courtyard sparring with Glitch or just prowling the halls of the castle. In the early days of our marriage, especially, I'd wake up in the middle of the night to find him gone, the hyperawareness of his warrior days making it impossible for him to stay in one place, even to sleep. He'd grown up in the Unseelie Court, where you had to watch your back every second of every day, and centuries of fey survival could not be forgotten so easily. That paranoia would never really fade, but he was gradually starting to relax now, to the point where sometimes, though not often, I would wake with him still beside me, his arm curled around my waist.

And given how rare it was, to see him truly unguarded and at ease, I hated to disturb him. But I walked across the room to the side of the bed and gently touched his shoulder.

He was awake in an instant, silver eyes cracking open to meet mine, never failing to take my breath away. "Hey," I greeted, smiling. "Sorry to wake you, but we have to be somewhere soon, remember?"

He grunted and, to my surprise, shifted to his back and put the pillow over his head. "I don't suppose I could convince you to go without me," he groaned, his voice muffled beneath the fabric. "Tell Mab I've been eaten by a manticore or something?"

"What? Don't be ridiculous." I snatched the pillow off his head, and he winced, peering up at me blearily. "It's our first Elysium together, Ash. They'll be expecting us. Both of us." He moaned and grabbed another pillow, covering his eyes. "No playing hooky and insulting the Winter Queen. I'm not doing this by myself." I took the second pillow, tossing it on the floor, and mock-glowered at him. "Up."

He regarded me with a wry smile. "You're awfully perky for someone who kept me up all night."

"Hey, you started it, remember?" I feigned defiance, but it still made my heart soar to see him like this. It was like tiny pieces of his wall crumbled every day, showing me the bright, beautiful soul that lay beneath. I knew it was there, of course, when he had returned from his quest at the End of the World, but it had been new and fragile and overshadowed by his past, by his Unseelie nature and ruthless upbringing. Now, though, I could see more of it every day. He was still Ash the ice prince to everyone else in the castle, and sometimes that frozen barrier sprang up when he was angry or upset, but he was trying.

"So, come on." I poked him in the ribs, making him grunt. "If I have to suffer through this, you do, too. That was part of the deal when you married me."

I went to poke him again, but his hand shot out faster than I could see, grabbing my wrist and pulling me forward. I gave a startled yelp and fell on top of him, and his arms immediately snaked around my waist, trapping me against him.

"I don't know," he mused, giving me a lazy smile, as my heart started pounding in my chest. "What would you do if I just kept you here all afternoon? We could send Glitch to Tir Na Nog in our place—I'm sure he'd smooth things over."

"Oh, yeah, that would go over well—" But my voice was lost as Ash leaned up and kissed me, cutting off any protest. My eyes closed, and I melted into him, savoring the feel of his lips on mine, breathing in his scent. God, he was like a drug; I could never get enough. My fingers roamed over his bare shoulders and chest, and he sighed against me, sliding his hands up to tangle in my hair.

"This…isn't going to get you out of it," I breathed, shivering as Ash gently kissed my neck, right below my ear. "You're still...going to Elysium..." He chuckled, low and quiet, and brushed his lips across my cheek.

"I am yours to command, my queen," he whispered, making my heart clench in complete, helpless love. "I will obey, even if you order me to cut out my own heart. Even if you order me to the hell that is the Winter Court Elysium."

"It's...not that bad, is it?" I managed to get out. Ash gave a rueful smirk.

"Well, let's put it in perspective, shall we?" he mused, brushing a strand of hair from my eyes as he gazed up at me. "How many Elysiums have you been to?"

"Three," I said immediately. "At least...this will be my third one."

"And how many Elysiums do you think *I've* been to?"

"Um. More than three?"

"I do appreciate your gift for understatement." Ash kissed me once more and let me go, shaking his head. I stepped back, because if I stayed there any longer, staring into that gorgeous face, I wouldn't be going anywhere. "Very well." He sighed, putting on a mock-affronted air. "I guess I can suffer through another Elysium." He shifted to an elbow, watching me beneath the covers, looking so sexy I was tempted to say the hell with it and miss Elysium myself. "You do realize that I'm probably going to be challenged at least once by some Winter Court thug who thinks I've turned traitor."

"Yes, well, try not to kill anybody, Ash."

"Majesty?" A soft tap came on the door. I opened it a crack to find three wire nymphs gazing up at me. "We are here to help you prepare for Elysium, your majesty," one said with a deep curtsy. "Councilor Fix insisted that we arrange a dress for you, one suited for your status as queen."

"Did he now?" I smiled. Fix, my chief packrat adviser, had been quite busy of late, researching Elysium, the other courts and all the customs that went with it. He was incredibly efficient and probably knew more about the event than most of the traditional fey did.

The wire nymph shuffled her feet, looking uncomfortable. "Yes, your majesty. He also wished us to remind her highness that it would be highly inappropriate to wear human jeans and a T-shirt to the Winter Court, and that sneakers are not considered proper court attire."

A quiet noise came from the bed, sounding suspiciously like a snicker. I spared Ash a quick glare over my shoulder, and he gazed back innocently. Last night, when Fix was going over the rules with me one more time, I *jokingly* had mentioned the event was so stuffy and formal, maybe I could go in casual clothes this year. Then I'd at least be comfortably frozen. I'd thought Fix was going to have a heart attack squeaking in horror, and quickly assured him I was kidding. Packrats were wonderful little fey and fiercely loyal, but they tended to take everything seriously. Puck would have a field day with them.

Puck. I felt a twinge of sadness at the memory of him. Where was he now? What was he doing? I hadn't seen my best friend since the day we defeated the false king and I claimed the Iron throne. Ash had; Puck had accompanied him to the End of the World in his quest to gain a soul so he could be with me in the Iron Realm. But they'd parted ways soon after, and no one had seen any sign of the Great Prankster since.

I wished I knew where he was. I missed him.

"All right," I told the wire nymphs, smiling to ease their nervousness. "Then I'm at your mercy, I suppose. Lead the way."

An indefinite time later, after being poked, prodded, stuffed into a gown, my hair teased into curls and my face touched with makeup, I went back toward the bedroom, relieved that it was done. This was one of the things I didn't particularly care for; these extremely formal affairs that required me to look the part of a powerful faery queen. I understood Ash's reluctance. Faery politics were tricky, conniving and, if you weren't careful, extremely dangerous. I'd had to learn the ropes fast. Thankfully, Glitch and Fix were there to offer guidance when I needed it, and now Ash was here, as well. And the youngest son of the Unseelie Queen was no slouch when it came to the power struggles between the faery courts.

Speaking of which...

He was waiting for me outside our chamber doors, leaning against one of the pillars, arms crossed. Seeing him, I paused to collect myself. Ash in his black-and-silver uniform cut a striking figure against the white marble column, his cloak draping his shoulders and his sword at his side. It reminded me of our first dance together, my first Elysium, when I'd seen the cold, dangerous son of Queen Mab up close for the first time and was completely lost. Call it fate, destiny or just blatant hardheadedness on both our parts, from that moment on, there was no turning back.

As I approached, he smiled and pushed himself off the column, extending a hand. He had this uncanny ability to see everything about me in a single glance without taking his eyes from my face. I sensed he was doing that now. His expression looked a bit dazed, for just a moment, before he took my hand and kissed the backs of my knuckles, a perfect gentleman even now.

"Well." I sighed, ignoring the butterflies set loose in my stomach. "Here am I, all fancied up and ready to go to Elysium." I glanced down at the metallic gray-and-white fabric of my dress, befitting colors for the Iron Queen, and shook my head. "I hope this gown is heavy enough. Mab's palace isn't exactly the warmest place in the Nevernever."

"You look beautiful," Ash said, pulling me close. I blushed, and a slightly mischievous look crossed his face. "I'm glad Fix was able to talk you out of jeans and a T-shirt."

I swatted his stomach with the back of my hand. He laughed softly, offering an arm, and together we walked through the long hallways of the Iron palace. Gremlins scurried over the walls and ceilings, cackling, and Iron knights lowered their heads as we passed. Hacker elves, Cog dwarves, wire nymphs and clockwork men all bowed as we went by, before continuing their duties. My Iron fey. It was hard to believe that a few years ago I was a normal teenager living in the Louisiana swamps, and the Iron fey were slowly making their move to destroy the Nevernever. Now I was their queen, and they, while not really welcome in the wyldwood and the other courts, were no longer considered abominations to be eradicated. So much had changed. *I* had changed, and so had everyone around me.

I snuck a glance at my knight, walking quietly at my side. He seemed truly at ease now, comfortable and content in the Iron palace. Though his gaze constantly swept our surroundings, taking everything in, and he watched every faery I spoke to with searing intensity, ready to spring into action if needed, he'd acclimated to the Iron Realm surprisingly well. I'd been worried at first, that he would miss Tir Na Nog and the Winter Court and would have a hard time adjusting to the alien nature of the Iron realm and the fey within it. But he'd slipped into his role here surprisingly well, almost like it was familiar. Like he'd done it all before.

And, strangely enough, maybe he had. I didn't know what Ash had gone through on his voyage to the End of the World to earn his soul. He'd told me the gist of it, without going into too many painful details, and what he *had* told me seemed almost too crazy to believe. One section in particular, the part where he'd seen a future version of us, he didn't speak of much at all. It wasn't that he was being evasive, but he'd explained that he didn't want to color our future with what-ifs and things that might never happen.

Truthfully, I wasn't worried. I knew he would tell me everything, down to the last detail, if I really wanted him to. But Ash was here, in the Iron Realm. He had found a way to survive, to be with me. That was all that really mattered.

"You're staring at me again," Ash murmured without turning his head, though one corner of his lips quirked up. His silver eyes danced mischievously. "Is it the uniform? Perhaps I should remove it if it's so distracting."

"Behave, Ash." I wrinkled my nose at him, smiling. "And don't think I don't know what you're doing. Your little ploy to get out of Elysium isn't going to—"

I gasped as, without warning, my stomach turned over and a bout of dizziness made the walls spin. I tried to say something to Ash, to ease the alarm and worry on his face, but the ground beneath my feet tilted, and the floor rushed up at me.

CHAPTER TWO

"Meghan!"

Groaning, I opened my eyes.

I lay on my back on the cold floor, the walls still swaying slightly, the last of the dizziness fading. Ash knelt beside me, his arms under my shoulders, gently easing me down. He'd caught me, of course, and was now watching me with a pale, alarmed expression. The hand suddenly gripping my own was painfully tight.

"Meghan."

"I'm...all right, Ash." Wincing, I sat up, breathing deep as the world went normal again. "I just...fainted, I guess." Well, that was humiliating. Here I was, the Queen of the Iron Fey, passing out in my own hall. Good thing we weren't in Tir Na Nog yet; showing weakness like that in front of the Unseelie was asking for trouble.

"Are you sick? What happened?" Ash took my elbow and gently helped me stand, eyes bright as he stared at me, appraising. "Should I call for a healer?"

"No. I'm fine." I put a hand on his arm, squeezing once. "It's nothing. I guess I've been working too hard lately. I feel perfectly all right now, promise."

"Maybe we shouldn't go to Elysium," Ash said, sounding

unconvinced of my all-rightness. "Have Glitch send Mab and Oberon our apologies. If something is wrong—"

"No." I faced him, my voice firm. "I'm the Iron Queen, and this is something I cannot miss. It's not negotiable. I have to go."

"Meghan…"

"If I don't show up, it will make this realm look weak, and we can't afford that. You know what Mab will think, Ash. You, of all people, know what she's like."

Ash nodded once. "I know," he murmured darkly.

"I won't put my people in danger." Turning from him, I gazed down the hall, watching the gremlins and the Iron knights and the packrats and everyone. "I can't fail them, Ash," I said. "I won't. I won't have the other courts thinking the Iron Queen isn't strong enough to come to Elysium, to protect her own people."

"No one will ever think that." Ash stepped up behind me, his strong hands on my shoulders. "But you're going to Tir Na Nog no matter what I say, aren't you?" He sounded resigned, and I didn't have to answer. Sighing, he lowered his head, his lips brushing my ear. "I've never been able to stop you, my queen," he murmured, "but I do want you to know that I might be a little overprotective tonight. These are your people, so that makes them mine as well, but my first and only duty is to you. Always."

"Majesty!"

Glitch strode toward us before I could answer. Neon lightning snapped in his hair, throwing purple shadows over the walls as he bowed. "The carriages are here," the First Lieutenant said with a nod to Ash, who inclined his head in return. "We are ready to depart for Tir Na Nog, with your approval."

"Then let's go. We shouldn't keep Mab waiting." Before either of them could reply, I strode forward with my head up and my back straight as Fix had instructed. The walk of a queen, regal and confident. After a moment, Ash fell into step beside me. I could sense he wanted to say something, argue with me, but he kept silent and didn't bring it up again during the long, cold ride to Winter.

To put it mildly, the court of the Winter Queen was not my favorite place in the Nevernever. The last time I'd been to Tir Na Nog, I'd been a prisoner of Queen Mab and the Unseelie Court. My own doing, of course. It was part of a deal I'd made with Ash in exchange for getting my brother home safely. And though I'd do it all again if I had to, it was, as I remembered it, the worst few weeks of my life. Mab despised me, her middle son, Rowan, constantly tormented me and her Unseelie subjects either wanted to kill, freeze, torture or eat me.

Then there was Ash. He had been there as well, but he had turned cold and cruel, abandoning me to the mercy of his brother and queen. Or so I'd thought at the time. The Winter Court is brutal and unmerciful, viewing emotion as a weakness that must be destroyed. Ash had been keeping me safe the only way he knew how: by playing the part of a heartless Winter prince. He'd played it well; he'd hinted to me about how he would have to treat me when we got there, and I'd still believed his act wholeheartedly. I'd thought he had turned on me, used me, and my heart had broken into little pieces. I didn't realize until later how much Ash had sacrificed to keep me safe.

God, I was so naive, I thought, watching crystalline stalactites roll by the carriage windows. Mab's palace resided in an enormous icy cavern, the ceiling so high you couldn't see it through the darkness. *I'm lucky I didn't get eaten the very first day I was there. If I could go back to that moment and talk to my-*

self, I'd probably smack me. Thinking of that shy, uncertain girl now made me sigh. *You can't afford to wear your heart on your sleeve anymore, Meghan. Not in the Winter Court. You're the Iron Queen now. You have a whole kingdom counting on you to be strong.*

The palace came into view through the carriage windows, a pristine, glacial blue castle with ice hanging off every tower, coating every step, as beautiful as it was deadly. Just like its queen.

Who, admittedly, was not terribly pleased with me for marrying her favorite—and now only—son.

I looked at Ash, who was gazing toward the palace, his eyes distant and his face blank. Remembering, just like me. I felt a twinge of sadness, empathy and guilt. This had to be hard for him.

"Hey." I touched the back of his palm, where a gold band entwined with silver vines and leaves circled his third finger, a twin of my own. He turned almost guiltily, and I smiled at him. "You all right?"

"Yes." He nodded. "I'm fine. Just…" He nodded out the window, to the frozen spires looming above the rooftops, and shrugged. "Memories."

"Do you miss it?"

"The court? The squabbles and backstabbing and constantly having to watch what I said or did? Hardly." He snorted, and I smiled, relieved to hear it.

"But…" He sighed, looking out the window again. "There are *some* things that I miss. I lived here such a long time, I knew the Winter Court better than almost anyone. I still do. But now…" His brow furrowed. "Now, when I look at Tir Na Nog, all can I see are the missing pieces. The family who's no longer there. Sage is gone. Rowan is gone." His eyes clouded over, and I could feel his regret, the gnawing ache of remorse and guilt. "I never thought I would miss them,"

Ash mused in a soft voice. "I never thought…I would be the very last of my line."

I took his hand in both of mine, squeezing gently, the cool metal of his wedding band brushing my skin. "I'm sorry, Ash," I whispered, as his bright soulful gaze shifted to me. "I can't even imagine what that's like. I miss my family like crazy, and they're still alive."

"It's a little different." Ash gave me a faint smile, though his eyes were still shadowed. "Your family loves one another—you would do whatever it takes to keep them safe. My family… well, you've seen them. I could never drop my guard around my brothers, especially Rowan. And Mab…" He shook his head. "Mab was always the Winter Queen, and she never let us forget that."

"But you still miss them."

"Yes," he admitted. "I was still a part of that circle. It was familiar, safe. I belonged there. Even with all the cruel games we used to play, the countless times we used each other, I still knew that Rowan and Sage and Mab would always be there." He gazed down at his hand, still trapped in mine. "But things are different now. My brothers are gone, and the Winter Court will no longer welcome me, not like it did before."

"Feeling homesick?"

"Tir Na Nog is no longer my home." Ash finally looked up again, meeting my gaze. His eyes lightened, back to that gorgeous silver. "I'm whining, aren't I?" he said with a rueful look, and shook his head. "No, I'm not homesick. I might miss my kin, but my home is Mag Tuiredh, or wherever you wish to rule from. The Nevernever, the Iron Realm, even the mortal world, it doesn't matter to me. Meghan…" He shifted closer, closing the distance between us, and one hand rose to brush my cheek. "My home…is with you."

Dammit, don't cry, Meghan. I bit my lip to keep the tears in check. It would not do to show up to the Winter Court with blurry eyes, but sometimes Ash would surprise me with quiet, sincere statements like these and I couldn't help it.

"I'm sorry," he murmured, mistaking my tears for remorse, perhaps. "I'll stop talking about the Winter Court. I knew I had to come back and face Mab eventually. You shouldn't have to hear me go on and on about it—"

"Ash," I interrupted, placing a finger against his mouth, making him arch his brows. "Just kiss me."

He smiled. Slipping an arm around my shoulders, he drew me forward, lowered his head and brought his lips down to mine.

We kissed each other in that dark carriage, our lips moving in rhythm, both of us uncaring of the Unseelie city right outside the windows. Ash was gentle at first, keeping himself under control, but when I leaned against him, tracing kisses down his jaw, he groaned and tilted his head back, whispering my name. I pushed him into the corner, my hands tangling in his hair, his running the length of my back, pulling us closer. Our kisses were hungry now, devouring. My tongue parted his lips, sweeping inside; his pulled away to press to my neck, making me shiver and gasp. My hand slipped down his chest to his lean, hard stomach, and then slid beneath the fabric, tracing his ribs. He jerked, exhaling raggedly, before his cool lips seared over mine again.

Pulling back, he watched me, those clear silver eyes gleaming brightly in the darkness. "My queen," he breathed, one hand reaching up to frame my cheek, making my stomach jump and twirl. "I belong to you. No matter what Mab says, no matter how long I've been in Tir Na Nog, my life is yours. Nothing will ever make me leave your side."

"You're going to make me cry," I warned him, as my eyes went blurry again and his gorgeous face shifted in the darkness like water. "And Mab is either going to be very happy to see me in tears, or very disgusted with us." He laughed softly and drew me close, wrapping his arms around me in a fierce, protective way. His heart pounded beneath my fingers, and I felt the lightest brush of his lips against my ear.

"I love you, Meghan," he whispered, and I gave a tiny, happy sob, hiding my face in his shirt. Ash held me tight, resting his chin atop my head, gazing out the window. "I don't have to hide anything anymore," he murmured above me, sounding content and defiant at the same time. "Not from Mab, not from anyone. Let them talk and stare. This Elysium will be very different."

The carriage jerked and shuddered to a halt at the front gates of the Winter palace. Ash reluctantly let me go as I pulled back, composing myself for the ordeal ahead. The carriage driver hopped down from the seat and opened the door for us, letting in a swirl of chilly wind. Ash exited first, then turned to help me down.

"Ready for this?" I asked him as I stepped out into the cold, snowy courtyard. Icicles hung from everything, and the air was bitingly cold. Oh, yes, lovely Unseelie weather. I remembered this quite well. Glitch and a squad of Iron knights stepped forward, flanking us, ready to follow. Ash nodded, offering his arm, and together we stepped into Mab's cold, frozen domain.

The first thing I noticed, as we crossed the courtyard full of frozen statues and huge, multicolored crystals, was that it was full of Winter fey. Considering this *was* the heart of Unseelie territory, that wasn't surprising, but what made me wary was the fact that they were all staring at us. Sidhe nobles watched us with barely concealed smirks, goblins and redcaps followed us hungrily, though they still kept their distance from the knights, and bogies lurked in the shadows, watching intently as we passed.

Ash's grip on my arm was tight as we wove our way through the courtyard, ignoring and yet unable to ignore our inhuman audience. As we began climbing the steps into the palace, one of the sidhe nobles, a lanky faery with spiky crystalline hair, gave Ash a mocking salute and murmured a sarcastic "Prince." Ash didn't acknowledge him; his face stayed blank. The mask of the Winter prince.

It dawned on me what was happening. They were all here to see the new queen and her supposedly mortal husband. Not to be welcoming or polite; they were testing for weakness, wondering if this new, half-human queen would be easy to manipulate and take apart. And they were also here for Ash, to see if their former ice prince would be weak as a mere mortal. Which would make the queen he served weak, as well.

Oh, that had to end. Here and now. Not only for the future of my kingdom, but if Ash was to have any peace in Tir Na Nog, he was going to have to prove himself to his own people. Prove to everyone that neither the Iron Queen nor her knight—though both had mortal blood—were ever to be underestimated.

"Ash," I whispered as we neared the top of the steps. "Remember what I said this morning, about not getting into any duels?"

"Yes."

We'd reached the top of the steps, a few feet away from the open door into the hall, and I pulled him to a stop. Glitch and the knights paused as well, but I motioned for them to keep going. He gave me a worried look, but bowed and went through the arch, stopping on the other side to wait for us.

I turned to my knight, who looked vaguely worried, as

well. "I take it back. The mob behind us is itching for trouble. I want you to oblige them."

Ash blinked. "You want me to start a fight?" he asked in disbelief. "Now?" When I nodded, he frowned, lowering his voice. "Mab and Oberon are expecting both of us," he said. "It might send the wrong message if you go in alone."

"I can handle them." I glanced at the crowd at the bottom of the steps, seeing their wide smirks, their hungry gazes, and felt my resolve grow. "I'm the Iron Queen—I should face the other rulers by myself first. And I want you to send another message, Ash. The Unseelie Court is no doubt wondering if their former prince is as strong as he was. They're curious to see if a mere mortal can protect himself and his queen in the Winter Court. If there is any doubt, word will spread, and the other courts might see the Iron Court as weak, easy to exploit." I reached out and squeezed his arm, smiling fiercely. "That doubt ends right here. I want you to make sure that everyone knows that we are *not* weak, that the Iron Queen's knight is not someone to cross. Ever."

Ash's eyes gleamed, the shadow of an evil grin crossing his face. "As you command, my queen," he said in a low voice, barely hiding his glee. "I will carry out your wishes. Please send Mab and Oberon my apologies. I will rejoin you as soon as I am able."

I nodded and went through the door, nodding at Glitch to follow, leaving my knight to turn and face the trailing crowd. I heard the rasp of his ice-blade as it was unsheathed, and the shouts of the mob in the courtyard. Footsteps scuffled over the ground, no doubt Winter fey scrambling to attack…or flee. I felt an icy burst of glamour, probably from Ash, and another yell of utter shock.

"What *are* you?" something howled, and then there was a crash, and the sound of shattered icicles tinkling to the ground.

Laughter rang out, *Ash's* laughter, jubilant and defiant, making me pause.

What are you?

A good question. One that I'd asked myself on more then one occasion. Physically, Ash was no different than before; lean and graceful, with the same command of Winter magic and sword skills that made him such a lethal warrior. He was still fierce, loyal, protective and could level an icy glare that could make your insides freeze. In that regard, he hadn't changed.

And yet, sometimes, he was so different. It would be insane to ever think of Ash as soft, but the frozen shell that had always surrounded the Winter prince was gone. He was... kinder now, able to empathize in ways he couldn't as a pure Unseelie. There were times when he seemed so human in little, subtle ways I'd never noticed before, that I'd forget he had ever belonged to the Winter Court.

It made me wonder. Was Ash human like me, a mortal with faery glamour and magic left over from his life as a Winter prince? Or was he still fey? A faery...with a human soul?

I didn't know. And really, I didn't care. Ash was Ash. You couldn't put a descriptor on him; there was no one who had done what he had, no other like him in the entire realm of Faery. He was...unique.

Another yell echoed through the door. I continued down the hall with Glitch and the knights as the clamor of battle rang out behind me, followed by howls of pain and dismay. And I smiled to myself. Whatever Ash was, he was the best at what he did. It wouldn't take him long.

This year's Elysium was held in Queen Mab's ballroom, and the place was already filled with fey. I left Glitch and the knights in the hall just outside the entrance, and an Unseelie herald announced my arrival in clear, high tones: "Her maj-

esty Meghan Chase, monarch of Mag Tuiredh, sovereign of
the Iron territories and Queen of the Iron Fey."

He paused, as if expecting to announce Ash as well, but of
course Ash was not with me at the moment. After a heartbeat, the herald nodded, and I stepped into the room, to the
stares of dozens of fey.

A long white table waited at the end of the room, with
three figures already seated and two empty spots farther down.
Queen Mab, King Oberon and Queen Titania waited for me
as I walked across the room, my back straight and my chin
held high.

"Meghan Chase." Mab's greeting could not exactly be
called a welcome. The Unseelie monarch sat in the middle of
the table, her long black hair styled elegantly atop her head,
pinned in place with icicles. "How fortuitous of you to join
us."

"Queen Mab," I said politely, and nodded to my father, to
her left. "Lord Oberon, Lady Titania." The Summer Queen
pursed her lips and pointedly ignored me, but Oberon gave
a solemn bob of his head. Not unfriendly, but not really ac-
knowledging me as a daughter, either. I stifled a sigh. This
was going to be a long night.

"Where is Ash?" Mab inquired, her dark gaze flicking to
the door behind me. "Has he not come? Is he not anxious to
see his old court and kith?" Her voice lowered, turned slightly
dangerous. "Has he forgotten us so quickly?"

"No, Queen Mab. Ash is here." I was quick to reassure her,
knowing Mab took insult easily and held grudges forever. "He
was...held up...for a few minutes in the courtyard. I'm sure
he'll be here soon."

"I see." Mab sat back, apparently mollified. "Good. I wish
to hear how Ash is getting along in the poisoned realm."

I was about to reply that Ash was doing just fine, thank

you, when every light in the place—torches, the icicle chandeliers, flickering blue candles in the columns—sputtered and went out.

Snarls and cries of alarm filled the air. Chairs overturned as fey leaped to their feet, drawing weapons and glaring into the shadows. I spun, searching for hidden dangers, for anything stupid or crazy enough to attack during Elysium when the most powerful fey in all the Nevernever were in the very same room.

"Silence!" Mab stood up, her voice booming through the darkness, and instantly everything went completely mute. You could've heard a pin drop. "Whoever is responsible for this will soon wish they had never been born," she rasped into the still darkness. "You will not embarrass me in my own court in the midst of Elysium. Show yourself, now!"

She waved her hand, and lights sprang up again, candles and chandeliers flaring to life. The faeries in the room blinked and cringed and glanced around, wary of attackers and one another.

They didn't immediately notice the old woman standing in the middle of the room, where nothing had been before. But I spotted her almost at once, and my stomach went cold with dread.

The oracle, ragged, dusty and as brittle as old newspaper, turned the hollow pits of her eyes on me and didn't look away. I heard Titania's sharp gasp, just as the other fey discovered the ancient creature standing in their midst and surged away from her like she had a disease. But the oracle's sightless gaze never wavered, and she seemed to float over the ground like a dusty wraith, until she stood a few yards from me.

"Oracle," Mab stated in a flat voice. "Why are you here? What is the meaning of this disturbance?"

The oracle ignored the Winter monarch, however, drifting closer to me. "Meghan Chase," she whispered, and the stench of centuries-old dust filled the air, the smell of a grave or a tomb. "Iron Queen. Do you remember me?"

"What do you want, Oracle?" I stood tall, keeping my voice calm.

"Old Anna brings a warning," the oracle whispered. "One that has been ignored before. Do you remember what I told you, Meghan Chase? You and your Winter prince. Do you recall what I said would happen?"

A murmur went around the room, and Mab's glare sharpened; I could feel it searing into the back of my head. Goose bumps prickled over my skin, but I kept my voice firm. "No," I said, taking a step forward. "You told us a lot of things, and I gave you what I could. I did what I had to do, to save my family. That's all that was important."

"You remember," the oracle insisted. "Do you not? The one thing you refused to give up. That which would cause you nothing but grief. Do you remember now, Meghan Chase?"

For second, I didn't know what she was talking about.

Then it hit me, and were it not for the hundreds of fey watching, including the rulers of the other courts, I would have fallen as my knees gave out. I remembered her words, so long ago, when I had first come to Faery. I had traded away a memory for her help, but that wasn't the only thing the oracle had wanted.

"You will not give it up, even though it will bring you nothing but grief?"

"Oh, God," I whispered, and my hand slipped to my stomach. The nausea, the sudden weakness and fainting spells. It couldn't be.

"Yes," the oracle whispered, and raised a withered hand, pointing at me. "You know of what I speak. And you have a decision to make, Iron Queen. What you carry will either unite the courts, or it will destroy them. I have seen it. I know one of these will come to pass."

"No," I said in a shaky voice. No one in the room seemed to hear us now. It was as if we were in our own small world, the oracle and myself, and everything around us had faded into obscurity.

The withered hag watched me with the pitiless holes in her face. "You know I speak the truth, Meghan Chase," the oracle went on. "You know the great power resting inside you. Power that can destroy, turn everything we know into dust. But all is not lost." She raised a shriveled claw. "I have a proposition for you. We must speak further, but not here. Not like this." She drew back, the hollow pits of her eyes never leaving my face. "Time is of the essence. Find me. You have friends who will show you the way. I will be awaiting you, and your decision."

A sudden wind rushed through the ballroom, resnuffing candles and causing a few chandeliers to crash to the ground in a ringing cacophony. Fey jumped and howled, and by the time Mab restored order and reignited the lights again, the oracle was gone.

CHAPTER THREE

"Explain yourself, Iron Queen!"

Shivering, I turned to face the Unseelie monarch, on her feet and glaring at me over the table. Mab's eyes glittered with distrust, and Oberon didn't look very reassuring, either. Titania, of course, was staring at me like she was hoping my head would explode.

But they were the least of my worries, now. The oracle's words rang through my head, over and over again, staggering me with the implications.

You know the great power resting inside you.

What you carry will either unite the courts, or it will destroy them.

You have a decision to make, Iron Queen. Find me.

"I have to go."

That wasn't well received. Mab straightened, every inch of her bristling with offense. "You dare, Iron Queen?" she asked in her scary soft voice. "You dare insult me in my own court? In front of my own people?" Her black eyes narrowed, and she leaned across the table, coating the glasses with frost. "You will tell me what is happening, or you will prepare for the wrath of Winter."

I stared her down. "No, Queen Mab. You will not threaten me or my kingdom for this." Mab didn't move, but I could sense her shock; the daughter of Oberon was no longer a cowering little girl. I gestured to the room behind us. "You heard what the oracle said—this affects all the courts, not just my own. I will not adhere to some ridiculous, outdated protocol when my realm could be in danger."

"The girl is right, Lady Mab," Oberon said, *finally* coming to my defense. Better late than never, I supposed. "A Summons from the oracle cannot be ignored. If she knows something that threatens the stability of the courts, we must be prepared."

"And what of Ash?" Mab snapped, a bit peevishly now. "I have not seen my son in months. The Iron Queen makes decisions that affects them both. What does Ash think of all this?"

"Ash," said a cool, deep voice, suddenly at my shoulder, "stands with the decision of his queen."

I didn't move, though my heart leaped and I wanted to glance at him in relief. But I kept my gaze on the Unseelie monarch in front of us. "Ash," Mab said, switching her attention to my knight, standing tall at my side, "you have not been home in months. Do you not care that your queen is breaking the ancient traditions of Elysium? Do you not care that she would pit you against your own court, if it came to war between us?"

I felt a blaze of fury at the Unseelie Queen's manipulative ways, but Ash's voice remained calm. "This is not my home any longer," Ash said in a clear voice, making sure everyone heard him. "And if it came to war, I would be the first on the front lines, defending the Iron Court."

Mab looked stunned. I took advantage of her silence to bow and step back. "We'll be taking our leave now," I told the rulers of Faery, ignoring my pounding heart. Of the three, only Oberon nodded. Titania snorted in disgust, and Mab continued to watch me with her dark, eerie glare. "I apologize for the inconvenience, Queen Mab, but we must return to Mag Tuiredh. Please excuse us."

And, without waiting for an answer, I turned and left the ballroom with Ash at my side, feeling the Winter Queen's frosty gaze skewering the back of my neck.

That was the easy part.

As soon as we were in the hallway, out of sight and sound of the rulers, Ash turned on me, silver eyes bright. "I heard the commotion in the ballroom," he said, his voice low and intense, nothing like the cool, composed nonchalance he had shown in front of Mab. "What happened? Why are we leaving Elysium? What's going on, Meghan?"

My legs were shaking. Now that I was away from the rulers, the oracle's words came back in a rush, threatening to drown me. I couldn't think, couldn't explain. I needed time to compose myself, to sort this out. Ash had to know, he was the other part of this equation, but the Unseelie Court was not the place to break this kind of news. I couldn't tell him now. Not like this.

"Home, Ash," I said finally, desperate to get out of Tir Na Nog, back to the familiar comfort of my realm. "Please. I'll tell you everything when we get home."

He wasn't happy, but conceded to my wishes, though I could feel his eyes on me the entire ride back to Mag Tuiredh.

How am I going to tell him? What is he going to think about all this? I gazed out the window, Ash's worried, intense stare burning my cheek. *Oh, Ash, I wanted this day to come, but I never thought something from our past would come back to haunt us. What are we going to do now?*

Glitch didn't say anything when the carriage pulled to a halt outside the palace, and no one tried to stop me as I strode down the halls; even the gremlins, who would normally swarm around me like happy, psychotic puppies whenever I entered a room, kept their distance. Only Ash kept pace with me, saying nothing, though I knew that would end the second we reached our chambers. I still didn't know how I was going to tell him.

Beau glanced up from the bed as we entered the room, thumping his tail against the mattress. I went to the dog and scratched him behind the ears, still trying to collect my scattered thoughts. He pushed his nose against my palm and whined, and I buried my face in his soft fur. My heart was going a mile a minute, and my stomach twisted nervously as Ash's footsteps followed me into the room.

"All right," Ash said, closing the door firmly behind us, "I've kept quiet long enough. What's going on, Meghan? What happened at Elysium?"

My mouth went dry. With Beau trailing worriedly behind me, I walked to the glass doors across the room, opened them and stepped onto the balcony, breathing in the night air. Far below, Mag Tuiredh, the city of the Iron fey, sparkled under the full moon. My city. My Iron fey. The realm I had sworn to protect from any and all threats, from without…and within.

What you carry will either unite the courts, or it will destroy them.

"Meghan." Ash was behind me in the door frame, his voice firm yet pleading. "Please. Tell me what's happening."

I took a deep breath and walked back into the bedroom.

"I… We had an unexpected visitor," I began. Ash came to my side, not bothering to shut the balcony doors, and a cold breeze ruffled the curtains. "In the ballroom. It was the oracle. She showed up out of nowhere and freaked everyone out. Do you remember her?"

"I remember," Ash said, sounding puzzled. "New Orleans. We went to that cemetery to get a Token for her, to exchange for your memory. The Church Grim chased us all the way to the edge of the grounds. What did she tell you?"

I gripped the back of a chair to keep myself upright. My

heart was pounding against my ribs, and I could barely get the words out. "She...she came to me with a warning. She reminded me that the thing that I refused to give up will bring me nothing but grief. That—" my stomach cartwheeled; I swallowed hard and continued in a whisper "—that what I'm carrying will either unite the courts, or destroy them."

"What you're..." Ash stopped. Stared at me. I felt the energy in the room shift the moment he got it.

"Meghan." His voice was calm, controlled, but so many emotions swirled just below the surface. "Are...are you...pregnant?"

I shivered and closed my eyes, not knowing whether to laugh or cry or scream. "I think so."

Ash exhaled slowly. I heard him sit, rather suddenly, on the bed.

Silence fell. Beau whined and nudged his hand, but when that yielded no reaction, he hopped up and sank down next to him with a groan, laying his head on his paws. I closed my eyes and waited.

"What else did the oracle say?" Ash finally whispered, sounding dazed.

"She has a proposition for me," I replied, afraid to turn around, to face him. Afraid that I would see fear, dismay or disappointment in his eyes. "She wants me to find her, said that I have 'friends who can show me the way.' She said she'll be waiting for me, and my decision."

"Decision?" I heard the frown in his voice. "What kind of decision?"

"She didn't say." I was shaking, trying to hold back frustrated tears. I needed to be strong, but I had just received the news that I was pregnant, and not only that, my child could end up destroying everything I'd worked so hard to protect. To top it all off, I didn't know if Ash wanted a kid, or was ready for a kid, or if *I* was ready for a kid. "I didn't have a chance to ask about the details," I said, attempting to keep my voice steady. "After reminding me of that little prophecy, she disappeared, and I decided it was time to go home, screw what the other rulers thought."

"Hey." Ash's low, soothing voice finally made me turn around. He sat on the edge of the mattress, his eyes and face calm, and held out a hand. "Come here a second."

I stepped forward and put my hand in his. He drew me close and wrapped his arms around my waist, pressing his forehead to my stomach. "I'm here," he murmured, as I gave a shaky sob and bent over him, hugging him in relief. "You're not alone in this. We'll figure it out."

I buried my face in his hair, letting the cool, soft strands brush my cheeks. He was my rock, the one thing I could lean on when the world was crumbling around me. "I guess I made a rather strong impression for my first Elysium as queen," I murmured, finally starting to feel a bit steadier, like the ground wasn't cracking under my feet. "I just hope I'm invited back after this. Mab is never going to forgive me for walking out on her."

I felt him smile. "She'll get over it."

"You think so?"

"Not really."

I groaned, and we both fell silent.

We stayed like that for a while, holding each other, offering comfort and support, yet lost in our own thoughts. Ash was quiet; I wondered what he was thinking, if he was pleased or terrified at the notion of becoming a father. Not only that, the father to a child who might or might not grow up to destroy the courts. How did one reconcile that? Was there a way to ever be prepared for something that extreme?

I couldn't ask him yet. I still didn't know how *I* felt about it.

"When do you want to leave?" Ash murmured at length. And his voice, though it shook ever so slightly in the beginning, was steady by the end. I took a deep breath.

"Tonight," I said. "I don't think I'll be able to sleep until this whole thing is resolved." He nodded, and I pulled away to pace the room. Ash watched quietly from the bed. "Though, I'm not even sure how to find the oracle," I mused, turning to face him. "She didn't say where she would be. I guess we could go back to the Voodoo Museum in New Orleans—"

"You will not find her there, human."

I spun, my heart leaping at the familiar, bored voice. Through the open doors, silhouetted against the night sky, a furry gray cat perched on the balcony, watching us with moonlike golden eyes.

At the sight of the intruder, Beau jerked upright, bristling and showing his teeth. He tensed to lunge, but Ash put a hand on his neck and murmured a quiet word, and Beau calmed instantly, sinking back to the bed. The gray cat yawned, unimpressed, and gave his paw a couple licks.

"Hello, Iron Queen." Grimalkin sighed, as if this meeting was encroaching on his valuable time. "We meet yet again. Sooner than I had anticipated, but I suppose it is to be expected." He shook his furry head, contemplating us both. "Why is it that neither of you can manage to stay out of trouble for a single season?"

Ash rose from the mattress, his expression wary and puzzled. "How did you get in here, cat?" he asked, frowning. Grimalkin sniffed.

"I climbed."

"That's not what I meant."

It hit me then, what Ash was saying. "Wait a minute," I echoed, striding out to the balcony, where the cat regarded me lazily. "How *are* you able to be here, Grim? You're not an

Iron faery, you still can't be in Mag Tuiredh without being poisoned, and I'm certain you didn't take that journey to the End of the World for *yourself*." Grimalkin snorted, as if such a thought was highly offensive. "How are you doing this?" I continued, frowning at him. "And if you say 'I am a cat,' I swear I will throw you off this balcony."

Grimalkin sneezed with amusement. "Worry not, human," he stated, slitting his eyes at me. "I am in no danger. It is all part of the deal I worked out with the former Iron lieutenant."

"Ironhorse?"

"Mmm, yes." Grimalkin scrubbed a paw over his ear. "You can say his…hmm…spirit still inhabits the amulet I procured, that as long as it remains intact, I am exempt from the poison of the Iron Realm." He yawned again, curling his whiskers. "I do not know how long it will last, how much time I have left in the Iron Realm, but the former lieutenant was one of the stronger fey, after all. His last wish was to protect you, even if he could not be there himself." He sniffed and yawned again, showing a flash of pointed teeth. "Still, I doubt it will last forever, and I certainly do not intend to stay here any longer than I have to. Time is of the essence." Flicking his tail, he gazed up at me. "Shall we get on with it, then?"

"Then, you know," Ash said from behind me. "You know about the oracle's prophecy."

"You humans are so very adept at stating the obvious."

"Do you know where she is?" I asked. "Where we're going?"

Grimalkin blinked at me. "I do," he purred, holding my gaze. "And I will ask no favor to lead you there. That has already been taken care of. I am to guide the Iron Queen, her knight and one other through the wyldwood, to a place called the Wishing Tree."

I could tell by the way Ash went motionless that he knew

about this place. "What's the Wishing Tree?" I asked, looking back at him.

"Do you really wish to stand around and discuss it?" Grimalkin said before Ash could reply. "We are wasting time. We
must meet one other before the night is out, and if we do not
hurry, we will miss our window. Let us go." He stood, waving his plumed tail. "I will be waiting for you at the southern
edge of the wyldwood, past the bridge into the Iron Realm.
Do hurry, human."

And, in true Grimalkin fashion, he vanished.

Ash and I spared only a few minutes to change—me into
jeans and a sweater, him into his long black coat—and to pri-
vately call Glitch into the room. The First Lieutenant was
not happy about me traipsing off into the wyldwood in the
middle of the night. I was the Iron Queen; I had responsibilities to my people and my realm. What if I didn't come back?

"I'll be back," I assured him, grabbing my sword from the
wall and buckling it around my waist. The curved steel blade
settled comfortably against my hip. You could never be too
careful in the wyldwood. "Ash will be with me. There's nothing out there that will keep us from returning. I have to do
this, Glitch. I can't explain it, but I have to go. I'm trusting
you to take care of things while we're gone."

Glitch looked unconvinced, but bowed. "Yes, your majesty."

Beau whined and nudged my hand. I knelt to scratch the
dog behind the ears. "You be good, too," I told him. "Take
care of Glitch and Razor while we're gone, okay?"

Beau panted and wagged his tail. I gave him one last pat and
rose, the breeze from the open glass doors ruffling my hair.

"Let's go," I told Ash, who waited quietly next to the balcony, sword at his side. "I don't want to be away longer than
we have to."

I walked onto the balcony and put my hands on the railing, ignoring the city spread like a map of stars below. Instead, I closed my eyes, calling up my glamour, the magic of Summer and Iron that swirled through every part of me, tying me to the realm. It was the essence of science, logic and technology, but also nature and warmth and life. It was how I could look at a clock and see every intricate gear that made it turn and function, but also the painstaking attention to detail that fit beauty and function together seamlessly. It was how I could listen to a song and hear the rigid lines and perfectly timed notes that made up the score, carefully woven through the pure emotion of the music itself.

And it was how I could sense my Iron fey. How, by focusing my consciousness outward, I could feel their thoughts and know what they were doing.

I sent my glamour through the castle, invisible tendrils reaching out, searching. I felt Glitch, walking back into the hall, his worry for me carefully concealed. I sensed the guards, standing rigid at their posts, unaware that something was wrong. I caught frantic blips of movement from the gremlins, scurrying about the palace walls, constantly looking for trouble. I kept searching, moving through the walls, searching up and up until…there. On the far eastern tower, hanging sleepily from the rough stones, were the creatures I was looking for.

I sent a gentle pulse through our connection and felt them respond, buzzing excitedly as they woke up. Opening my eyes, I stepped back from the railing, and a moment later two insectlike gliders crawled down the wall and perched on the edge of the balcony, blinking huge, multifaceted eyes at us.

I glanced at Ash. "Ready?"

He nodded. "After you."

I walked to the edge of the balcony, held my arms out from

my sides, and one of the gliders immediately crawled up my back, curling thin jointed legs around my middle. Stepping over the railing, I gripped the insect's front legs and dove off the tower, feeling a rush of wind snap at my hair. The glider's wings caught the air currents, swooping upward, and we soared over Mag Tuiredh, its distant lights glimmering far below.

Ash swooped down beside me, his own glider buzzing excitedly at mine, as if they hadn't seen each other in days rather than seconds. He gave me an encouraging nod, and we turned the gliders in the direction of the wyldwood.

CHAPTER FOUR

The Wishing Tree, as I learned from Ash, was one of those oddities in the Nevernever that sounded too good to be true. And, like the old saying warned, it usually was. The tree stood in one of the deepest regions of the wyldwood and was probably as old as the Nevernever itself. There were stories about humans going on quests to find it, for the legend stated that if you could get past the dragon or giant snake or whatever nasty thing was guarding the tree, you could wish for anything your heart desired.

But of course, as with all things in Faery, a wish never turned out the way the wisher expected. A dead lover might be brought back to life with no memory, or married to a rival. The wealth the wisher asked for might belong to someone else, someone very large, very powerful and very angry. Wishing for someone to fall in love with you almost ensured that they would die soon after, or become so manically obsessed, all you wanted to do was escape them, cursing the day you ever heard about the tree.

"So, why does Grimalkin want to meet us *there?*" I asked, as we landed our gliders a little way from the edge of the Iron Realm. As the new treaty dictated, no Iron fey could cross the border into the wyldwood without permission from Summer or Winter. As Iron Queen, I could probably have ignored the rule this once, but the peace treaty was still new, and I didn't want to rock the boat, so I would oblige them for now. The gliders made disappointed clicking sounds when I told them to go home, but eventually went swooping back toward Mag Tuiredh. "I hope he doesn't expect us to make a wish on the thing," I continued, as Ash scanned the surroundings, wary and alert as always. "I've learned my lesson, thanks. I'd rather go to tea with Mab than make a wish on something called the Wishing Tree in the middle of the Nevernever."

"You have no idea how relieved I am to finally hear you say that." Ash was still gazing around the clearing, looking solemn apart from the grin in his voice. When I glared at him, he turned, and the smile finally broke through. "I don't think we'll have to worry about that," he said easily. "Though I would still advise you to be cautious. This is Grimalkin we're talking about, after all."

"Yeah." I sighed as he closed the distance between us, not touching, but always close. "And he won't tell us anything until he's good and ready and I'm about to strangle him."

Ash's smile faded as he raised his head, tilting it to the side as though listening for something. "Do you hear that?" he asked.

We fell silent. Through the trees, faint at first but growing steadily louder, voices rose into the air—shouts and curses, mixed with the clang of weapons.

"Sounds like a fight," Ash stated calmly, and I exhaled. Of course it was. This was the Nevernever, where nothing was ever simple.

"Come on," I muttered, drawing my sword, "we'd better see what's happening. I swear though, if I catch any more Winter knights this close to the border, Mab is going to get an earful."

We headed into the trees, which quickly grew dark and tangled as the Iron Realm faded into the uniform murk of the wyldwood. The sounds of battle grew louder, more consistent, until we finally broke through the trees and stood at the edge of the wyldwood proper. A large chasm ran the length of the perimeter, separating the wyldwood from the Iron Realm, and a bridge spanned the gulf between territories. At one point, the bridge had been made of wood, but the wyldwood kept dragging it down, as if it didn't want anyone coming or going into the Iron Realm. So finally, I'd spoken to my father, King Oberon, and another bridge had been constructed, this time made of stone and fashioned in place by trolls and rock dwarves. Moss and vines still curled around the heavy posts and railings, but dwarves knew stonework better than anyone, and this bridge wasn't going anywhere for a long time.

Just as well.

A fight raged in the middle of that bridge—at least, I thought it was a fight. It might've been a crazy, twirling dance for all I knew. A hoard of small, dark faeries in wooden masks jabbered and danced around a tall figure in the center of the bridge. Spear points flashed, and I realized the little men were trying to stab the stranger, who was doing a fantastic job of dodging or blocking every strike with his daggers. His hair gleamed a shocking red in the darkness, and my heart leaped to my throat.

"Puck!"

The redheaded faery in the middle of the chaos shot me a quick glance. "Oh, hey, Meghan!" Robin Goodfellow paused a split second to wave before dodging back as a midget stabbed at him. "Small world! And ice-boy's here, too! What a coincidence, I was just coming to look for you. Hey!" He ducked as a spear flew over his head. "Jeez, take it easy, you guys! I already told you, it was a simple misunderstanding." The midgets chattered angrily and surged forward, jabbing with their weapons. Puck grimaced. "Uh, ice-boy, a little help?"

Ash instantly drew his arm back and sent a flurry of ice daggers spinning toward the bridge, striking several of the small
figures, though not hard enough to kill them. They shrieked
and whirled on us, dark eyes flashing, then bounded forward
with raised spears.

I tensed, but at the edge of the Iron Realm, they skidded
to a halt, gazing up at me with wide eyes. Crowding close,
they jabbered to one another in that strange, unfamiliar language before turning to shout something to the few who still
swarmed around Puck. They paused, then came forward to
babble at one another in low voices, pointing fingers at me,
then Puck.

"What's going on?" I whispered to Ash, who was following the strange conversation with a slight frown. He sighed.

"They're Aluxob," he said, to my utter confusion. "Mayan
nature spirits. They protect the ancient forests of the Maya,
but are usually fairly tolerant of outsiders." He shot a look at
Puck. "Unless the trespasser does something to anger or insult them."

"Ah."

"What do you mean, 'ah'?" Puck said, still keeping a wary
eye on his former attackers. "I told them before, it was a
teensy tiny misunderstanding with an old headdress and an
ancient burial ground. How was I supposed to know it was
so important?"

"Puck—" I groaned, but one of the small men had crept
close, watching us carefully. As I waited, he gave a jerky bow.

"Goddess?" he asked in a clear, high-pitched voice. "You...
goddess of place, yes?"

I looked down at the tiny men, keeping a straight face even
as I recalled the line from a favorite movie. *When someone asks
you if you're a god, you say...yes!*

"I am Meghan Chase, Queen of the Iron Realm. What do you want here?"

"Command," the Alux-whatever went on, pointing back to Puck. "Command this one. Return to us what was stolen. Return, and we go."

Ash sighed and shook his head. I blinked at the midget, then turned to glare at Puck. "What did you steal?"

"I didn't steal it," Puck said, sounding affronted. "I was just borrowing it for a while. I was going to give it back."

"Puck!"

"Okay, okay. Jeez." Reaching back, Puck pulled a long feather out of his hair. It shimmered as it caught the light, a rainbow of different colors, shifting gorgeously in the wind. Begrudgingly, he handed it to the nearest little man, who snatched it from his fingers, scowling. "Man, take one feathered serpent's wingtip and you're marked for life. It's not like they don't shed them every decade or so."

The Aluxob bared their teeth at Puck, bowed to me and, as quickly as they had come, melted back into the trees. We watched until their small forms had completely disappeared into the tangled shadows, leaving the three of us standing alone at the edge of the wyldwood.

For a few heartbeats, we just stared at each other. The last time I'd seen Puck, I had been normal Meghan Chase, the girl he'd looked after for years at the command of my father, Oberon. That was before I nearly died saving Faery from the false king, took the throne for myself and married Puck's archrival. Before I became the Iron Queen.

Things were different now. After the final battle, Puck had vanished, first to help Ash in his quest to earn a soul, then disappearing from the Nevernever completely. No one knew where he'd gone, but I suspected he'd wanted to put some distance between us, take some time to think. I'd desperately hoped to see him again soon, if only to let him know how grateful I was. Puck had loved me, but he'd gone with Ash to help him earn a soul so that his archrival could return to the Iron Realm to be with me. Robin Goodfellow, for all his pranks and mischief, was the sweetest, most noble person I'd ever known, and I'd missed him terribly.

"Well." Puck finally broke the silence, scratching the back of his neck. "This is awkward. And here I thought I would have to rescue you and ice-boy from something again. That's normally how these little reunions go." He gave me a sheepish grin and stood uncomfortably next to the bridge, shoving his hands into his pockets. "Not sure what to do here, your highness. I'd give you a hug, but that might not be proper, and bowing just seems weird. Think I'll just stand here and wave. Or, I could give you a salute—"

Shaking my head, I walked up to him, reached out and pulled him into a hug. He hesitated only a second, then returned it tightly.

"Hey, princess," he murmured as we drew apart, and I smiled at his old, stupid nickname for me. It seemed everything was back to normal between us, or at least on its way. His gaze flickered to Ash, who stood by calmly, watching us both. I spared a glance at my knight, but there was nothing cold or hostile in his expression. He almost appeared happy to see Puck. Almost.

"We missed you at the wedding," he said.

"Yeah." Puck shrugged. "I was in Kyoto at the time, visiting some old kitsune friends. We were traveling up to Hokaido to check out this old temple that was supposedly haunted. Turns out, a yuki-onna had taken up residence there and had scared off most of the locals. She wasn't terribly happy to see us. Can you believe it?" He grinned. "Course, we, uh, might've pissed her off when the temple caught fire—you know how kitsune are. She chased us all the way to the coast, throwing icicles, causing blizzards…the old hag even tried burying us under an avalanche. We almost died." He sighed dreamily and looked at Ash. "You should've been there, ice-boy."

"So, how did you end up here?" I asked, promising myself to get the rest of that story out of him later. Right now, I needed to focus on what we were doing.

Puck scratched the side of his face. "Well, after the, erm, *misunderstanding* in Hokaido, I decided I should probably put some distance between myself and temperamental snow-maidens. So, I headed out to Belize and was poking around these cool Mayan ruins, when all of a sudden the oracle pops in outta nowhere, being all mysterious and spooky. I think she tried to scare me with the dust and the light show, but I've seen so many things jump out and go *boo,* it's just kinda sad, now."

I started. "The oracle?"

"Yeah." He shrugged. "She said I needed to hightail it back to the Nevernever, because you and ice-boy were gonna need my help soon. Didn't give me much else to go on, only that the three of us had to be together to get past some big nasty coming up in our future. Naturally, I thought the two of you had gotten into some kind of trouble, so here I am. Uh, minus a few hitchhikers I picked up in Belize." Puck crossed his arms, giving me an appraising look. "So, what's the big emergency, princess? You and ice-boy look fine to me, and the Nevernever isn't crumbling around us. What's going on?"

"I'm pregnant, Puck," I said quietly, and watched his eyebrows shoot into his hair. Briefly, I explained what had happened at Elysium, the oracle's mysterious appearance and invitation, and Grimalkin's instruction to meet him at the Wishing Tree. By the time I was done, Puck was still staring at me openmouthed, struck mute for maybe the second time in his life, and I would've laughed if the situation wasn't so serious.

"Oh," he finally managed. "That's, uh…wow. That's not something you hear every day. Not exactly what I was expecting, though the entire prophecy thing does get old after a while." He shook himself, seeming to regain his composure, and glanced at Ash. "So, it's the ever so popular Firstborn Child of Doom prophecy, huh, ice-boy? How very cliché. Why can't it ever be the third nephew twice removed who's fated to destroy the world?"

I felt a twinge of exasperation that Puck was being so flippant about a very serious matter, again…but that was Puck. His way of coping with the situation. I guess you couldn't blame him. I *had* just dropped a rather large bombshell in his lap; it *wasn't* every day that your best friend told you she was pregnant with the future Destroyer of the World.

Oh, great, now I'm *making jokes.*

Ash gave Puck a weary look. "We don't know anything yet," he said, glancing at me as if he knew what I was thinking. "We have to find the oracle and see what she can tell us, what she's offering. Until then, it's useless to worry about something that hasn't happened yet."

I marveled that he could be so calm. Did he know something I didn't, something he had glimpsed in that future version of us? But that couldn't be right; surely he would tell me if he'd seen something like *that:* our child growing up to destroy the courts. That was kind of a big thing not to mention.

Or was that all a part of the "future what-ifs" he didn't want to talk about?

"Well," Puck said cheerfully, forcing a rather pained smile, "it's just like old times, isn't it? You, me, ice-boy, the future of the Nevernever hanging in the balance…we just have to wait for Furball to show up and then it'll be perfect."

"He is already here, Goodfellow," came a familiar voice behind us, sounding bored and offended all at once. "Where he has been for much of the conversation, waiting for you to see past the end of your nose."

"Yep." Puck sighed as we all turned to face Grimalkin. "Just like old times."

CHAPTER FIVE

"So…why are we going to the Wishing Tree again?" Puck asked as we followed Grimalkin through a section of the wyld-wood that was even darker and more tangled than most. Trees crowded together and vines and branches interlocked like clutching fingers to block the path. It would've been diffi-cult to navigate, except the tangled vegetation shifted and uncoiled to let us through as I approached. The Nevernever recognized a queen of Faery; Ash had explained when this first happened. The rulers of the courts were all, in some way, tied to the land, and the Nevernever responded to their very presence, even out here in the wyldwood.

"Oy, Furball," Puck called when Grimalkin ignored him. "I know you can hear me. Why are we going to the freak-ing Wishing Tree, of all places? Is creepy oracle lady going to meet us there?"

"She is not."

"She is not," Puck repeated, wrinkling his nose. "Of course she's not. That would make too much sense, right?" Grimal-kin didn't answer, and Puck rolled his eyes. "So, where *is* she meeting us, cat?"

"The Dreaming Pool."

"Okay, if anyone else is as confused as me, raise your hand," Puck said, putting his arm in the air. "Do I have to ask the obvious question, then? If she's meeting us at the Dreaming Pool, why the heck are we going to the Wishing Tree?"

Grimalkin looked over his shoulder, twitching his tail disdainfully. "I would have thought the answer obvious, Goodfellow," he said in a very slow, annoyed voice. "If you recall, the Dreaming Pool lies somewhere in the Briars. Very deep in the Briars, and never in the same place twice. To reach it normally, one very nearly has to stumble upon it by accident. And I do not wish to go floundering about the thorns with the lot of you for who knows how long. The Wishing Tree will get us there much faster."

"How? Don't tell me you're gonna *wish* us there." Puck looked faintly alarmed for a second, and glanced at Ash. "That didn't work out so well for us last time, huh, ice-boy?"

I blinked at them in shock, but Ash snorted. "You were the one who made the wish, Goodfellow. I seem to recall telling you not to do it. Of all people, you should've known better."

"Really?" I looked at the grinning prankster. "Do I even want to know?"

"You really don't, princess."

"He was trying to make Oberon forget about a certain prank that went off in Titania's bedchambers," Ash answered for him. "I don't even remember what it was, but it backfired and caught Oberon instead of Titania. The Erlking was about ready to tear his head off."

"Oh, great, ice-boy, make it sound like the worst thing ever."

I rolled my eyes at him. "It's a wonder you've survived this long. What happened with the tree?"

Puck scratched the back of his head. "Well—and this was a long time ago, understand—we made it to the tree—"

"Which took no small amount of effort, because Oberon was hunting us all over the wyldwood," Ash broke in.

"Who's telling the story here, ice-boy? Anyway…" Puck sniffed. "We made it to the tree. And I wished that Oberon would just…forget about that little misunderstanding. I thought I phrased it very well, didn't leave anything to chance. And, it worked…sort of."

"Sort of?"

"*Everyone* forgot us." Ash sighed. "The entire Nevernever. No one remembered who we were, that we'd ever existed." He leveled a piercing glare at Puck. "I very nearly faded away, thanks to you."

"He'll never let me forget that," Puck told me, rolling his eyes. I stared at him in alarm, and he grimaced. "But yeah. It was a pain in the ass to get that wish reversed. Not something I'd want to do again. Wishing Tree equals bad news. And that's not even counting the stupid thing guarding it."

"Which is why *I* am here, Goodfellow." Grimalkin sighed from up ahead. "Do not worry about the phrasing of the wish—I will take care of that. All you must concern yourself with is getting the queen past the sentinel of the tree. That is why you are here, I assume."

"Sentinel?" I frowned as a thick wall of bramble and thorns peeled back for me, revealing a small clearing beyond. "What sentinel?"

Puck winced and nodded into the glen. "That sentinel."

A tree stood in the center of the clearing. It was large and pale, bare of leaves, with crooked branches reaching up to claw the sky. However, only the top limbs were visible above the coils of a massive snake curled around the trunk. The huge serpent, black and shiny with thick, armorlike scales, shifted its huge body into an even tighter coil, looking like it wanted to suffocate the tree. I could see its head, resting on the ground, an arrow-shaped viper skull with lidless red eyes. A forked tongue, almost as long as me, flicked out to taste the air.

"Jeez, that thing has gotten huge," Puck muttered, crossing his arms as we stared at the gigantic creature. "I don't remember it being half that big the last time we killed it, do you, ice-boy?"

I started, frowning at him. "You *killed* it? Then, how is it…still here?"

"It doesn't stay dead," Ash replied, watching the monster over my shoulder. His hands came to rest lightly on my waist as he moved close. "If someone wants to use the Wishing Tree, they first have to kill the guardian. If they're successful, they get their wish, but the sentinel returns to life soon after, even bigger and harder to kill than before."

"Oh." I glared at Grimalkin, calmly washing his paws on a nearby rock. "That's just fabulous. And you expect us to kill that thing? It's the size of Walmart."

The cat yawned. "I do not expect you to do anything, Iron Queen," he said, examining his claws. "I am simply to guide you to where you need to go. If you do not wish to get to the oracle and inquire about the future of your child, that is your decision." He gave the paw a final lick, then set it down. "But the only way to the oracle is through the Wishing Tree. And the only way to the Wishing Tree is through the sentinel."

"He's right." Ash sighed, and drew his blade. Puck followed suit with his daggers. "If the only way to the oracle is past that serpent, then we're cutting a path straight through. We did it before—we'll just have to do it again."

"I love it when you talk my language, ice-boy." Puck grinned.

I drew my sword as well, but Ash put a hand my arm. "Meghan, wait," he said softly, pulling us back a step. I hesitated, then followed him back into the trees, out of sight of the serpent. "I don't want you to fight this time," he said as he bent close, his expression intent and serious. "Stay back with Grimalkin. Leave this fight to me and Puck."

I scowled. "What, you don't think I can handle myself?" I asked, vaguely aware that Puck had moved away, giving us some space. Grimalkin had also disappeared, so it was just me and my knight. I glared at him, hurt and indignant. "Afraid I'll get in your way or slow you down?"

"It's not that—"

"Then what is it?" I faced him calmly, drawing on the persona of the Iron Queen. I would not act like a whiny teenager. I was the ruler of Mag Tuiredh, the queen of thousands of fey, and I would not throw a tantrum in the middle of the Nevernever. "You know I can fight," I told him. "You were the one who taught me. We've fought side by side against Machina, Virus, Ferrum and an entire army of Iron fey. I've fought more battles than most have seen in a lifetime, and I know I'll have to fight more in the future. This is part of my duty, Ash. I'm not helpless anymore."

"I never said you were!" Ash pressed his hand to my cheek, peering at me intently, silver eyes bright. "I never meant to imply that," he continued in a softer voice, running his thumb over my skin. "It's just…you're carrying our child now, Meghan. I can't risk anything happening to you. To both of you."

My anger vanished. It was impossible to stay mad when he said things like that. But still, I was the Iron Queen. I would not let those I loved put themselves in danger while I watched from the sidelines. I'd done far too much of that already.

"Ash," I said, meeting that bright, soulful gaze. "I can't. I can't hang back and do nothing. Not anymore." He let out a quiet breath, and I placed my hands on his cheeks, gazing up at him. "Our life, our world, is always going to be dangerous, and there will always be something that wishes us harm.

But if this is for the future of our child, and the future of our kingdom, I will stand with you and fight. That is my promise, and my duty as queen. I won't let anything come between us or stand in our way."

Ash's eyes grew smoldering. "As you wish, my queen," he said in a low voice, bending close. "If this is your will, then I will fight beside you with everything I have." And he brushed his lips to mine.

We kissed until Grimalkin's impatient sigh filtered through the brambles around us.

"Goodfellow is getting uncomfortable," the cat said, as we reluctantly pulled away. "And the guardian is waiting for you. Perhaps we can refrain from celebrating until after it is defeated." He sniffed as I rolled my eyes, grabbing my sword from where I'd jammed it into the earth. "Also, I feel obligated to point out that the sentinel is very near invincible now. Its scales will turn away most sword blows, and it is impervious to magical attacks. A frontal assault would be most unwise."

"Okay, so how are we supposed to kill the thing?"

Grimalkin sniffed. "How was Achilles finally defeated? How did the dragon Smaug meet his end? There is always a chink in the armor, human. It is small, but it is always there."

A piercing hiss rent the relative silence of the glade, making me flinch, and Grimalkin disappeared. The huge snake had uncoiled, and was towering in front of the tree, its tongue flicking the air rapidly. And then *another* arrow-shaped head rose up where the tail should've been, identical to the first and just as frightening. The two-headed serpent hissed again, sounding angry and defiant, flashing twin pairs of very long, curved fangs.

"Uh, guys?" Puck glanced over his shoulder at us. "Not to be rude and all, but this thing is starting to eye me like I'm a big tasty mouse. I hope you two are planning to join the party soon."

I shared a glance with Ash, who waited quietly, not looking at the snake or Puck or Grimalkin, but at me. "Ready for this?" I asked him, and he nodded, gesturing with his sword.

"Lead the way, my queen. I'm right beside you."

We left the trees, walking calmly across the field, side by side. The monstrous, two-headed snake hissed a challenge and reared up into a coiled S, ready to strike.

"How you wanna do this?" Puck muttered as we got closer. The sentinel's beady eyes followed us as we approached, never blinking, and it had gone perfectly, dangerously still. I felt the tension lining its huge body, like a rubber band stretched to breaking, and my heart pounded.

"You take one head," Ash replied, his narrowed gaze on our opponent. "I'll take the other. Meghan, that will give you enough of a distraction to look for the weak spot. And let's hope Grimalkin knows what he's talking about."

"Weak spot?" Puck echoed, looking confused. "What weak spot? Last time we fought this thing, we just hacked it to—"

One snake head lunged. Insanely fast, it darted in, jaws gaping, a dark blur that took me by surprise. Puck, however, was ready for it. He leaped straight up and, as the snake's jaws snapped shut in the place he had been, landed on the flat, scaly head.

The sentinel hissed and reared back, shaking its head, trying to dislodge its unwanted passenger. Puck whooped loudly, clinging like a leech, dagger flashing as he hacked and stabbed when he could. Where the dagger edge met scales, sparks flew, but the blade was unable to pierce the thick hide. Still, it must've pissed the snake off royally, because the head went crazy trying to dislodge him.

"Meghan, watch out!"

I jerked back, cursing myself. In the split second my gaze had been on Puck, the second head had streaked toward me. Ash lunged in front of me and met the attack with his own, the ice-blade slashing down to catch the serpent in the eye. The snake screamed, in pain this time, and recoiled. Hissing furiously, it turned on Ash, who stepped forward to meet it, his blade held up before him.

Too close, Meghan. Focus, dammit.

I took a deep breath and felt the glamour of Summer and Iron rise up in me. With Puck and Ash keeping the sentinel busy, I closed my eyes and sent my magic into the ground, into the wyldwood itself. I felt the roots of the ancient Wishing Tree, extending deep into the earth, the power that hummed through it and all the Nevernever. I could even feel the heart-beat of the sentinel itself, the sudden fear as it realized the two warriors it fought were just a distraction. That the small, insig-nificant human on the ground, glowing with sudden power, was the real threat.

"Meghan!"

I heard Ash's warning shout, sensed that both heads had broken off their attacks and were now coming for me. I felt the speed of the heads as they darted in, lethal fangs extend-ing to pierce me and swallow me whole, and smiled.

Too late, I'm afraid.

The roots of the Wishing Tree, thick and gnarled and an-cient, erupted from the dirt around me, surging into the air. They shot forward to meet the sentinel, wrapping around the huge coils, pinning it to the ground.

Hissing, the snake thrashed and flailed its powerful body, snapping the tough, thick roots and wiggling free. It was strong, stronger than I expected. Triumphant, the heads reared up again, ready to strike. But an ice-spear flew through the cage of branches, striking one head, and a huge raven swooped in to peck at the eye of the second. The heads flinched, distracted for a brief moment, and that was all the time I needed.

I called the roots again, but this time, my Iron glamour surged forth, infusing the wood as it wrapped around the snake. The sentinel hissed and thrashed again, trying to break free, but the ancient roots were streaked with iron now and as strong as cables. The snake's thrashing slowed as the iron roots coiled around it, and it shrieked in frustration.

Gripping my sword, I walked forward, still sending power flowing into the tree, the merged glamour of Summer and Iron. I passed the first head, which hissed and tried to snap at me, failing. I walked calmly past the second, to the same result, until I stood in the center of the coil of roots and snake. And I closed my eyes again, searching for the heartbeat, the pulse of life that pounded through the huge sentinel. I followed that beat, the coils of both snake and tree thrashing wildly around me, until I found it. A chink in the snake's armor, a hole barely the size of my fist. The sentinel wailed, beady red eyes glaring at me through the branches, and I gave it a sad smile.

"I'm sorry. But I am the Iron Queen, and you are in my way."

Raising my sword, I drove it, point down, into the crack between scales, sinking it deep. The sentinel screamed, a high piercing wail, and convulsed madly, shaking the roots of the tree. I staggered away, clutching my sword, as it wailed and thrashed, fighting the inevitable. At last, its struggles slowed, the light went out of its crimson eyes and it finally stopped moving.

I slumped against a branch, breathing hard, my body spent from using so much power. Pushing myself off the root, I sheathed my blade as Ash and Puck came through the web, both their expressions blank with disbelief. I grinned at them tiredly.

"There, that wasn't so bad," I said, still trying to catch my breath. "So, why did you guys have such a hard time, before?"

Puck blinked at me, and Ash approached until he stood only a few feet away. Silently, he met my gaze and, lowering his head, gave me a very solemn bow. "You are truly a queen of Faery," he said in a voice only I could hear. "I am honored to be your knight."

A lump caught in my throat, but at that moment, the Wishing Tree flared up and blazed with light. I flinched and turned away as hundreds, if not thousands, of candles sprang to life along the branches, making the entire tree glow in the darkness like a beacon.

"Oh, yeah," Puck commented, staring up at the galaxy of flickering lights. "I remember this. Bit of advice, princess— only blow out the one candle. Bad things happen if you try to wish for more than one thing."

Warily, we stepped beneath the limbs of the tree, feeling the heat from a thousand tiny flames against our faces. I caught a flash of gray fur overhead, and Grimalkin peered down at us from one of the branches, the candlelight reflected in his golden eyes. "The wish has already been spoken," he purred, waving his tail. "The way to the oracle is clear. When you are ready, simply douse a candle and close your eyes. The tree will do the rest."

"Yeah, and what else will it do, I wonder?" Puck muttered, giving both Grimalkin and the flickering candles a dubious look. "You sure you voiced the wish *exactly* right, cat? No loopholes or funny turns of phrase that could be used against us? I don't wanna wake up as a frog or find myself on the bottom of the ocean or something crazy like that."

The cat scratched an ear, unconcerned. "I suppose you will have to take your chances."

I spotted a candle on a low hanging limb, its orange flame

dancing weakly in the shadows. "Come on," I told the boys quietly. "If this is the only way to the oracle, we have to do this. No turning back now."

Ash moved beside me and took my hand. "We don't want to get separated," he murmured, lacing our fingers together. "There will be a cost, later, that's how it works. The Wishing Tree always demands a price, no matter what Grimalkin says."

My stomach twisted, but Ash gave me a reassuring smile and squeezed my hand. I felt the smooth metal of his wedding band press against my skin, and I smiled back.

Half turning, I held out the other hand to Puck. He hesitated, still eyeing the tree, and I wrinkled my nose at him.

"Robin Goodfellow," I said, giving him a challenging smile, "don't tell me you're afraid."

His green eyes flashed with familiar defiance, and he stepped close, taking my hand. "Not on your life, *princess,*" he returned, smirking. "Though don't think I don't know what you're doing. If we all end up as llamas, I'm going to spend the rest of my life following you around saying 'I told you so' in llama-ese."

I quickly pushed away the thought of Puck as a llama before I started laughing. I needed to stay serious, focus on what lay ahead. The oracle waited for me, and she held the answers about my child. But I wasn't afraid anymore. Not with Ash and Puck beside me, their fingers wrapped tightly around mine, protective auras glowing strong. Just like old times, as Puck said. The three of us had been through so much together and always won; this wasn't going to be any different.

I squeezed their hands, raised my head and blew out the candle. A thin wisp of smoke curled into the air, and that was the last thing I saw.

CHAPTER SIX

I opened my eyes, blinking in confusion. I didn't remember closing them, but I must have, because everything was different. The glen and the Wishing Tree were gone, as was the body of the monstrous snake. A tunnel of thick black brambles surrounded me, bristling with thorns, the branches creaking and slithering against one another like they were alive.

"Well, we're here," Puck said, releasing my hand to pat himself down, as if making sure he was all there. "Looks like we made it in one piece, too." He peered past me to where Ash stood on the other side, squeezing my fingers in a death grip. "*And* all together. I was half expecting us to land in different corners of the Nevernever, or at the very least surrounded by nasties wanting to tear our heads off. Looks like Furball actually pulled it off."

"What did you expect, Goodfellow?" Grimalkin sauntered by, tail in the air, and did not look at us. "I am a cat."

I stole a glance at Ash. He looked relieved as well, though I could tell he was worried about the whole situation. He, too, had been expecting trouble the moment we arrived.

"Stay alert," he told us softly as we moved forward, following Grimalkin down the tunnel of thorns. "Just because there are no surprises now doesn't mean there won't be some later."

Ahead of us, the ceiling of the tunnel began to shimmer,

rippling with waves of blue light. As we reached the end of the corridor, the passage opened up, and we stood at the edge of a small grotto surrounded by thorns. Overhead, the Briars shut out the sky, branches woven so tightly together the area felt more like a cave than anything else. The walls were filled with human clutter: toys, books, picture frames, trophies, stuffed animals, all dangling from the thorns or speared upon a long black spike. Grimalkin had vanished within the clutter, like another stuffed animal in the huge pile of toys. A porcelain doll with a missing eye stared at me as I ventured past the lip of the tunnel into the chamber.

"Well, that's just all kinds of creepy," Puck muttered at my side, giving the doll a look of alarm. "If you see any clowns, do me a favor and don't point them out, okay? I'd rather live without the nightmares."

I was about to snap at him for putting the thought of killer clown dolls in my head, when Ash touched my arm and nodded to something ahead of us.

In the center of the grotto, a bright, glowing pool threw hazy reflections over the walls and ceiling. But the pool itself was perfectly still, like the surface of a mirror, and you could see everything reflected in it. The walls full of clutter and the ceiling of the grotto plunged down like a hole in the pool's surface. At the edge of the water, slumped in an ancient rocking chair like a pile of discarded rags—or a long desiccated corpse—was a familiar old woman.

For few seconds, the oracle was so very still that I thought she was dead, after all. Then her head slowly turned, and those empty, eyeless pits fastened on me.

"You have come." She rose from the chair as if she were on strings and raised a withered hand, beckoning us forward. I squared my shoulders and marched toward her, Ash and Puck close behind me. The Briars seemed to hold their breath, the dolls and other toys watching intently, until we stood just a few feet from the ancient hag, the now-familiar stench of grave dust and old newspapers clogging the back of my throat.

For a second, nobody moved.

I cleared my throat. "All right," I announced, meeting that eerie stare head-on. Or, hoping I did, anyway. It was difficult to glare at an eyeless face—you didn't really know if it was looking at you or not. "I'm here, Oracle. We came as fast as we could. Now, what is this offer you were speaking of at Elysium? What do you know about my child?"

"Your child," the oracle mused, almost dreamily. "Your *son*. Yes, I know much about him," she continued, smiling at my shock. "Many futures have I glimpsed, and in all, he is a remarkable creature, born of Summer, Winter and Iron, an anomaly among all his kind. Human and fey, with the magic of all three courts flowing through his veins, he will possess a power none have ever seen." She paused then, her forehead creasing like wrinkled paper. "And here is where his future becomes cloudy. Something is out there, Iron Queen, something dark, and it has the power to turn your son from you. I cannot see what it is, perhaps it is not even in the world yet, but *he* is balanced on a very fine edge, able to fall either way. And what comes after…" She shook her shriveled head. "I have seen death and destruction on a grand scale, many lives lost, the courts destroyed, and in the center of it all is your son."

I was having trouble breathing. My legs felt shaky, and I locked my knees to keep myself upright. Beside me, even Puck looked stunned, his face pale beneath his red hair. Ash didn't say anything, but he stepped close and placed a steady hand on the small of my back, just to reassure me he was still there. I leaned into him and drew strength from his touch.

"You…still haven't told me your offer," I whispered, reeling from the flood of information the oracle had thrown at me. "You could have told me this at the Voodoo Museum, or anywhere in the Nevernever. Why did you call us here?"

The oracle's thin lips curled in a grim smile. "Because, I have something to show you, Iron Queen," she whispered back, and turned to gesture at the water behind her. "The Dreaming Pool can show anyone their future, or the future of another, if one knows where to look. Come…" She beckoned me with a talon. "Step forward, into the waters, and I will show you your son."

I shared a glance with Ash, and he nodded. But before we could step forward, the oracle spoke again. "Only the Iron Queen," she said, as I looked up sharply. "I can take only one with me into the pool. This is the queen's decision, no others'."

"This is Ash's son, too," I protested. "He deserves to see this."

"I cannot," the oracle said simply. "I can show only one, and you are the queen. This responsibility, and the choice that comes with it, falls to you."

Ash took my arm, gently drawing us away from the shimmering light of the pool. Puck nonchalantly moved between us and the oracle, crossing his arms and smirking at her, making sure she didn't follow, but she did not move.

I looked up at Ash, and he offered a faint smile, taking my hands. "It's all right," he murmured, gazing into my eyes. "I trust you. I know you'll do what's best for our son, even if I can't be there. Just remember this, Meghan." One hand rose to cup my cheek. "Whatever the oracle shows you, no matter how bleak or terrible or frightening, it hasn't happened yet. Don't let her terrify you into doing something we'll both regret."

I nodded, my heart pounding. Ash lowered his head and kissed the side of my neck, right below my ear, and I shivered. "I love you," he whispered. "Know that I'm with you always, even if you can't see me." He pulled back just enough to place a soft kiss on my lips, his gaze intense. "Whatever you discover, you're not alone. You have me, and Puck, and a whole kingdom, ready to stand beside you at a word. There is nothing the oracle can reveal that will make us abandon you."

My throat felt tight. I wanted to fall into him, to curl into his arms and shut out the whole world. But the oracle was watching us; I could feel the hollow pits of her eyes on the back of my head, and I could not appear weak, not now. So I pressed a palm to Ash's cheek, trying to convey what I felt without words. He covered my hand with his own and smiled.

Then I turned, raised my chin and walked back to the oracle.

She was no longer in the same spot but had drifted out into the center of the Dreaming Pool, still watching my every move as we joined Puck at the edge. Our reflections gazed back at us, perfect mirror images on the glassy surface: the Iron Queen, her knight and the infamous Robin Goodfellow, smirking at the hag in the center of the pool. The oracle stood on top of the water, as if the pool was only an inch deep. Though the water was so still, it was impossible to discern the bottom; all I could see was the brambly roof of the grotto, reflected back at me.

"Step forward, Iron Queen," the oracle beckoned. "Come to Anna, and I will show you your son. Remember, only you are allowed this privilege. Your knight and the Summer prankster must stay behind. Do not worry, it will not take long."

"Oracle," Ash said in a deadly calm voice as I took a step forward, halting at the water's edge. "I am trusting you with the well-being of my wife and a queen of Faery," he continued as I hesitated. "If she returns harmed in any way, not only will you face the wrath of the entire Iron Court, you will have to deal with me, personally."

"Yeah, and he won't be alone, either," Puck chimed in, sounding more serious than I'd heard in a while. "You'll have to deal with both of us, not to mention a very pissed-off Summer King. And probably the entire Seelie Court." He grinned then, but it was one of his scary, evil smiles. "Just a friendly warning to bring her back unscathed."

The oracle pursed her bloodless lips. "Your queen's physical body will be in no danger," she said reluctantly, as if being forced to read the fine print of a contract. "However, glimpsing the future, even a small part, is a serious matter, and can be traumatizing for weaker minds. I cannot promise that your queen will not be *changed* by what she will see. I can only show her the future. I cannot be responsible for how it affects her."

Puck turned a worried gaze on me. "Sure you wanna do this, princess?"

I felt Ash at my back, remembered his words, the look in his eyes, and felt no fear. "Yes," I said firmly, facing the pool again. Ash had seen our future, a possible one, anyway, and it hadn't stopped him. I needed to do this, to discover everything I could about my child, our son. "I'm ready," I told the oracle. "Show me what you've seen. I want to know."

"Then, come," the oracle whispered, holding out a hand. "Step into the Dreaming Pool, Meghan Chase. Step into the pool, and I will take you to your son."

I walked forward, expecting the sink below the surface, to wade out to where the oracle floated above the water. But the pool was only an inch deep, after all, because the water didn't even come past my ankles, barely soaking the hem of my jeans as I walked out to the middle of the pool. The water barely rippled as I passed, maintaining its near-perfect glassiness even when my footsteps broke the surface. By the time

I reached the oracle, waiting in the center, the pool had returned to absolute calm once more.

The oracle's eyeless holes scanned my face. "Are you certain this is what you wish?" she asked, as if this was the last formal courtesy she had to get out of the way. "You cannot unsee what you are about to discover."

"I'm sure," I said.

She nodded once. "Then look down, Iron Queen. Look straight down, into the water."

I looked down.

My reflection stared back at me, perfectly clear. I felt like I was standing on a piece of glass or a giant mirror, rather then the surface of a pool. But, then I stared past my image, past my head, to where the ceiling of the grotto should've been reflected in the water's surface.

The brambly ceiling of the chamber now blazed with stars, and a full silver moon beamed down from a cloudless sky.

Startled, I looked up. The shadowy grotto had disappeared. A puddle still soaked my feet, but I now stood in the middle of a grassy field, gentle hills rolling away on either side. In the distance, at the bottom of a slope, fluffy white creatures moved through the grass like stray clouds, and their faint *baas* drifted to me over the breeze.

"Where am I?" I asked, turning in a slow circle. A hint of dust and decay abruptly caught in my throat and sent the sheep bolting over the hills in terror.

"The mortal realm," the oracle whispered, appearing behind me. "Ireland, I believe it is called now. The birthplace of many of our kind."

I was about to ask what we were doing in Ireland, when another scent on the wind made me stop, my heart jumping to my throat. It was faint, but I recognized it immediately;

live through enough war and battles, and the smell becomes impossible to ignore.

Blood.

I followed the direction of the breeze and saw a lone figure several yards away, standing beneath the light of the moon. His back was to me, but I could see he was tall and lean, his loose silver hair gleaming in the darkness, tossed gently by the wind. He stood in the middle of a ring of toadstools, huge white bulbous things that formed a near-perfect circle around him.

As I approached, my heart began a strange thud in my chest. The figure didn't turn around, his attention focused on the ground at his feet. As I got closer, I saw the sword, curved and graceful, held loosely in one hand. The blade and the arm that held it were stained with blood, dark streaks all the way past his elbow.

As I drew close, the figure turned, and I gasped.

I couldn't see his face; it was blurry and indistinct, his features hidden as if in a fog. But I knew him; I recognized him as surely as I knew my own shadow, my own heartbeat. Bright, tall, achingly handsome, even if I could not see his face. I sensed piercing, icy-blue eyes, somewhere in the haze between us, felt him smile at me.

My son. *This is my son.*

And he was covered in blood. It stained his hands, his arms, was splattered in large streaks across his chest. My heart gave a violent lurch, thinking he was fatally wounded, dying perhaps. Was this what the oracle wanted to show me? Was this the grief she was talking about, the death of my child? But how could that be, when he was standing right there, and I could still feel his smile, directed at me?

Then I realized the blood was not his own.

And I saw what was lying in the grass before us.

The world seemed to stop for a moment. My legs shook,

and I sank to my knees, unable to hold myself up any longer. No, this couldn't be. This was a cruel joke, a nightmare.

A body lay at my son's feet, sprawled on its back in the grass, gazing sightlessly at the moon. Another boy, my age perhaps, with messy brown hair and smoky blue eyes. A pair of short blades were clutched loosely in his hands, though the edges were clean. Blood pooled from a gaping slash in his chest, right over his heart, staining his once-white T-shirt nearly black.

I felt sick, and covered my mouth to keep from screaming. I'd never seen this boy, not like this, but I knew him. I recognized his face, his eyes, the tug on my heart. Though he was years older now, and had changed so much, I'd know him anywhere.

"Ethan," I whispered, touching his arm. It was cold, sticky, and I yanked my hand back, shaking my head. "No," I said, trembling. "No, this isn't true. It can't be." I looked up at my son, who was no longer smiling, and I sensed his cold blue eyes, appraising me. *"Why?"*

My son didn't answer. Sheathing his sword, he stared down at the body, and though his face remained hidden and blurred, I could sense tears running down his cheeks. A voice, low and soft, clear and high, filled with infinite possibilities, drifted over the grass.

"I'm sorry."

Then he turned and walked away, leaving me shaking with grief and horror and confusion, staring at the lifeless shell of my baby brother.

"That is always the trigger," the oracle whispered behind me. "No matter what your son chooses afterward, be it savior or destroyer, this scene is the catalyst that heralds the entire event. The death of Ethan Chase brings with it a storm unlike any Faery has seen, and in the eye of the hurricane stands your son."

"This can't...be his only future," I whispered, unwilling to believe that my son was destined to kill my brother. "There have to be other paths, other outcomes. This can't be for certain."

"No," the oracle said, almost reluctantly. "It is not the only path. But this is the future that is the most clear. And it becomes clearer with every passing day. Be forewarned, Iron Queen, your brother and your son are on a collision course toward each other, and if they ever meet, the fate of the Nevernever dangles in the balance. As do the lives of your family. But...I can stop it."

I finally tore my gaze from Ethan's body and looked at her. "You? How?"

The oracle's eyes were pitiless holes as she watched me, the wind fluttering her clothes like old rags. "I offer a contract," she whispered. "A bargain, for the sake of the Nevernever and your family. For all the lives it will save, including your brother's."

A cold hand gripped my stomach. I suddenly knew what she was going to ask, but I continued nonetheless. "What kind of contract? What do you want from me?"

"Your child," she replied, confirming my hunch and making my insides recoil. "Promise me your firstborn son, and all the futures I have glimpsed with him will melt away. Your brother's life will be spared, and the Nevernever will be in no danger, if you remove his string from the tapestry."

"No!" The response was swift and automatic, without thinking. No way I was giving my firstborn son to this creepy faery. It was out of the question. But the oracle held up her hands in a placating gesture, claws glinting the moonlight.

"Think about it carefully, Iron Queen," she whispered. "I know your initial response is to refuse, but think about the implications of your choice tonight. The fate of the Nevernever, and your human family, hangs on this one string. You are a queen of Faery—you have responsibilities now, to your subjects and your kingdom. It is your duty to protect them, from *all* threats, whatever form they wear. If this was not your son, if this was a random stranger threatening the future of the Nevernever, of countless lives, would you not choose to stop it?"

"But it's *not* a random stranger," I said in a shaking voice. "It's my child. Ash's child. I can't do that to him."

"You are his queen," the oracle went on. "He will understand, and he will support any decision you make, regardless if he agrees or not." She held out a hand, her voice earnest. "I promise you, Meghan Chase, your son will want for nothing with me. I will be like a mother to him. He will grow up unaware of his true heritage, far from the courts and any influences they might have over him. He will be safe, and he will never grow into the threat you saw tonight. That is my offer, and my solemn vow. So, Meghan Chase..." She drifted closer, her hollow gaze burning into me. "The fate of your world hangs on this reply. What is your answer? Do we have a deal?"

I closed my eyes. Could I do this? Give up my son, to save the Nevernever? Was I being selfish, dooming everyone to chaos and destruction, if I refused? And what of my family? My brother, the one who had started the entire adventure, in a way. I'd do anything to keep him safe. Just...not this.

I clasped my hands in front of my face, thinking, and my fingers pressed against something cool and hard. Opening my eyes, I looked down at my hand. My ring sparkled in the moonlight, gold and silver, reminding me of its twin and the knight it was attached to.

Ash saw his future, I thought suddenly. *He saw* our *future. Or, one of them, anyway, when he was trying to earn a soul. Did he see this? Our son killing Ethan, destroying the Nevernever? If he did...*

If he had…he hadn't let it stop him. He had finished what he'd set out to do: he'd earned his soul, and come back to the Iron Realm to be with me.

"I trust you." His voice echoed through my head, like he was right there, standing behind me. *"I know you'll do what's best for our son. Remember, whatever the oracle shows you, no matter how bleak or terrible or frightening, it hasn't happened yet."*

"No, it hasn't," I whispered.

The oracle wrinkled her forehead. "What was that?" she asked, frowning. "I did not hear you. Have you come to a decision, Meghan Chase?"

"I have." I straightened my shoulders and stared her down. "And the answer is no, Oracle. No deal. I'm not giving up our son, because of a future that *might* come to pass. And you have some nerve, trying to force this decision on me without the father of my child present to hear it, as well. We're a family now. Whatever happens, we will deal with it, together."

The oracle's withered, eyeless face crumpled with rage. "Then I am sorry, Iron Queen," she hissed, floating back several paces. "If you will not accept my offer, you give me little choice. For the future of the courts, and all of Faery, you will not leave this place."

I drew my sword, and the oracle hissed, raising her steely talons. "You gave your word," I told her as she circled me like a dusty, ragged phantom, her hair writhing in the breeze. "You promised Ash and Puck that I would not come to harm."

"I said your *physical* body will not be harmed," the oracle replied, baring rotten yellow teeth. "But we are not in the physical world anymore, human. This is more a dream, or a nightmare, depending on how you see it."

Damn faery word games. I should've seen this coming. "Ash and Puck are still waiting for me," I told her, keeping the point of my blade angled in her direction. "If I don't return, you'll have the entire Iron Realm coming after you. This isn't worth it, Oracle."

"Your protectors know nothing of what is happening now," the oracle replied, darting back like a marionette whose strings were jerked. "They see only your physical body, and the death of your dream self will not affect it. Though they will take an empty husk back to the Iron Court tonight, and by that time, I will be long gone. I did say your mind might not be *unchanged* by this little encounter."

I growled a curse and lunged at her, stabbing with my sword. She jerked back, baring her rotten teeth. "This is *my* realm, Meghan Chase," she spat. "You might be a queen of Faery, and have an entire kingdom ready to fight for you, but here, the dream obeys me!"

Snarling, she waved a claw, and the landscape twisted around us. The moonlit hills disappeared, and black, gnarled trees rose up around us, clawing and grasping. I dodged, cutting away branches that slashed at me with twiggy claws, and the oracle hissed a laugh.

I smacked away a limb reaching for my head and spun to face the withered hag. My arms shook with anger, but I kept my voice calm. "Why are you doing this?" I asked, watching her glare at me balefully. "You were never spiteful, Oracle. You helped us a great deal before, why turn on me now?"

"You do not see, do you, child?" The oracle's voice was suddenly weary. She waved a claw, and the trees retreated a bit. "I do not take pleasure in this. I truly do not wish your death. It is for the good of the Nevernever, for all of us. Your human sentiments make you blind—you would sacrifice the courts to save one child."

"*My* child."

"Exactly." The oracle shivered, seemed to ripple in the air. Then, like she was being torn in half, her dusty, ragged body split, became two, six, twelve copies. The duplicate oracles spread out, surrounding me, their wrinkled mouths speaking as one. "You make decisions as a human and a mother, not a true queen. Mab would not hesitate to give up her progeny, even her beloved third son, if she thought he put her throne in danger."

"I am *not* like Mab. And I never will be."

"No," the oracles agreed sadly, and raised their claws. "You will not be anything."

They came at me all at once, a dozen ragged, jerky puppets lunging at me from all sides. I dodged one attack and lashed out with my sword at the next. The blade sheared through the thin body and the duplicate wailed, exploding into a cloud of dust. But there were so many of them, slashing and clawing at me; I felt talons catch my skin, tearing through my clothes, leaving bright strips of fire in their wake. I danced around and through them, dodging and parrying their blows like Ash had taught me, striking back when I could. But I knew I couldn't keep this up forever.

The oracles drew back. Their numbers were smaller now, little swirls of dust dissolving in the wind, but I was hurt, too. I could feel the gashes their claws had left behind, and took deep, slow breaths, trying to focus through the pain.

One of the oracles gestured, and the tree behind me bent entirely in half and tried crushing me beneath its trunk. I dove away, feeling the impact rock the ground, and rolled to my feet, panting. The trees were groaning and swaying at weird, unnatural angles, and the oracles shuffled forward again, trying to drive me back into the forest.

This is just a dream, I thought, trying to stay calm. *A dream world that the oracle controls, but a dream nonetheless. I am not going to die here. I am the Iron Queen, and if the Nevernever responds to my wishes, then I can control this nightmare, too.*

The oracles surrounded me, trapping me between them and the swaying trees at my back. I took one step back and, for just a moment, closed my eyes and sent my will through the Dreaming Pool, just like I had in the Iron Realm.

"Know that I'm with you always, even if you can't see me."

I heard the oracles' piercing wail as they lunged to attack me again, and jerked my eyes open.

A flash of blue light erupted between me and two of the duplicates, shearing through them as easily as paper. The rest of them jerked to a halt, as Ash lowered his sword and turned to give me a brief smile.

"You called, my queen?"

The oracles shrieked, skittering backward, arms flailing. "Impossible!" they howled as Ash stalked forward, his face hard. "How? How did you bring him here?"

"That's a good question," came another voice, as Puck stepped out from the trees behind me, daggers already in hand. "One minute I'm trying to decide if that doll is looking at me funny, then next, *poof,* here we are. And just in time, too." He turned and smirked at the oracles, eyes gleaming. "That," he stated, waggling his knife at one of them, "is *my* trick."

The oracles screeched and flew toward us again, claws slashing. We met them in the center of the glade, the three of us, fighting side by side. Dust flew, swirling around us, as one by one, the duplicates vanished, cut down by my sword, stabbed with Puck's daggers or pierced through the heart with a shard of ice. Until, finally, only one was left.

"Wait!" the last oracle, the real one, cried, throwing up her hands as Ash stalked toward her. "Iron Queen, wait! Spare me, I beg you! I have not told you everything. I know one last secret. Knowledge of your son and your brother, something that could save them both!"

"Ash, wait," I called, and Ash halted, keeping his sword at

the oracle's withered chest. "More secrets, Oracle?" I asked, walking up to her, keeping my blade drawn. "Why didn't you tell me this before?"

"Because it is a small thing," the oracle whispered, her sightless gaze shifting from me to Ash and back again. Puck joined us, arms crossed, a disbelieving smirk on his face. "The tiniest lynchpin, in a huge, complicated machine. But, if it is removed, the entire structure could fall, sending our world into chaos. It is the domino that begins the collapse of everything."

"Enough," I said, as Puck rolled his eyes dramatically. Ash didn't move, still keeping his blade inches from the oracle's heart, waiting for my orders. "Speak, then, Oracle. How do I stop this? Tell me, right now."

The oracle sighed. "To save your brother, you must—"

A deafening crack ripped the branches of the tree behind us, and a giant limb came smashing down, barely three feet from where we stood. I flinched, taking my eyes off the oracle for the briefest of seconds—

—and the scene disappeared. Blinking, I gazed around, wondering what had happened, where we were. Ash and Puck stood close by, also glancing around in confusion. The oracle was nowhere to be seen.

"What the hell?" Puck exclaimed, throwing up his hands. "What the heck just happened there? I'm getting a little tired of being *poofed* about whenever it strikes someone's fancy."

I saw an arched stone bridge standing a few yards away and drew in a short breath. "We're back in the wyldwood," I said, stunned. "At the edge of the Iron Realm. But…how?" I looked at Ash and Puck. "We were in the Briars, the Dreaming Pool. The oracle was just about to tell us how to save Ethan."

Ash let out a long sigh and sheathed his blade. "The Wishing Tree," he said, and I frowned in confusion. "There's al-

ways a cost for using it," he went on. "Something unexpected
and unexplained that happens at the worst possible moment.
This was the price that it took."

"Mmm, not a bad price if you ask me," came Grimalkin's
voice from the top of the bridge railing. The cat perched on
a post like he'd been there all morning, licking a paw. "Usually the cost is much more entertaining. But then, I was the
one who voiced the wish, after all. There was very little room
for error."

"So that's it?" I asked. "The oracle gets away, we don't know
where she is and I still don't know anything about Ethan or
my son. Or how to save them." I rubbed my temples, feeling
a headache pound behind my eyes. "Why did we come here?"
I whispered, feeling the dark unknown loom up before me.
"It seems kind of pointless now. I'm going to be a paranoid
wreck from now on."

"That is the danger of too much knowledge, human," Grimalkin said quietly. "Knowing the future is far too great a
burden for most of your kind. However, once you do possess
a bit of that knowledge, the question becomes, what do you
do with it?"

"Nothing today," Ash said, drawing me against him. Surprised, I glanced up, and he gave me a weary smile. "Right
now, I think we should go home. We can deal with whatever
this brings, tomorrow."

I nodded and sagged against him. "Yeah, you're right.
Glitch is probably having a minor breakdown about now.
We should head back." I pulled away and looked at Puck,
watching us with a small smirk and his hands behind his head.
"What about you, Puck? I've missed you. Are you going to
be sticking around?"

"Well, I was thinking of heading up to the Alps and tracking down this yeti tribe that's been seen around the area."

Puck grinned and shrugged, putting his hands in his pockets. "But, with all the excitement cropping up, I think I might hang around. For a little while, anyway." He sniffed and made a face. "Wonder if Titania has cooled down any? I'll have to visit Arcadia and see what's been going on in my absence. I'm sure they'll be thrilled to have me back."

Smiling, I walked up to him, and he opened his arms. "Don't be a stranger, Puck," I whispered in his ear, pulling him into a hug. "It's not the same without you."

"Oh, I know," he replied cheerfully. "I don't see how anyone survives without me, it must be terribly dull." He pulled back and kissed my cheek. "I'll be around, princess. If you ever need me, just send a note. Or a gremlin. Or whatever." Stepping back, he raised a hand to Ash, who nodded solemnly. "Catch ya later, ice-boy. Maybe next time I see you, you'll be changing diapers and reading bedtime stories." He snickered and shook his head. "Ah, who would've thought you'd be the one tied down with a family, prince? How the mighty have fallen."

I smacked his arm, but Ash only shook his head. "I wouldn't want to be anywhere else," he said calmly. "Maybe you should try it, Goodfellow."

Puck laughed and backed away. "Me? Robin Goodfellow, a family man? Ha, not likely, ice-boy. I mean, think of what that would do to my reputation." Glamour shimmered around him, and he gave us a wink. "Later, lovebirds. Gimme a heads-up when the kid arrives. 'Uncle Puck' will be waiting."

With a cascade of glamour and black feathers, Puck transformed into a huge raven. Beating powerful wings, he rose above us with a mocking caw, swooped into the branches of the wyldwood and was lost from view.

I didn't have to turn around to know Grimalkin had vanished, as well. The railing was empty, both Grim and Puck were gone, but I wasn't sad. We would see them again, both of them. We had forever to catch up.

Ash held out a hand, and I stepped into him with a sigh, feeling his arms wrap around me. I closed my eyes, and he kissed the top of my head.

"Let's go home," he whispered.

EPILOGUE

I stood on the balcony of my room, letting the cool night breeze toss my hair, gazing down at Mag Tuiredh, far below. Beau sat beside me, tall German shepherd ears pricked to the wind, wary and alert. It was near midnight, and most of Mag Tuiredh was still. Peaceful. I wished I could find some of that tranquility.

Soft footsteps came onto the balcony, and a moment later Ash slipped his arms around me from behind. I reached back and buried a hand in his silky hair, and he nuzzled my neck, making me sigh. Beau gave me a sideways glance, huffed and padded back to the room, leaving us alone on the balcony.

"What are you thinking about?" my knight murmured against my skin.

"Oh, you know." I tilted my head as his lips trailed down my shoulder. "Oracles and prophecies and futures and such. Ash, can I ask you something?"

"Anything."

I turned to face him, taking his hands, and he waited patiently as I struggled with the question, wondering if I should really bring this up. But he did say I could ask him, and I didn't want us to hide anything from each other. "I…I know we haven't talked much about your quest at the End of the World," I began. "But…did you…see anything, when you lived that future life with me? Did you see anything about our son...destroying the courts?"

"Ah." Ash leaned back against the railing, drawing me with him. "I was wondering when that would come up."

"I'm sorry, Ash," I said quickly. "If you don't want to talk about it, I understand. I just thought...you've been so calm through all of this. I wondered...if you had seen anything..."

"No." Ash tightened his grip, stopping me from leaving. He met my gaze and smiled. "I didn't see anything of the oracle's prophecy, Meghan. If I did, if anything like that had happened to us, even in that dream, I would have told you. I swear."

"Oh." I was relieved, though a tiny bit disappointed, as well. If Ash had seen that future, we might know what was coming, what to expect. We might be able to prevent it.

Ash ran his hands up my arms, his gaze thoughtful. "It's strange," he mused, looking past me at the distant lights of Mag Tuiredh. "I can barely remember anything of that life anymore. I remember you, and our son, and ruling Mag Tuiredh, but...it's fading. I lose more of it every day." He gave his head a tiny shake, looking back at me. "I think that's how it's supposed to be. That life, it wasn't real. This..." He framed my cheek, his silver eyes intense as they met mine. "This is real. This is what's important to me now. I'm not worried about the future, whatever it brings. I have all I need, right here."

"I wish I had your confidence." I sighed.

Ash pulled me closer, his eyes gentle as they gazed into mine. "Meghan, I'm going to tell you something someone once told me, when I was afraid of what was to come." He lowered his head, soft strands of his hair brushing my skin. "Nothing is certain," he murmured. "The future is constantly changing, and no one can predict what happens next. We have the power to change our destiny, because fate is not set in stone, and we are always free to make a choice." His fingers came up to brush my hair back, tucking it behind one ear. "A very powerful seer told me that, once. And she was right. That's why I'm not afraid of the oracle's prophecy, or the future. We are only slaves to fate if we let it control us. There is always a choice."

I sniffed. "I wish you had told me that earlier," I mock grumbled at him. "It would've saved me a lot of freaking out."

Ash chuckled, low and deep. "I didn't know it would shake you so badly. The Meghan I know doesn't let small things like oracles and Prophecies of Doom stand in her way." I pinched his ribs, and he grunted a laugh. "I do know one thing," he continued. "Whatever this child will be, whatever it grows into, it will be loved. No prophecy, oracle, warning or pre-monition will ever change that."

He was right, and in that moment, I didn't think it was possible to love him more than I did right then. Leaning into him, I closed my eyes, and he gathered me close. Tilting my chin up, he kissed me gently, and I wrapped my arms around his waist. No matter what happened, if he was beside me, if we stood beside each other, we could face whatever the world threw at us.

"Ash," I whispered, my heart soaring with happiness, with relief and love, as I pulled back to face him. "Can you believe it? You're going to be a father."

His hand slipped down to my belly, palm gently pressing against my stomach, as his eyes shone with wonder and awe. He was going to be a father. We were going to be a family. "So," I ventured, smiling at him through my tears. "I guess the only question left is, what are we going to name him?"

Ash raised his head, meeting my gaze, and smiled back.

"I've always liked the name Keirran."

GUIDE TO
THE IRON FEY

A WORD OF CAUTION

This guide contains spoilers.

If you have not yet read all of The Iron Fey novels, the characters and the author highly recommend that you read all the books and novellas before proceeding further.

[Human, I do not recommend you read it at all. Stay where you are and do not concern yourself with matters of Faery. Or when you blunder into the Nevernever and find yourself at the wrong end of a goblin's spear, I shall be called upon by a certain all-too-softhearted queen to rescue you, no doubt. Yawn.]

User ID: 20835000223003
Library name: LENOIR

Call number: OCLC ILL
CHECKOUT
Title: OCLC ILL CHECKOUT
Date charged: 6/27/2016,12:21
Date due: 7/21/2016,23:59

Total checkouts for session:1
Total checkouts:5

To renew call 527-6223 Ext 507

THE ORIGINAL SURVIVAL GUIDE TO THE NEVERNEVER

Written in the hopes that others might avoid the many terrible predicaments in which Meghan Chase found herself during the course of The Iron Fey series.

Read at Your Own Risk.

DISCLAIMER

This guide is intended to give intrepid travelers into the realm of the fey a minimal chance at surviving the creatures and denizens that dwell within. Please note, the author of this guide is in no way responsible for lost or damaged souls, ensnarement or accidental or intentional death. Entering the realms of fey can, and likely will, be hazardous to your health and is not recommended. You have been warned.

PREPARATION

One can never prepare adequately for entry into the Nevernever. There are, however, a few rules that one can follow to help increase the chances of surviving.

WHAT SHOULD I WEAR?

Dressing for the Nevernever means blending utility with comfort. If you have questions about whether or not an item is appropriate, ask yourself the following: If running for my life, would this slow me down? And: If caught while running for my life, would this protect me? If the answer to the first question is yes, and the second question is no, then the item is inappropriate. Here are a few suggested items to wear to help you make it out of the Nevernever alive.

- **A light pack** (either a backpack or large satchel) can be helpful for storing other necessary items. Make sure to avoid large, bulky or heavy packs, as they will slow you down when (not if) you need to run for your life.

- **Comfortable clothing** that covers the arms and legs (the Briars have thorns, after all). Be sure to wear muted colors, as bright or flashy colors will attract the fey. Layers are also strongly recommended, as the temperature can vary quite drastically from one part of the Nevernever to the next.

- **A protective charm** may reduce the chances of being eaten. Cold iron blessed by the druids during a new moon works best, but if that is not available, a twist of Saint John's wort, a four-leaf clover or a rabbit's foot might help. If you have none of the above, wearing your clothing inside out may work in a pinch.

- **A high-quality pair of cross-trainers or running shoes.** Remember, buying the shoes is not enough. A strong cardio program is highly recommended before crossing into the Nevernever.

WHAT SHOULD I PACK?

It is a common mistake to take a large number of gadgetry (cameras, cell phones, portable computers, etc.) into the Nevernever. The second problem with these devices is that they will not work well (if at all) in Faery. The first and larger problem is that any fey you chance across will not take kindly to the presence of so much mortal technology, which, in turn, could lead to a situation where the running shoes mentioned previously are needed. Better to stick with a few simple items.

- **Food.** Any type of small, high-caloric, portable food items will suffice. Energy bars, candy bars, trail mix, dehydrated foods, etc., will extend the amount of time you can spend in the Nevernever. (Note: Extending the amount of time spent in the Nevernever is not recommended.) It is recommended that you do not eat anything you find or are offered while in the Nevernever. Side effects of faery food include, but are not limited to, mood swings, inebriation, memory loss, shape-changing, obsession, coma, inability to leave the Nevernever and death.

- **Weapon of steel or cold iron.** Modern steel (e.g., a knife, sword or other implement of death) is serviceable in this regard, but cold iron (e.g., a spike from a wrought-iron fence, a length of pig iron, etc.) is preferable as it has a more direct impact on the fey. Before entering Faery, an intense training program with your chosen weapon is strongly encouraged. Several years of training should be enough to adequately protect yourself from the weakest fey. If you wish to protect yourself from the strongest fey, you will need several mortal lifetimes.

- **Gifts for the fey.** If you encounter creatures of the Nevernever, many can be won over by offering gifts, free of obligation. Suggested items include jars of honey, bags of candy, bronze weapons and young children. Please check with the laws of your home country before procuring any of these items.

- **Water.** While most of the water in the Nevernever is drinkable without direct side effects, it is also the home of many aquatic fey of the nastier variety and drinking it or venturing too near it may result in numerous indirect side effects: nausea, vomiting, sudden blood loss, inexplicable need to flee and death.

ENTERING THE NEVERNEVER

This guide will not lay out explicit instructions on how to enter the Nevernever. The publishers consulted with their legal team and determined that the associated liability of such an act was, as one attorney put it, "Certain to lead to financial ruin for this company, reprisals from the Summer and Winter courts and, quite possibly, the end of the world as we know it." Suffice it to say, one enters Faery through trods, paths between the mortal realm and the realm of the fey. Finding those trods is, per Legal, up to you.

Should you, despite all warnings, somehow stumble your way into Faery, the following information might be useful while traversing the different realms. However, the author of this guide assumes no responsibility for any who are captured, eaten or driven mad.

THE GEOGRAPHY OF THE NEVERNEVER

The Nevernever is a diverse and wild realm populated by strange creatures and ancient powers. The land itself is said to have a consciousness and a sometimes-malicious will. When traveling through the Nevernever, there are four primary realms with which one may have to contend.

- **Arcadia, the Summer/Seelie Court.** Thick forests, ancient hills and flowering grasslands dominate Arcadia, home of the Summer fey. Newcomers to the land of the Summer King might falsely believe that Seelie territory is not as dangerous as the rest of the Nevernever, but do not be deceived. Arcadia is sunny and beautiful year-round, but it is not safe. Satyrs, dryads and trolls roam the forests of Arcadia, and the lakes teem with mermaids and nixies. The Seelie Court rests beneath an enormous

faery mound, where King Oberon and Queen Titania rule
without opposition.

- **Tir Na Nog, the Winter/Unseelie Court.** The territory
  of Mab, the Winter Queen, is as hostile and icy as the fey
  that dwell there. Snow covers everything, and the frozen
  woods, fields, streams and lakes all rest beneath several
  inches of ice. All sorts of vicious creatures call the Winter
  Court home, from goblins and redcaps to bogeymen
  and ogres. The Winter palace lies beneath an enormous
  cavern, home of the terrible Winter Queen. Few mortals
  who set eyes on the Unseelie Court and Mab ever live to
  tell of it.

- **The wyldwood.** The dark, tangled forest called the
  wyldwood is the largest territory in the Nevernever,
  completely encircling both courts and extending into the
  Deep Wyld. It is neutral territory; neither Summer nor
  Winter hold sway here, and the wyldwood denizens owe
  allegiance to no one. The wood is vast and endless, and
  the creatures that roam there come from every corner of
  the imagination. Not only does this make the wyldwood
  one of the most dangerous places in the Nevernever, but
  one of the most mysterious, as well.

- **The Iron Court.** Until recently, not much was known
  about the mysterious emergence of a new court within
  the bounds of Faery. One would think that a realm called
  the Iron Realm, born from the very substance most
  harmful to the fey, would be a rumor at best and quickly
  exterminated at worst. But such a court does exist, and is
  now ruled by a young faery queen called Meghan Chase.
  The Iron Queen is said to be half faery and half human,
  and it is within her realm that you will find the strange

and wondrous species known as the Iron fey. These
faeries—for they are indeed true fey—are thought to have
evolved from mankind's love of technology and progress.
Currently, however, not much information is known
about them.

DENIZENS OF THE NEVERNEVER

If you are wise, you will do as little as possible to draw the attention
of the fey. Sometimes, even if you are a quiet observer, the fey will
find you. If this occurs, there are a few steps you can follow that may
allow you to escape with your free will and, if you are lucky, your life.

- **Always be polite.** Discourtesy is a deep insult to the fey
  and will not be well received, no matter how cool you
  think it will make you look.

- **Do not be deceived by the politeness of the fey.** Fey
  are almost always polite. This does not mean they will not
  happily remove your head. They will, however, be grateful
  for the entertainment you provided. Or, if you are very
  unlucky, the sustenance.

- **There is no such thing as a free lunch.** In the
  Nevernever, there is no free. Accept no gifts, no matter
  how sure you are that there are no strings attached.
  There are always enough strings attached to tie you up
  in a pretty bow and deliver you to someone who will be
  grateful for the sustenance.

- **Give gifts freely.** The fey will either think you are a
  masterful manipulator and respect you more, or be
  completely befuddled by the notion of a gift with no
  obligations.

- **Never, ever, under any circumstances, enter into a contract with the fey.** It always ends badly and often fatally. In the rare cases where it does not end badly, that is because it does not end. You will be bound for eternity.

- **If you have to run, zig and zag.** Many faeries carry bows and arrows.

- **If you chance upon a big, gray cat, you probably owe him a favor.** Even if you do not remember the favor, do it, anyway. In the long run, you will do it, but it will be far less painful if you do it up front.

HOW DO I LEAVE FAERY?

The best answer to this question is, quickly. Spending a lot of time within the realms of the Nevernever can lead to many strange effects. A few minutes in Faery may be years in the mortal realm, or the reverse may be true. If you leave by a different trod than you entered, even one only a few feet away, you may find yourself on the other side of the world, or at the bottom of the ocean. Here are a few things to remember when attempting to leave the Nevernever.

- Always keep track of how to return to the trod by which you entered.

- Never, ever ask for directions or a way out. Most fey will help you, but they will charge a steep price, most commonly your tongue, as they do not want you to share this information. Note: if they ever catch on to texting, they may start asking for thumbs, as well.

- If you cannot find your way back to your original trod, purchase a way out by using the gifts mentioned earlier in this guide. If you enter into this type of bargain, make sure to phrase things appropriately. "I'm lost and can't get home" is sure to lead to trouble. Try something different, like "I'll pay two jars of honey to a fey who will take me to the mortal realm, alive and whole, with my mind and soul intact, neither physically or mentally harmed, to be placed on solid ground at an altitude and in an environment that can readily sustain human life, no farther than a mile from a human settlement, at a time not more than thirty minutes from now." Even then, be careful.

CONCLUSION

The above procedures should afford you the barest chance at survival in the Nevernever. There are, of course, no guarantees and any and all interactions with the denizens of Faery must be handled with the greatest of care. If, however, you proceed according to the above, you will have a leg up on the other mortals who wander from time to time through the Briars and into the heart of Faery. You have been warned repeatedly. Proceed at your own risk.

CHARACTER BIOGRAPHIES
AND USEFUL INFORMATION

Knowing the life stories of a few
key members of Faery may come in handy
should you find yourself at their mercy,
begging to be returned home—
or to stay forever.

Main Characters

MEGHAN CHASE
(Meggie, princess, half-blood,
daughter of Oberon, the Iron Queen)

Meghan Chase is a half human, half fey girl with white-blond hair and blue eyes. She grew up in the Louisiana bayou with her mother, stepfather and half brother, raised as a normal teenage girl. She was often ignored and overlooked, and didn't realize that this was due to her fey heritage.

Meghan's biological father is Oberon, the Summer King, though she doesn't find this out until traveling into the Nevernever to rescue her brother, who has been kidnapped. Before this revelation, she believed herself to be fully human, and had a father who disappeared when she was six years old. She later discovers that the man she believed to be her father, Paul, was abducted by the Exile Queen Leanansidhe at the behest of Puck to keep him safe from a jealous Queen Titania and is reunited with him.

Meghan is incredibly loyal and willing to sacrifice herself to protect the people she loves. It is this strength, and many other qualities, that causes Ash, Prince of the Winter Court, to fall in love with her, even as she is falling in love with him in return—a sentiment that is forbidden by both the Summer and the Winter courts.

Meghan's best friend growing up was the mischievous and often secretive Robbie Goodfell. When her brother was kidnapped, Meghan discovered that Robbie is actually Robin Goodfellow, the infamous faery Puck best known from Shakespeare's *A Midsummer Night's Dream*.

As the daughter of the Summer King, Meghan has the ability to call upon Summer glamour. She can summon roots and vines to her aid, wrapping them around her enemies. She can also make life erupt from even the deadest of woods, and while wielding the Scepter of the Seasons, she is even able to produce lightning bolts. After she killed the Iron King, Meghan inherited all of his powers and became the true heir to the Iron throne. While her Iron and Summer glamours initially clashed, making her sick when she tried to use them individually, she was eventually able to merge the two, bringing life to the Iron Realm and ending its destructive spread through the Nevernever.

Throughout her time in the Nevernever, Meghan made an enemy of both Titania, the Summer Queen, and Mab, the Winter Queen, but after defeating both the Iron King and later the false king, she ended her journey as a queen of her own realm, respected and powerful.

Good to know: If you're in a tight spot, Meghan is the perfect queen to seek out for help. She is loyal to those she loves and wired to help humans in need, and the least likely person in all of Faery to require a favor in return.

ASH
(the Winter Prince, ice-boy,
son of Mab, Ashallayn'darkmyr Tallyn)

❄

Prince Ash is the youngest son of Mab, the Winter Queen. He has dark hair, silver eyes and an angelic face. His father is unknown, but he has two older brothers, Sage and Rowan. Growing up in the Unseelie Court, Ash learned early on that feelings were a weakness that could be used against him, so he learned to close himself off.

In his youth, Ash was close friends with Robin Goodfellow, hunting with him in the wyldwood despite the fact that friendship between Summer and Winter fey is forbidden. But when Puck accidentally caused the death of Ash's beloved, Ariella, by leading them into a wyvern nest, Ash swore that he would one day kill Puck.

After years of mourning Ariella and fighting back the darkness that rose inside him on the day she died, Ash met Meghan and, while accompanying her into the Iron Realm to defeat King Machina, began to fall in love with her. Later, after helping Meghan to escape Tir Na Nog and take back the Scepter of the Seasons from the false Iron King's lieutenants, Ash confessed his love in front of both courts. Refusing to be separated from her, Ash chose exile from the Nevernever, only to be pulled back in when Meghan agreed to go back into the Iron Realm and defeat the false king before he could spread his iron plague across the Nevernever.

Ash is an expert swordsman, and he wields an icy-blue sword made for him by the Ice Archons of Dragons' Peak. His blood, glamour and a tiny piece of his essence went into its creation and he doesn't like anyone touching it but him. Ash is also a master of Winter glamour, often shooting ice shards from his hands at his enemies during battle. He was also able to free Meghan from the block of ice his mother had encased her in.

When Meghan asked Ash to be her knight, invoking an ancient ritual that shows ultimate trust and would tie his life to hers, Ash made the vow instantly, bestowing upon Meghan his True Name. When she defeated the false king and lay dying in the Iron Realm, Meghan released Ash from his vow of knighthood in order to save his life, and used his True Name to order him out of the Iron Realm. As he left, he made a new vow—to find a way for him and Meghan to be together once again.

With the help of Puck, Grimalkin and some unexpected new companions, Ash set out for the End of the World, where it was said he might earn a soul and become human, thus allowing him to live in the Iron Realm free from harm. Along the way, he discovered a secret that changed much of what he believed about himself and his former friendship with Puck. Working as a team, Ash and his companions made their way to the Testing Ground at the End of the World. There Ash faced tests that no faery had passed before, earning a soul and becoming something between human and fey, so that he could return to the Iron Realm, to Meghan Chase, and marry her.

Good to know: Since gaining a soul, Ash has become more sympathetic to the human condition. He is still not the easiest person to ask for help, unless you are one of his respected acquaintances or friends, but his moral code in the end compels him to do the right thing. Unless you threaten his wife in any way. Then you're frozen toast.

PUCK
(Robin Goodfellow,
Robbie Goodfell, the Great Prankster)

Puck is a Summer fey, a servant of the Summer King, Oberon, and a maker of mischief. He has red hair and green eyes and a trickster personality; he is best known for cracking jokes, playing pranks and angering older, stronger fey just to see if he can get one up on them.

When Meghan Chase was born, Puck was charged with watching over her and keeping her blind to the faery world. Disguised as human Robbie Goodfell, Puck kept his secret hidden until the Iron King kidnapped Meghan's brother and replaced him with a changeling. Defying direct orders from his king in order to help his best friend, Puck revealed his true nature and guided Meghan into the Nevernever.

Along with the standard Summer glamour, Puck can shape-shift into various animals, including a horse and a raven. He is also able to create clones of himself made of leaves and twigs, and often throws balls of fur at his opponents in battle, which transform into animals such as bears or badgers.

Puck is a formidable fighter, small, fast and cunning, and rather than a sword, he wields two daggers. His long-standing rivalry with his former best friend, Ash, often leads to duels, which he doesn't take seriously, often sending clones to fight for him while he makes sarcastic comments from a safe distance.

Puck defied orders to help Meghan, his best friend, at least three times, and eventually professed his love for her. When he was forced to accept that Meghan would choose to be with Ash, Puck withdrew from them both. Yet when trouble followed Meghan and Ash into exile, Puck came to help despite their rocky relationship. While preparing Meghan to fight the false king, their friendship was almost destroyed when Meghan discovered a secret Puck kept about her family. In the end, Puck and Meghan reconciled and Puck stood by her and Ash as Meghan fought her way into the false king's fortress to save all of Faery.

After Meghan became the Iron Queen and Ash set off on his quest to find a way to be with her, Puck tagged along with Ash, with the explanation that he wanted Meghan to be happy, even if it wasn't with him. He accompanied Ash to the End of the World to help him earn a soul and become human, and the two friends reconciled their long-standing rivalry.

> **Good to know:** Puck is loyal to his court and even more loyal to anyone who earns his respect. He will go to the ends of the earth for his friends and make them laugh the whole way. He can also drive even the most even-tempered person utterly

mad with his pranks. He makes the best friend and the worst possible enemy. Do not get on his bad side lest you be turned into a hedgehog.

GRIMALKIN
(Grim, Cait Sith,
Devil's Cat, Furball)

[Human, if you don't know who I am by now, there is no hope.

Oh, all right. Some editor type insists on including detailed information about me. Honestly, I live in fear for the future of your kind. If you must know...]

Grimalkin is a mysterious faery cat with long, wispy gray fur and golden eyes. [Well, human, I suppose this could be worse. *Mysterious* is not a half-bad start.] Like most cats, Grimalkin is self-assured to the point of arrogance [you are walking a thin line, human] and despairs of others for their lack of intelligence. He has a talent for direction, though it is not clear if he is very good at remembering the places he's been or if he is able to sniff out the things he's seeking [your lack of perception is showing; do put the pieces together and realize it could *possibly* be a bit of both, hmm?] and he prides himself on always being right. [There is no pride involved. A fact is a fact.]

Grim has the ability to disappear from sight, which he often does the moment he senses trouble—when Grim vanishes, it is almost a sure sign there is danger nearby. He usually reappears once danger has been averted, waiting impatiently for his companions to "hurry up." [I will never understand the propensity for humans and love-struck fey to dawdle about when clearly there is danger at hand.] When asked how he is able to do the things he does, Grim often answers simply, "I am a cat." [And really, that is all you needed to say in the first place. Why the long-winded biography, human? Whom are you trying to impress?]

Grimalkin is also responsible for the creation of an amulet that allows Winter and Summer fey to enter the Iron Realm without consequence for a limited time. Creating these amulets requires the essence of an Iron fey, however. Grimalkin's is quite powerful and contains the essence of Ironhorse, who sacrificed himself to help Meghan Chase. [Let us move on, human. Let the dead rest.]

Being a cat, Grimalkin has a somewhat understandable rivalry with the Wolf, whom he calls "Dog," and the two often threaten and insult each other. [Yawn. How much more of this must we dredge through? Old news, human. Old news.] Some, like Ash, suspect that they just enjoy playing at being rivals, since their banter never leads anywhere.

Grim deals in favors and often uses his ability to find things in order to procure promises from anyone he comes across. He has guided Meghan Chase into the Iron Realm at least twice, as well as through the Briars, the human world and the wyldwood. He also accompanied Ash and Puck on their quest to the End of the World. [As if those two could have found it on their own. Please.]

When confronted with a doppelganger of his true nature, Grimalkin was not surprised to find that his inner self was not that much different from his outer self, suggesting that Grimalkin doesn't suppress his true nature. [Are we finished? I see a butterfly....]

Good to know: When Grimalkin speaks, listen and do as he says. Do not question him unless you wish to either wind up dead at the hands of some dangerous creature or feel like the stupidest being ever to enter Faery. If Grim vanishes, run away from wherever you are immediately and quietly.

The Faery Rulers

LEANANSIDHE

(Lea, the Dark Muse,
Queen of the Exiles, Ruler of the Between)

At one time, Leanansidhe was one of the most powerful beings in the Nevernever. She inspired many great artists, including James Dean, Kurt Cobain and Jimi Hendrix, helping them to produce their most brilliant works. Of course, there was always a price to be paid for her gifts. She would occasionally kidnap mortals who were especially gifted and keep them until she got bored.

Allegedly, Leanansidhe was banished from the Nevernever by Oberon for growing too powerful and having too many mortal worshippers. However, her banishment was actually due to the jealousy of Titania. Setting up residence in a mansion in the Between, Leanansidhe gathered new followers and crowned herself Queen of the Exiles, taking in stray faeries who had nowhere else to go.

Leanansidhe likes expensive things and has clients with unusual tastes, and she uses half-breed "employees" to procure these items. She also has the habit of abducting male human musicians and turning them into musical instruments. She calls all of these men Charles, as she finds it hard to remember their real names. She is the one responsible for abducting Meghan's human father, though she did it at Puck's request and did not know at the time who he was connected to.

Leanansidhe is incomparably beautiful, with wavy, waist-length hair that shimmers like strands of copper. She is tall and pale and carries herself like the queen she knows she is.

Good to know: Leanansidhe's mesmerizing beauty and charm can turn on you in an instant. If you enter into a bargain with her, do so with the greatest of caution, lest you end up as a violin or grand piano.

MAB
(the Winter Queen, Queen of Air and Darkness, Sovereign of the Autumn Territories)

❄

The Queen of the Unseelie Court draws the eye of everyone in the room. Her hair is so black it appears blue, and spills down her back like a waterfall of ink. Her eyes are pitch-black.

Mab is a cruel queen, forcing her three sons to compete for her favor and using their emotions and weaknesses against them whenever possible. However, despite this, it is obvious that Mab loves her sons and her grief is mighty when she loses Sage to betrayal, Rowan to his own folly by Ash's hand and Ash to love.

Mab wields the power of an arctic winter, calling forth snow, ice and subzero winds to slay those who displease her. She has a tendency to encase individuals in blocks of ice, either because they have annoyed her or as a way of preserving them forever so she won't have to see them get old. Being trapped in Mab's ice, victims live forever, all the while gasping for breath that never comes.

Good to know: Mab is one of the four most powerful fey in the Nevernever. She is highly protective of Winter and may look well upon one who has information to help her realm. But she does love her ice sculpture garden and is as likely to add you to it as she is to reward your services.

OBERON

(the Erlking, King of the Summer Court,
Ruler of Arcadia, Lord Oberon)

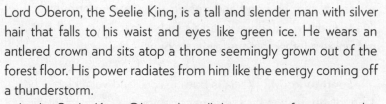

Lord Oberon, the Seelie King, is a tall and slender man with silver hair that falls to his waist and eyes like green ice. He wears an antlered crown and sits atop a throne seemingly grown out of the forest floor. His power radiates from him like the energy coming off a thunderstorm.

As the Seelie King, Oberon has all the powers of summer at his disposal. He can call vines and plants to his aid, wield fire and lightning and turn into a formidable treelike giant. He also has the ability to trap Robin Goodfellow in a form of his choosing, and often keeps him in a cage in raven form when he is displeased with him.

Oberon fell in love with Meghan's mother while watching her paint and draw in a local park, describing her as beautiful and artistic.

Good to know: Oberon is the most powerful faery in Arcadia and one of the four most powerful fey in the Nevernever. Do not cross him, unless your name is Puck and you can talk the rain out of falling during a storm.

TITANIA

(the Summer Queen, Lady Titania)

Titania is a fey of otherworldy beauty, willowy-thin with long hair that shifts between silver and gold, glittering blue eyes and an aura of arrogance and power.

Titania is an extremely jealous faery, and has been known to be vindictive when her jealousy is provoked. She had Leanansidhe banned from the Nevernever for daring to rival her queenliness. She also tried to go after Meghan's human father as a way to get revenge for Oberon's fidelity without harming the human woman he loved and stoking his ire. Upon meeting Meghan, she attempted to turn her husband's daughter into a hart. When commanded to stop by her husband and denied the pleasure of hunting hart-Meghan down with dogs, Titania sent her to toil away in the kitchen not unlike another famous fairy-tale princess.

Good to know: Titania is both jealous and vain. Flatter her and you may go far. Cross her and you will go nowhere ever again once her hounds hunt down your new rabbit-self and tear you to pieces.

The Extended Cast of Characters

ARIELLA TULARYN
(The only daughter of
the Ice Baron of Glassbarrow, The Seer)

❄

Ariella was Ash's first love, an innocent and naive soul who he met when she came to court for the first time as a representative of her father. Vowing to protect her from the cruel politics of the court, Ash quickly fell in love with her and found she was the only person he could be himself around. While hunting in the wildwood, Ariella discovered Puck and Ash's friendship, a relationship forbidden by their rival courts, but didn't seem fazed. She and Puck also became great friends, and the three spent much of their time together hunting in the wyldwood. She was tragically killed by a wyvern's sting when Puck's playful nature led the group into its nest, leading to the deadly rivalry between Puck and the Winter Prince.

Unbeknownst to everyone, Ariella was resurrected by the Nevernever, her prophetic abilities heightened so she could aid Ash and Meghan in their destiny to save the courts from the encroaching Iron Realm. Using her magical foresight, she manipulated such events as the exile of Leanansidhe, Puck's guardianship of Meghan and the first meeting of Meghan and Grimalkin in the wyldwood.

Reunited with Ash and Puck on their quest for the End of the World, she guides them to the Testing Ground. When Ash has passed all three of his trials, Ariella sacrifices herself to create a soul for him so that he can be with his true love, Meghan, and so that she can be with him, in a sense, forever.

ETHAN CHASE

Meghan's half brother, the son of her mother and stepfather, Ethan is a sweet four-year-old with curly brown hair and big blue eyes. He has the Sight, which means he can see the fey that most humans naturally overlook. He is kidnapped by the Iron King and replaced with a changeling, but later saved by Meghan. He worships his big sister and doesn't understand why she leaves and cannot come home. He ultimately blames Ash for her abandonment.

FERRUM
(the Old King,
the false king, the Iron King)

Ferrum was the Iron King before Machina. Power-hungry and terrified of losing his throne, his fear was corrupting the land and he refused to accept that he was obsolete and that it was time for a new Iron King to rise. When Ferrum tried to stab him in the back, Machina, his First Lieutenant, defeated him and stepped up to rule in his place, absorbing all of his powers per the rules of the Iron Realm. However, Ferrum did not fade away, but rather hid out in the tunnels under the Iron Realm, worshipped only by packrats.

When Meghan first encounters him, Ferrum is an old, old man sitting on a throne of junk. His skin is metallic-gray, his eyes are green and his white hair flows past his feet. When she meets him again, he wears voluminous black robes and there is an iron crown upon his head. He glows with a dark purple aura of power. Ferrum has sharp, clawlike fingers, which he uses as weapons, and he is super-fast. Meghan must defeat him to save all of Faery and become the Iron Queen.

GLITCH
(the Rebel Leader, the First Lieutenant)

Glitch was King Machina's First Lieutenant. He has a sharp, angular face and pointed ears, and wild black hair, spiked up like a punk rocker, with neon threads of lightning flickering between the strands. He wears ripped jeans and a studded leather jacket. He has the ability to cause electrical glitches with a single touch. When Machina fell and the false king took his place, Glitch led the revolution against him. He originally wanted to hide Meghan away, but later follows her and joins with the armies of Summer and Winter against Ferrum's forces. When Meghan becomes the Iron Queen, he becomes her First Lieutenant.

IRONHORSE
(Rusty)

Ironhorse is one of King Machina's lieutenants. He is a massive black horse with eyes that glow like hot coals and flared nostrils that blow steam and fire. His body is made of iron, with pistons and gears jutting out from its ribs. His mane and tail are steel cables, and a great fire burns in his belly, visible through the chinks in his hide.

Ironhorse is loyal to the true ruler of the Iron Realm. He was initially an enemy of Meghan's, working for Machina to bring her to his fortress. When Meghan killed Machina and inherited his powers, and therefore his throne, Ironhorse sought her out under the guise of helping her take back the Scepter of the Seasons, when in fact he was serving and protecting her as the rightful ruler of the Iron Realm.

Ironhorse is a very large and outdated machine, and when he speaks it is in a booming voice. Despite his ferocious appearance, he is also very loyal and he did eventually sacrifice himself to help Meghan overcome her enemy Virus. At the time of his death, he agreed to give his essence to Grimalkin to create an amulet that would allow the faery cat to travel through the Iron Realm and continue to aid Meghan without being poisoned.

As the Lord of the Obsidian Plains, Ironhorse rules over a clan of similarly built horselike iron fey. He has the ability to take the form of a monstrous black man with glowing red eyes.

MACHINA
(the Iron King)

King Machina was the true Iron King, the predecessor of the first king, Ferrum. When Ferrum became obsolete and refused to abdicate his throne, becoming hostile and paranoid, Machina rose up and overthrew him, absorbing his powers.

Tall and elegant, with flowing silver hair and pointed ears, Machina is refined and graceful, yet unmistakably powerful. He wears a stark black coat, a metal stud in one ear and a Bluetooth headset in the other. Energy crackles around him and electricity occasionally crackles across his black eyes. His face is beautiful and arrogant, all sharp planes and angles, but when he smiles, it lights up the whole room. He wears a strange, silvery cloak across his shoulders that wriggles slightly as though it were alive. In actuality, this cloak is a network of silver cables, a halo of metal wings wickedly barbed on one end.

He kidnaps Meghan's brother, Ethan, replacing him with a changeling, in order to lure her into the Nevernever in the hopes of making her his queen. When Meghan kills him by stabbing him in the heart with the Witchwood arrow, he becomes a massive iron oak tree. Upon his death, his powers transfer to Meghan, and he begins to appear to her in dreams.

MELISSA AND LUKE CHASE
Melissa (Meghan's and Ethan's mom),
Luke (Meghan's stepfather and Ethan's father)

Meghan's mother, Melissa, is a former artist who, despite being married to a mortal man, was seduced by the power of the Summer King. Meghan was raised as a human by Melissa and her husband, Paul, a piano prodigy, until she was six, when Paul mysteriously disappeared.

Unbeknownst to Meghan, Paul had been abducted by Leanansidhe. Fleeing to the Louisiana Bayou, Melissa met Luke, a pig farmer and "true hick" as Meghan describes him. Due to her half-fey nature, Luke often tended to overlook Meghan, and his frugal ways frustrated her. Nevertheless, her mother never forgot her and when she becomes the Iron Queen, Meghan returns one last time to say goodbye to her family.

RAZOR
(Buzz-saw)

A typical gremlin with long, thin arms, huge batlike ears and slitted, electric-green eyes, Razor is one of the first to realize who Meghan is and try to help her claim her rightful throne as the Iron Queen. He first helps her escape from Glitch and the rebel Iron Fey in her attempt to join the fight against the false king. Later, Razor travels to Mag Tuiredh and rallies the gremlins at Meghan's behest, swarming Ferrum's moving fortress and short-circuiting the electrical defenses and halting it in its progress toward the wyldwood.

ROWAN
(Traitor, second son of Mab)

❄

Prince Rowan, leader of the Thornguards, is the middle son of Queen Mab. The games his mother played, pitting her sons against one another for centuries, formed Rowan into a jealous and power-hungry prince. His greatest resentment fell against his younger brother, Ash, who is often seen as Mab's favored son.

Rowan betrayed the Winter Court to side with the Iron fey, convinced he could become immune to Iron's effects and ultimately survive when the Iron Realm completely took over the Nevernever. However, the iron ring he wore on his finger caused him to begin to rot and severely weakened him. He was eventually killed by Ash while trying to protect the false king.

SAGE
(First son of Mab)

❄

Prince Sage is the eldest and tallest of the three sons of Mab. As gorgeous as his brothers, he is pale with high cheekbones, eyes like chips of green ice, slender brows and long, black hair that ripples behind him like a waterfall of ink. His constant companion is a large, golden-eyed wolf.

Sage is killed by Tertius while defending the Scepter of the Seasons. When he dies, his body turns completely to ice.

VIRUS

Virus is the second of King Machina's lieutenants, and when he is killed by Meghan, she sides with the false king against Meghan and the rest of the Nevernever. She has poisonous green eyes, hair that appears to be made of wires and thin network cables in green, black and red, and often wears lipstick and nail polish in shades of blue and sickly green. She wears a poison-green business suit and three-inch high heels. Virus controls small insectlike creatures called drones, which burrow into a person's head and gives her the ability to control their actions. She is responsible for setting the chimera loose in the Summer Court during Elysium, and is also the mastermind behind the theft of the Scepter of the Seasons. While holding the scepter hostage, Virus implants one of her drones in Ash and sends him to kill Meghan's human family. She is later killed by Ash, split in two after being distracted by Meghan's use of Iron glamour.

THE WOLF
(the Big Bad Wolf, the Eldest Hunter, Wolfman)

One of the oldest, strongest and most legendary of the fey, Wolf is best known for his role in several oft-told mortal fairy tales. The ultimate hunter, Wolf will sometimes take on a personal hunt for the right favor. He first encounters Meghan and Ash when he hunts them at the request of Oberon, in order to save Meghan from her supposed abduction into the Winter Realm. He later accompanies Ash on his quest to find the End of the World and prove himself worthy of a soul.

Underneath Wolf's frightening exterior beats a loyal heart, as he shows when he sacrifices himself to keep the door to the Gauntlet open long enough for everyone else to get out. Wolf favors the openness of the Deep Wyld and has a long-standing offer to eat Grimalkin, should the faery cat ever give him the opportunity.

GLOSSARY

amulet: A pendant created with the essence of an Iron fey inside it that protects traditional fey from being slowly poisoned when they must go into the Iron Realm for any length of time. The Iron fey dies in the creation of an amulet.

bean sidhe: A faery that foretells death with an eerie, loud and terrifying wail. Hope that you never hear one.

boggart: A faery that attaches itself to a human household with ill intent, causing food to sour, animals to go lame and playing other nasty tricks on the inhabitants. Rumor has it a boggart will follow a family that tries to flee to a new home. You do not want one of these.

bogey: Often confused for a boggart, this faery hides under beds and in closets and jumps out to scare humans.

brownie: A shy faery who does household tasks in secret, often late at night, usually with other brownies. Brownies are said to love porridge and honey. They are quite wonderful to have around when you treat them well.

bug: A tiny, insectlike flying Iron faery that can be placed in a human's or faery's brain and used to control them. Traditional fey are poisoned and driven mad by a bug.

cait sith: A catlike faery often reported to be black with a white spot on its chest. Some legends say a cait sith is not a faery at all but a transformed witch. [Human, stop. You are getting it wrong and the best thing to do with a cait sith is to let it remain a mystery. Honestly. Black with a white spot? *A witch?* I despair.]

catoblepas: A four-legged animal with a bull or boarlike head that is so large and heavy, the animal can only look down.

changeling: A faery offspring that has been left in place of a human child. The changeling takes on the look of the stolen child, but may not initially show the correct characteristics, causing confusion, consternation and even danger. Should you suddenly begin to display mysterious, otherworldly behavior, you may be a changeling. Or a teenager.

chimera: A fire-breathing, three-headed monster with various animal heads—often a goat, a dragon and a lion—and the body of a lion.

dragon: A huge, lizardlike creature, with webbed wings, shining scales and sharp talons, that breathes fire.

dryad: A tree faery. Dryads depend on the health of their trees for survival.

dwarf: A short, stocky, strong being often with a long beard (males) and hair, known for mining and thought to live underground.

Elder Dryad: The oldest, most powerful and respected dryad in a forest.

Elysium: The yearly gathering of the most powerful fey at either the Summer or Winter court. Elysium is a time of wary accord when the court rulers meet to discuss any concerns affecting the Nevernever. A great feast is held with music, dancing and performances, with much pomp and ceremony. Traditionally, a prince of one house will lead a princess from the opposite house in the first dance.

faery death: The end of a faery's life, when it fades from existence. Because faeries do not have souls, if a faery is killed, its body soon disintegrates.

faery fire: Glowing blue light created in a faery's hand. Often used to light the way in darkness, or lure unsuspecting humans into danger.

faery knight: A faery that has pledged an oath to serve and protect a ruler or another being above all others. Once the vow is made it cannot be broken and ends only if the being pledged to releases the knight.

favor: A task granted in return for a promise to reciprocate, at a later time, in whatever way is agreed upon. Faeries *always* collect on favors. It is best never to owe one.

Fomorians: An ancient race of giants said to have been defeated and made extinct in war with the fey.

the Forgotten: Faeries mankind has forgotten that have nearly faded from existence. The Forgotten can exist by siphoning glamour from other fey, leaving the "donor" weak or possibly dead.

glamour: A faery's magic and the essence of its being.

glider: An insectlike Iron faery that carries passengers by attaching to their back and flying through the air. Steered by pulling on the front legs and shifting body weight.

goblin: A nasty creature with warty yellow-green skin and a bulbous nose, about two to three feet tall, that eats anything it can catch and is known for being sly and unreliable. Goblins are opportunists and always dangerous to be around.

gremlin: A small Iron faery with batlike ears and glowing, electric-green eyes and teeth, known for wreaking chaos. Gremlins are loyal to and under the command of the Iron ruler. Their presence may be heralding by buzzing noises.

the Grim: A graveyard spirit, in the form of a large, frightening dog, that guards the dead and does not take kindly to being disturbed.

hag: A water faery with green skin and hair thought to live in ponds and to pull in humans and drown and eat them.

hart: The faery term for a deer.

hedge wolf: A wolflike faery that takes the form of a hedge and waits for its prey. Hedge wolves live and hunt in packs. Avoid them unless you have mad fighting skills and a sharp fey weapon.

hobyah: A pale, slimy-looking faery with bulging eyes that attacks with poisoned spears and eats humans and other faeries if it can catch them. Hobyahs live in villages. To outside ears, their speech seems to be simply "Hobyah! Hobyah!" Should you be captured by hobyahs, chances are they will boil you alive and have a feast.

iPod: A small metal and plastic music-playing device—a formidable weapon in traditional Faery and a valuable bargaining chip in the Iron Realm. A good thing to bring with you so long as you don't mind that it will likely never work properly again.

jabberwock: A monster that lives in Faery. According to legend, one can only be permanently slain with an artifact known as the Vorpal Sword.

kelpie: A black, horselike faery with needle-sharp teeth that lives in the water and preys on humans and other beings foolish enough to swim near it. Do not be fooled by their beauty.

manticore: A creature with the body of a lion, the face of a human and wings, with three rows of very, very sharp teeth. Their tail is also spiked on the end, and they can hurl these spines at enemies or potential prey.

nixie: A water faery that looks nearly human but has shimmery scales around the throat covering its gills, needle-sharp teeth, webbing between the fingers and toes and sharp claws. Known to sing a mesmerizing song to humans to lure them underwater and drown them. Should you see one, plug your ears.

nymph: A female faery, descended from gods, that is attached to a certain natural area. Less likely to bother humans, so long as you do not disturb their homes.

ogre: A huge, strong creature that feeds on human flesh. Avoid.

packrat: One of the small, gentle Iron fey that carry all their worldly belongings—which is a lot of stuff—on their backs. Befriend the pack-rats. They are loyal and may help you unexpectedly when you need it most.

phouka: A shape-shifter faery. In their original form phoukas have furred ears and pointed canine teeth. They don't pay much attention to social rules and, in fact, take great pleasure in breaking them. Fun to be around, but never trust one.

piskie: A small, flying faery with gossamer wings and bright-colored skin and hair.

prophecy: A prediction of the future from an oracle. Often an unpleasant one that you will wish you had not heard.

redcap: A malicious faery bent on constant murder that wears a cap dipped in the blood of its victims.

satyr: A faery with goat horns and legs and a humanlike aspect that revels in physical pleasure.

Scepter of the Seasons: The staff that passes from Summer to Winter every six months to herald the changing of the season to either summer or winter. If the staff is not passed, weather is affected worldwide and chaos will ensue.

sidhe: The gentry—the aristrocrats of Faery.

soul: The essence of humanity that faeries lack.

sphinx: An intimidating creature with wings, the body of a lion and the face of a woman, known for requiring the answer to a riddle. Failure to answer correctly results in being denied passage or possibly a terrible death.

spider-hag: A spiderlike Iron faery with a bulbous body, spindly metal legs and a gaunt, womanly torso and head. Spider-hags spin webs of razor-sharp, thin wires that cut as well as contain prey. They are the assassins of the false king.

summerpod: A succulent Summer Court fruit that tastes like honey, nectar and everything delicious, and causes hallucinations in humans.

sylph: A faery with an elemental connection to air.

tatter-colt: A horselike faery with a shaggy coat and eyes like hot coals, known for luring humans to watery places and leaving them to drown.

Thornguard: One of Winter prince Rowan's deluded knights who believes that by wearing an iron ring and pledging loyalty to the Iron Court he will become immune to the effects of iron and flourish when the Iron Court takes over the Nevernever.

token: An object given power by a faery to be of use to the bearer, whether it be to transport him to Faery, protect him or cash in a favor owed by another fey.

Token: An object that has been infused with powerful glamour by its bearer, usually by an overwhelming and powerful emotion of its owner, such as true love.

trod: A passage between Faery and the human world, often found in places that inspire imagination in humans, such as children's closets, nightclubs and parks.

troll: A large, ugly, drooling, not-so-bright creature that may live in the mountains, in caves, under bridges or on rocks.

unicorn: A white, horselike creature with a single white horn growing from its head and cloven hooves. Legend says that a unicorn may be captured only by a virgin. Its horn may purify poisoned water.

wild hunt: A faery hunt led by fey hounds that does not end until the prey is run down and killed. No mortal has ever escaped a wild hunt without fey intervention.

will-o'-the-wisp: A small faery seen as a glowing light, famous for luring unwary humans into danger and probable death.

wiremen: Spindly Iron fey whose bodies are made of twisted wire. They are fast, nimble and have lethal talons that can slice through most anything.

wire nymph: A shy Iron faery that lives in places where there is lots of technology.

Witchwood arrow: The arrow created from the heart of the Elder Dryad's tree and given to Meghan Chase to kill Machina, the Iron King.

wood sprite: A small, lively faery that dwells in the woods.

wyvern: A cousin of the dragon, not as large or intelligent, but extremely dangerous and ill-tempered. They are covered in scales and have a poison stinger at the end of their tails that is highly potent.

REALMS OF THE NEVERNEVER (AND BEYOND)

The world of Faery—the Nevernever—exists parallel to the human world, and the two affect each other in ways humans may not be aware of. Human dreams and inspirations fuel the glamour that is the essence of the Nevernever. Faery wars and the exchange of the Scepter of the Seasons affect the weather and emotional climate of the human world. The rise of technology over the past few centuries has seeped into Faery and given rise to the Iron fey—and until a queen arrived to balance this new glamour with the traditional fey magic, all of Faery was in danger of being poisoned.

Should you somehow set foot in the Nevernever, the following are the places and the fey you might see. Proceed with caution.

ARCADIA
(the Seelie Court, the Summer Realm)

✿

Arcadia is the land of Summer, of powerful storms and lush foliage, of natural beauty and fierce passions. Filled with music, feasts and warmth, Summer is ruled by King Oberon and Queen Titania and is home to all the sun-loving fey.

The following are Meghan Chase's first impressions of the Summer Court, as described in *The Iron King*.

The entry to Arcadia:

We broke through the tree line, and ahead of us rose an enormous mound. It towered above us in ancient, grassy splendor, the pinnacle seeming to brush the sky. Thorny trees and brambles grew everywhere, especially near the top, so the whole thing resembled a large bearded head. Around it grew a hedge bristling with thorns, some longer than my arm. The knights spurred their horses toward the thickest part of the hedge. I wasn't surprised when the brambles parted for them, forming an arch that they rode beneath, before settling back with a loud crunching sound.

I was surprised when the horses rode straight at the side of the hill without slowing, and I clutched Grimalkin tightly, making him growl in protest. The mound neither opened up nor moved aside in any way; we rode into the hill and through, sending a shiver all the way down my spine to my toes.

The Summer Court:

A massive courtyard stretched before me, a great circular platform of ivory pillars, marble statues and flowering trees. Fountains hurled geysers of water into the air, multicolored lights danced over the pools, and flowers in the full spectrum of the rainbow bloomed everywhere. Strains of music reached my ears, a combination of harps and drums, strings and flutes, bells and whistles, somehow lively and melancholy at the same time.

The Throne Room:

The forest grew thick on the other side of the gates, as if the wall had been built to keep it in check. A tunnel of flowering trees and branches stretched away from me, fully in bloom, the scent so overpowering I felt lightheaded.

The tunnel ended with a curtain of vines, opening up into a vast clearing surrounded by giant trees. The ancient trunks and interlocking branches made a sort of cathedral, a living palace of giant columns and a leafy vaulted ceiling. Even though I knew we were underground, and it was night outside, sunlight dappled the forest floor, slanting in through tiny cracks in the canopy. Glowing balls of light danced in the air, and a waterfall cascaded gently into a nearby pool. The colors here were dazzling.

A hundred faeries clustered around the middle of the clearing, dressed in brilliant, alien finery. By the look of it, I guessed these were the nobles of the court. Their hair hung long and flowing, or was styled in impossible fashions atop their heads. Satyrs, easily recognized by their shaggy goat legs, and furry little men padded back and forth, serving drinks and trays of food. Slender hounds with moss-green fur milled about, hoping for dropped crumbs. Elven knights in silvery chain armor stood stiffly around the room; a few held hawks or even tiny dragons.

In the center of this gathering sat a pair of thrones, seemingly grown out of the forest floor and flanked by two liveried centaurs.

Another feature of Arcadia:

The Hedge

The Hedge is a tamer section of the Briars that lies within the Summer Court. Unlike the wyldwood, the Hedge is quite predictable and will usually take a person wherever they'd like to go within the court.

Denizens of Arcadia:

Tansy

This female satyr befriends Meghan during her time in the Summer Court. She has large hazel eyes and matching curly hair, and is at least a foot shorter than Meghan. Tansy is a bit skittish, but seems to warm to Meghan, acting as her guide in Arcadia and warning her about the rules and politics of the faery world.

Sarah Skinflayer

This troll is tall, green-skinned, with tusks and long brown hair. She runs the kitchens in Arcadia and, under Titania's orders, begrudgingly puts Meghan to work.

Lady Weaver

The tall, spidery seamstress with pale skin and long black hair designed the gossamer silver gown Meghan wears for Elysium.

TIR NA NOG

(the Unseelie Court, the Winter Realm)

The realm of Mab, the Winter Queen, is harsh and unforgiving to humans, with subzero temperatures, blizzards and miles of ice and snow. The fey who live here are cold and cruel, and even more deadly to humans than their Summer counterparts. While Summer fey might keep a human as a pet and play with them mercilessly,

Winter are more likely to tear out the human's heart and freeze it for fun. And then eat the rest of the body. If a human is lucky enough to find favor with Mab, she may freeze them alive for eternity and keep them in her sculpture garden, forever gasping for a breath that cannot come.

When Puck brings Meghan to Winter for the first time in *The Iron King,* he introduces the land quite succinctly:

> Puck stepped forward. "Ladies and felines," he stated grandly, grasping the doorknob, "welcome to Tir Na Nog. Land of endless winter and shitloads of snow."

Here is what Meghan sees as she first steps into Winter:

> A billow of freezing powder caressed my face as he pulled the door open. Blinking away ice crystals, I stepped forward.
>
> I stood in a frozen garden, the thorn bushes on the fence coated with ice, a cherub fountain in the center of the yard spouting frozen water. In the distance, beyond the barren trees and thorny scrub, I saw the pointed roof of a huge Victorian estate. I glanced back for Grim and Puck and saw them standing under a trellis hung with purple vines and crystal blue flowers.

In *Winter's Passage,* Meghan journeys to Tir Na Nog with Ash as his willing prisoner, thanks to the deal they made in *The Iron King.* This is how they enter Winter on horseback, after being picked up by knights of Winter, and Meghan's first sight of the Winter Realm:

> The mist cleared away for just a moment, and I saw the edge of the dock, dropping away into dark, murky lake water. The horses broke into a trot, then a full gallop, snorting eagerly, as the end of the dock rushed at us with terrifying speed.
>
> I closed my eyes and the horses leaped.

We hit the water with a loud splash and sank quickly into the icy depths. The horse didn't even try to resurface, and the knight's grip was firm, so I couldn't kick away. I held my breath and fought down panic as we dropped deeper and deeper into the frigid waters.

Then, suddenly, we resurfaced, bursting out with the same noisy splash, sending water flying. Gasping, I rubbed my eyes and looked around, confused and disoriented. I didn't recall the horse swimming back up. Where were we, anyway?

My gaze focused, my breath caught, and I forgot about everything else.

A massive underground city loomed before me, lit up with millions of tiny lights, gleaming yellow, blue and green like a blanket of stars. From where we floated in the black waters of the lake, I could see large stone buildings, streets winding upward in a spiral pattern and ice covering everything. The cavern above soared into darkness, farther than I could see, and the twinkling lights made the entire city glow with hazy etherealness.

At the top of a hill, casting its shadow over everything, an enormous, ice-covered palace stood proudly against the black. I shivered, and the knight behind me spoke for the first time.

"Welcome to Tir Na Nog."

In *The Iron Daughter,* Meghan is Mab's prisoner and has no idea how long she might be there or what Mab plans for her. This is her description of the throne room when Mab first calls for her in *Daughter:*

The corridor ended, opening up into a massive room with icicles dangling from the ceiling like glittering chandeliers. Will-o'-the-wisps and globes of faery fire drifted between them, sending shards of fractured light over the walls and floor. The floor was shrouded in ice and mist, and my breath steamed in the air as we entered. Icy columns held up the ceiling, sparkling like translucent crystal and adding to the dazzling, confusing array of lights and colors swirling around the room. Dark, wild music echoed through the chamber, played by a group of humans on a corner stage. The musicians' eyes were glazed over as they sawed and beat at their instruments, their bodies frighteningly thin. Their hair hung long and lank, as if they hadn't cut it for years. Yet, they didn't seem to be distressed or unhappy, playing their instruments with zombielike fervor, seemingly blind to their inhuman audience.

On the far side of the room, a throne of ice rose into the air, glowing with frigid brilliance. Sitting on that throne, poised with the stillness of an approaching glacier, was Mab, Queen of the Unseelie Court.

Other notable regions in Tir Na Nog:

Glassbarrow

Glassbarrow is a mountainous region in the Winter Realm, far removed from the court, and ruled over by an Ice Baron, known as the Duke of Glassbarrow. The mountains in this territory are inhabited by deadly ice wyrms.

The Ice Maw

The Ice Maw is a great chasm that separates the wyldwood and the Winter Realm. It runs for miles in either direction, meeting the Wyrmtooth Mountains in the north and the Broken Glass Sea in the south. The Ice Maw could at one time be crossed using an arched ice bridge, but this was destroyed by Prince Ash while being hunted by Wolf.

The Chillsorrow Manor

The Chillsorrow Manor is a sprawling estate blanketed in ice and snow. Inside, the stairways are slick, the floors resemble ice rinks and the air is frigid cold. The manor is served by creepy, pale-skinned, skeletal gnomes.

Even more wintery regions:

The Broken Glass Sea

The Frozen Bog

The Ice Plains

Icefell

The Wyrmtooth Mountains

Denizens of the Winter Court

The Thornguards

The Thornguards are Prince Rowan's elite guard, answering only to him and Queen Mab. Along with their prince, they betray their own people and side with the Iron fey, believing they can develop an immunity to the deadly metal and survive when the Iron Realm takes over the Nevernever. They wear rings made of iron that cause their flesh to slowly decay, thorny armor that bristles like giant porcupine quills and carry swords that are black and spiky with razor-sharp thorns running the length of the blade. When the Thornguards die, their bodies erupt into thorny brambles.

Tiaothin

This phouka befriends Meghan while she is being held in the Unseelie Court by Mab. They first meet when Meghan is being stalked through the library by a Jack-of-Irons. Tiaothin has dread-locked hair and yellow eyes, and she can take the form of a slinky black cat and a shaggy black goat, among other things. Tiaothin often jumps from subject to subject while in conversation, and acts as a messenger for Mab and the Winter princes. Meghan often gets the sense that Tiaothin is sizing her up, and though she is the one who discovers Meghan kneeling over the dead body of Prince Sage, she helps Prince Ash rescue Meghan from the Winter Palace by leading the guards on a wild-goose chase. Later, Ash admits he asked Tiaothin to keep an eye on Meghan while she was being kept in the Winter Court.

Dame Liaden

An ancient faery who lives in a small, dilapidated cabin beneath two rotting trees in the frozen wood of the Winter Realm. She wears a gray robe and cowl draped over her body like old curtains. She cares for a wrinkled, ghastly baby in a stained white blanket, a hideous child with a deformed head too large for its body, tiny, shriveled limbs and skin tinged an unhealthy blue. She must wash her child in the blood of human infants in order to make it healthy again, if only temporarily.

Narissa

This snow faery encounters Ash with Meghan and Puck as they make their way from the Chillsorrow Manor toward the trod to the Voodoo Museum in New Orleans. She overhears that Ash has made a bargain with Meghan and delights in the chance to tell Mab and the Unseelie Court about his potential betrayal.

THE IRON REALM
(the Iron Kingdom, the Iron Court)

When Meghan first enters the Iron Realm, then known as the Iron Kingdom, she sees a blasted wasteland, filled with old technology, scrap piles and acid rain that can burn through human and faery flesh. The encroachment of Iron is poisoning the traditional Nevernever and threatening the balance of Faery. Ultimately, it is Meghan who learns to balance the old and new and how one can complement the other, saving all of Faery and taking the throne as the Iron Queen.

This is Meghan's first view of Iron, from *The Iron King:*

A twisted landscape stretched out before us, barren and dark, the sky a sickly yellow-gray. Mountains of rubble dominated the land: ancient computers, rusty cars, televisions, dial-phones, radios, all piled into huge mounds that loomed over everything. Some of the piles were alight, burning with a thick, choking smog. A hot wind howled through the wasteland, stirring dust into glittering eddies, spinning the wheel of an ancient bicycle lying on a trash heap. Scraps of aluminum, old cans and foam cups rolled over the ground, and a sharp, coppery smell hung in the air, clogging the back of my throat. The trees here were sickly things, bent and withered. A few bore lightbulbs and batteries that hung like glittering fruit.

Here is Meghan's first impression of Machina's tower in *The Iron King:*

At last, the mountains of garbage fell away, and the lead packrat pointed a long finger down a barren plain. Across a cracked, gray plateau, spiderwebbed with lava and millions of blinking lights, a railroad stretched away into the distance. Hulking machines, like enormous iron beetles, sat beside it, snorting steam. And silhouetted against the sky, a jagged black tower stabbed up from the earth, wreathed in smog and billowing smoke.

Machina's fortress.

As Meghan lies dying at the foot of Machina's oak tree, her last act, the act that heals her and transforms her into the Iron Queen, is to infuse the combined powers of Summer and Iron into the land itself. Here it is, as described in *The Iron Queen:*

Movement swirled around me, flashes of color, showing a land both familiar and strange. Mountains of junk dominated the landscape, but moss and vines grew around them now, twisted and blooming with flowers. A huge city of stone and steel had both streetlamps and flowering trees lining the streets, and a fountain in the center square spouted clear water. A railroad cut through a grassy plain, where a huge silver oak loomed over crumbling ruins, shiny and metallic and alive.

"Summer and Iron," Machina continued softly, "merged together, becoming one. You've done the impossible, Meghan Chase. The corruption of the Nevernever has been cleansed. The Iron fey now have a place to live without fearing the wrath of the other courts."

More areas within the Iron Realm:

Machina's Tower

Machina's fortress was a jagged, black, iron tower stabbing up from the ground, surrounded by smog and billowing smoke. Huge, sharp and metallic, full of harsh lines and sharp edges, the tower is filled with ramparts covered in thorned metal creepers and jagged shards sticking out from the walls for no apparent reason. A staircase spirals hundreds of feet along the tower walls. At the top of the stairs is a large iron door bearing the insignia of a barbed crown; it leads into an enormous garden. Smooth iron walls surround the garden, topped with jagged spines, and the garden is filled with metal trees and stony paths. At the center of the garden is a water fountain made of clockwork cogs of varying sizes. The clockwork fountain opens a wall, behind which lies the enormous iron throne of King Machina.

The Obsidian Plains

This was Ironhorse's domain before his heroic death. A massive black plain made of volcanic glass, it is home of Ironhorse's kin. In the center of the Plains lies the Molten Pool.

The Molten Pool

This pool is a bubbling lake of liquid hot magma at the center of the Obsidian Plains. Close to the Molten Pool, the air is hot enough to peel skin from bone and is infused with the smell of sulfur and brimstone.

Caves of the Packrats

The packrats' caves run underneath the entire Iron Realm, a maze of tunnels that lead to the boiler room of Machina's black fortress. The tunnels converge on a giant, cathedral-like cavern filled with mountains of trash, at the center of which sits a throne made entirely of junk. It was from this cavern that Ferrum, the former Iron King, ruled the packrats until Machina's death.

The Desert of Lost Things

A vast desert filled of sand dunes, the Desert of Lost Things is where all things go that are lost in the mortal world.

Mag Tuiredh

Also known as the Fomorian city, Mag Tuiredh was once the home of an ancient race of giants. Formerly an evil place, full of curses and unknown monsters, it is one of the darkest places in the Nevernever and also the location of the Clockmaker's tower—the only place in the Nevernever where time is recorded. Everything built there is giant-size, with twenty-foot doorways, streets wide enough to drive a plane through and stairs as high as a normal-size human.

A massive city filled with black towers that belch smoke into a mottled yellow sky, Mag Tuiredh used to sit half in and half out of the mortal realm, in the country of Ireland. Eventually the city was pulled completely into the Nevernever and the Fomorians were driven into the sea, abandoning the city for thousands of years, until it was eventually corrupted by the Iron Realm and became home to the gremlins.

When Meghan takes the throne as the Iron Queen, she restores Mag Tuiredh and makes it the seat of her power.

Denizens of the Iron Realm:

Tertius

This Iron knight first served King Machina and later the false king, Ferrum. Having been created by Machina, along with his brethren, in the images of those in the Summer and Winter courts, Tertius is a physical replica of Prince Ash, but with eyes of gunmetal gray instead of silver. He is responsible for stealing the Scepter of the Seasons from Tir Na Nog, and the murder of Prince Sage, an act which begins a war between Summer and Winter. Tertius is killed by Puck, stabbed through the chest, while Meghan faces off against the false king, Ferrum.

Diode

Diode is a hacker elf, a timid member of the Iron fey who joins Glitch's revolution against the false king. He has huge black eyes with lines of green numbers scrolling across them. Diode has immense knowledge at his disposal and acts as an adviser and assistant to Glitch, and later Meghan.

The Clockmaker

The Clockmaker is a mysterious Iron fey who dwells in a giant clock tower in the city of Mag Tuiredh. He is a small, hunched creature, half the size of a human, wearing a bright red vest adorned with several pocket watches. His head is a cross between human and mouse, with large round ears, bright beady eyes and a mustache that looks suspiciously like whiskers. He also has a thin, tufted tail, and wears a pair of tiny gold glasses that perch on the end of his nose.

The Clockmaker has the ability to see how everything starts, and the exact moment its time runs out. He gives Meghan the key that allows her to enter Ferrum's iron fortress, as well as a pocket watch that saves her from one of the false king's lightning bolts.

Spikerail

The Iron horse who, at the request of the late Ironhorse, by way of Grimalkin, brings his herd of mechanical horses to the aid of Meghan and her followers in the final battle against the false king.

THE WYLDWOOD

This forest of perpetual twilight is the first area of the Nevernever Meghan sees when she enters the faery world to find her little brother. This vast space holds many mysteries and fey creatures never before seen by human eyes. The following are just a few of the known regions located within the wyldwood.

In *The Iron King,* Meghan enters the wyldwood for the first time through the trod that has formed in Ethan's closet. Here is what she sees:

> Pale silver light flooded the room. The clearing beyond the door frame was surrounded by enormous trees, so thick and tangled I couldn't see the sky through the branches. A curling mist crept along the ground, and the woods were dark and still, as if the forest was trapped in perpetual twilight. Here and there, brilliant splashes of color stood out among the gray. A patch of flowers, their petals a shocking, electric blue, waved gently in the mist. A creeper vine snaked around the trunk of a dying oak, long red thorns a stark contrast to the tree it was killing.
>
> A warm breeze blew into the closet, carrying with it a shocking assortment of smells—smells that should not be together in one place. Crushed leaves and cinnamon, smoke and apples, fresh earth, lavender and the faint, cloying scent of rot and decay. For a moment, I caught a tang of something metallic and coppery, wrapped around the smell of rot, but it was gone in the next breath. Clouds of insects swarmed

overhead, and if I listened hard I could almost imagine I heard singing. The forest was still at first, but I then caught movement deep in the shadows, and heard leaves rustle all around us. Invisible eyes watched me from every angle, boring into my skin.

Places you may encounter—or wish to avoid— while making your way through the wyldwood:

The Briars

Also known as the Brambles or the Thorns, the Briars is a giant black hedge maze that runs through the entire Nevernever, including both the Winter and Summer courts, reaching to the End of the World. The Briars are sentient and sadistic, a force that cannot be tamed or understood.

The Briars contain the highest concentration of trods anywhere within the Nevernever. There are doors hidden throughout the Briars, some constantly shifting, some only appearing at a special time under special circumstances. The hallways of the briar maze are filled with whispered voices and the walls are constantly moving, writhing and reaching for you. Deadly creatures watch you from the shadows and stalk the corridors, including giant spiders, dragons and swarms of wasp-fey. The Big Bad Wolf also claims to have stalked the Briars from time to time.

The Reaping Fields

The Reaping Fields are where all major battles between Summer and Winter are fought. Bisected by a frozen river and surrounded by the ruins of an ancient castle, the fields smell of blood from all the battles fought over the centuries.

The Bone Marsh

A murky gray swamp, filled with twisted green trees and a preternatural mist, the Bone Marsh is so named because of the bleached-white bones that stick out, intermittently, from its muddy depths.

A dangerous part of the wyldwood, filled with catoblepas, jabberwocks and various other predators, including the Bone Witch.

The Hollow of Death

A valley of darkness and thorns, the ground blackened and poisoned, pulsing with hate, blood and despair, the Hollow of Death was once home to a wyvern's nest. Silent as a tomb, this dark valley is the place where Ariella was killed, and the place where Ash vowed to kill Puck. A cursed place, decorated with the bleached skeleton of the deadly wyvern, this is where the resurrected Ariella dwelled while waiting for Ash to find her on his journey for a soul.

The River of Dreams

The River of Dreams supposedly runs forever, and no one has ever seen the end of it, or at least lived to tell the tale. It weaves through the wyldwood and the Briars, all the way to the End of the World. It always travels in one direction and can only be caught at specific points along its bank. The surface of the river is black as night and stretches on and on. It is littered with the physical manifestations of human imagination, dreams and nightmares, from such things as book pages, swords and butterfly wings to the most frightening of nightmare creatures. Swarms of fireflies and will-o'-the-wisps float and bob above the waves. The River of Dreams is the last familiar border of the wyldwood. On its far bank begins the Deep Wyld.

The Deep Wyld

The Deep Wyld is the vast, uncharted territory of the Nevernever, a place of old legends and forgotten myths. Light does not penetrate very far into the Dark Wyld. The Big Bad Wolf allegedly calls this territory home.

Phaed

Phaed is a town in the Deepest Wyld where old, forgotten fey go to die. It is a place void of belief and imagination. Sooner or later, every fey ends up in Phaed. The town itself consists of tired gray hovels and tilted wooden shanties built on top of stilts to avoid the marshy ground. Everything in Phaed is sagging, drooping or crooked, and is faded and gray. The fog in Phaed is thick and the streets are cluttered with items dropped and apparently forgotten.

The Gauntlet

The Gauntlet is the gateway between the Deepest Wyld and the End of the World. When the Guardian at the End of the World opens the doors to the Gauntlet, whomsoever wishes to pass through must do so before the doors at the other end close, otherwise they'll be stuck inside forever, left to become ghouls. The tests of the Gauntlet are different for everyone. When Ash and his companions passed through, they encountered two vicious stone fu dogs in an ancient courtyard, each with half a key around their necks, and a hall of mirrors, wherein they were confronted with the darker sides of their personalities.

The Gnashwood

The Gnashwood is a forest in the wyldwood, close to the borders of the Iron Realm, that is infested with goblins. Because goblin tribes are constantly at war with one another, and are intolerant of trespassers through their territory, the Gnashwood is a dangerous place to be.

Denizens of the wyldwood:

The Bone Witch

The Bone Witch dwells in an old, gray, wooden house on the edges of a scummy pond in the depths of the Bone Marsh. The house stands on a pair of massive, gnarled bird legs and is surrounded by a fence made from bleached-white bones, polished skulls topping the posts.

The Bone Witch appears to be an old woman, with tangled white hair, a lined, wrinkled face, sharp black eyes and crooked, yellow teeth. Incredibly powerful and unpredictable, she holds a grudge against Puck for tying the legs of her house together, causing it to fall over when she pursued him for stealing her broom. Despite this, Puck doesn't appear to be afraid of her; rather, finding vast amusement in his triumph and her subsequent rage.

Ash seeks out the Bone Witch on his quest to gain a human soul, as it is said in some legends that Grimalkin keeps company with a witch fitting her description. When Ash and Puck are reunited with Grim, she allows them to leave, but later pursues them to the edges of the Bone Marsh, vowing to hang Puck's skin from her doorway if she ever sees him again.

Twiggs

The tree-dwelling gnome offers Meghan and Puck hospitality on her first night in the Nevernever.

All manner of wild fey inhabit the wyldwood, from kelpies to catoblepas, hedge wolves to goblins, dragons, wyverns, the unicorn and many, many, many more. Grimalkin keeps a home there, too.

THE BETWEEN

There is no better introduction to the Between than Puck and Leanansidhe's conversation when he and Meghan first arrive at her mansion in *The Iron Daughter:*

"Where are we, Lea?"

"The Between, darling." Leanansidhe leaned back, sipping her wine. "The veil between the Nevernever and the mortal realm. Surely you've realized that by now."

Both Puck's eyebrows shot up into his hair. "The Between? The Between is full of nothing, or so I was led to believe. Those who get stuck Between usually go insane in a very short order."

"Yes, I'll admit, it was difficult to work with at first." Leanansidhe waved her hand airily. "But, enough about me, darlings. Let's talk about you."

Known locations in the Between:

Leanansidhe's Mansion

Leanansidhe's Mansion is a magnificent sight to see, complete with a double grand staircase sweeping toward a high vaulted ceiling, with roaring fireplaces and plush black sofas. The hardwood floors gleam red, the walls are patterned in red and black and gauzy black curtains cover high arced windows. Nearly every clear space on the wall is taken up by paintings—oil paintings, watercolors, black-and-white sketches. Music constantly echoes through the mansion, always played by one of Leanansidhe's many human pets. The vast dining hall sports a long table that takes up most of the left wall, surrounded by chairs of glass and wood. Candelabras float down the length of the surface, and the rest of the room is buried in shadow. The mansion also contains a library, which is red-carpeted with a stone fireplace and bookshelves that soar to the ceiling.

Despite the grandeur of the main house, the basement looks like a medieval dungeon, with damp stone walls, torches hanging from the walls, wooden portcullises and leering gargoyles decorating the walls.

Leanansidhe's Cabin

A wooden door in the basement of Leanansidhe's Mansion leads out into a forest glen, where across a stream lies a cabin, fully stocked and kept clean by brownies. Leanansidhe's "cabin" is an enormous, two-story lodge with a veranda that circles the entire upper deck. The front of it stands on stilts, twenty-or-so feet off the ground, giving the front deck a fantastic view of the whole clearing. Meghan, her companions and her human father stay in this cabin while Meghan learns to fight and to control her conflicting Iron and Summer abilities.

Familiar faces in the Between:

Kimi

Kimi is half Asian, half phouka, a follower of Leanansidhe who runs errands, and procures—and steals—items from the Nevernever in exchange for the Exile Queen's protection. She is tiny, with furry ears, hair that is hacked and messy, and she wears a ratty sweater that is two sizes too big. She and Nelson use their skills to obtain items that help Meghan break into the SciCorp facility housing Virus and the Scepter of the Seasons, including building blueprints and an ID tag. Kimi is taken over by one of Virus's bugs and, after being used to send a message to Meghan, has her brain scrambled.

Nelson

Nelson is a half troll, another of Leanansidhe's half-breed follow-ers. He is built like a linebacker, with muddy-blond hair and skin as green as swamp water. He helps Meghan break into SciCorp but like Kimi is later infected by one of Virus's bugs and has his brain scrambled.

Warren

Warren is a half satyr and one of Leanansidhe's followers. He betrays his queen, and Meghan, by joining forces with the false king. He attempts to shoot Meghan but is wounded when she uses Iron glamour to cause the gun to explode in his hand, and he is left to the mercies of an unhappy Leanansidhe. It is implied that she tortures him to death in an attempt to find out what he knows.

Charles

Charles is the name Leanansidhe gives to all of the men she kidnaps from the human world, since, as she claims, she is horrible with names. All of these men tend to be musical prodigies in one form or another, and when she grows bored with them, or when their minds have grown too addled, Leanansidhe has a tendency to turn them into musical instruments.

The man known as Charles whom Meghan meets in Leanansidhe's Mansion turns out to be Paul, the man she knew as her father until he disappeared when she was six. It is revealed that Leanansidhe took him and kept him safe at the behest of Puck, to protect him from the wrath of Titania. The Summer Queen, still mad at her husband's infidelity, couldn't lash out at Meghan or her mother without incurring Oberon's anger, and so Paul became her obvious target. Meghan initially trades her memory of him to the oracle for information on getting Ethan back, but buys the memory back later and, upon taking the title of the Iron Queen, rescues Paul from Leanansidhe's domain and eventually brings him to live in her palace at Mag Tuiredh.

Razor Dan

Razor Dan is the leader of Leanansidhe's redcap minions. They fled to Leanansidhe for asylum during the Goblin Wars, after angering every goblin tribe in the wyldwood by selling information to both sides. He and his band betray Leanansidhe by siding with Warren, but are not punished as they were only following their baser instincts.

THE HUMAN WORLD

Meghan was born and raised in the human world until her sixteenth birthday. The following are places she goes to during her adventures in and out of Faery. The human world is— [Human, I must interject once more. You live in the human world. If you do not realize this by now and know more about it than anyone could tell you in these pages, there is truly no hope for your kind. None. I know this. I am a cat.]

Fey hotspots in the human world:

Blue Chaos

This two-story dance club, lit with pink-and-blue neon signs, is located in Detroit, Michigan. It is owned by the faery Shard and houses a trod into the Winter Realm. Inside Blue Chaos, dry-ice smoke writhes along the floor, reminiscent of the wyldwood. Pink, blue and gold lights paint the dance floor as humans and fey dance together, the fey feeding off the heavy glamour. A door near the bar labeled Staff Only guards the stairs to the basement, and the ogre-guarded trod.

The City of the Dead

The City of the Dead is a cemetery in New Orleans. Rows upon rows of crypts, tombs and mausoleums line the narrow streets, some decorated with flowers, candles and plaques, others crumbling with age and neglect. Some of the tombs look like miniature houses, or even tiny cathedrals topped with spires and stone crosses. Statues of angels and weeping women adorn some of the rooftops.

The City is inhabited by bean sidhe as well as a ferocious and protective Grim. It was also the resting place of a Token before it was stolen by Meghan and Ash and traded to the oracle, Old Anna, in exchange for Meghan's memories.

Rudy's Pawn Shop

Rudy's Pawn Shop is another fey front hiding a trod into the Nevernever. It is owned by Rudy, a half satyr, and acts as a normal pawn shop, with dusty shelves filled with old televisions, video games and gold. One wall is dedicated to guns, protected by high counters and a blinking security camera. In the back, Rudy keeps a treasure trove of fey items to sell, including monkey paws, hydra poison, cockatrice eggs, glowing potions and magical tomes.

The Dungeon

This pub in the French Quarter of New Orleans houses yet another trod into the Nevernever. A sign above the thick, black entrance reads Ye Olde Original Dungeon, and there is red paint spattered against the frame in an attempt to mimic blood. Past the entrance, a narrow alley leads to a courtyard, where a scraggly waterfall trickles into a moat at the front of the building. A footbridge across the moat leads into a dark red room, a bar and nightclub catering to a more macabre crowd. The walls are brick, the lights dim and red, casting everything in crimson, and snarling monster heads hang on the walls over the bar. The Dungeon is considered Unseelie Territory and serves a rough crowd of humans and fey. The upstairs, Ash tells Meghan, contains skulls, cages and the dance floor.

In the back of the bar, bookshelves line the walls, floor to ceiling, one of which can either open up into a bathroom or become a trod into the wyldwood, close to the borders of the Winter Realm.

Fey you may find in the Human World:

The Elder Dryad

The Elder Dryad lives in City Park in New Orleans, where she and her family guard the lives of their trees. The Elder Dryad chooses to sacrifice her oak—and thus her life—to create the Witchwood arrow from the heart of her tree, in the hopes that Meghan can use it to kill the Iron King.

Old Anna, the oracle

A skeletal hag of a woman, smelling like dust, decay and old newspapers, with tangled white hair, twiglike hands, hollow pits for eyes and a withered face full of yellow, needlelike teeth. Anna has the ability to prophesize the future and can smell need and desire. She answers three questions in exchange for Meghan Chase's most precious memory, that of her father, and does not give the memory back until Meghan brings her a Token.

Rudy

Rudy is a pudgy half satyr. He owns a pawn shop that hides a trod into the wyldwood. He has had past dealings with Grimalkin, and allows Ash, Puck and Grim passage through his trod as payment for a favor he owed the cat.

Seedlit

This tiny piskie agrees to lead Meghan and Ash to the entrance to the Iron Realm in New Orleans. She is blue-skinned, with dandelion hair and gossamer wings.

Shard

Shard is an Unseelie fey who lives in the human world, guarding a trod to the Winter Realm. She is small and slight, with pale skin and neon-blue lips, spiky hair that sticks out at every angle and is dyed shades of blue, green and white, resembling ice crystals. She wears tight leather pants, a midriff tee and a dagger on one thigh. Her face and ears are covered in countless piercings, all silver or gold, and she has a silver bar through her bellybutton with a tiny dragon pendant dangling from it.

Shard's arrogance causes her to be outwitted by Meghan in a faery deal. When she tries to kill Meghan by luring her into the clutches of her imprisoned ogre, Grumly, Meghan outwits her again by agreeing to free the ogre in exchange for his protection.

THE END OF THE WORLD

Very few fey have ever seen the End of the World. In fact, none in recent memory outside of Ash and his intrepid company have made it that far. Here, in Ash's words, is what they saw in *The Iron Knight:*

> The vast emptiness of space stretched before us, endless and eternal. Stars and constellations glimmered above and below, from tiny pinpricks of light to huge pulsing giants so bright it hurt to look at them. Comets streaked through the night sky, and in the distance, I could see the gaping maw of a black hole sucking in the surrounding galaxy, billions of

miles away. Huge chunks of rock and land floated, weightless, in empty space.

At first, I thought I was looking at a continent floating beneath us; I could see lakes and trees and even a few houses scattered about. But then the continent twisted around with a flash of scales and teeth and drifted toward us, a leviathan so huge it defied belief. It spiraled up beside the bridge, a mountain of scales and fins and flippers, rising out of the void. Its eye was like a small moon, pale and all-seeing, but we were insects beneath its gaze, dust mites, too microscopic for it to know we were there. An entire city was perched on its back, gleaming white towers sitting at the edge of a glistening lake. Smaller creatures, as big as whales, swam beside it, looking like minnows compared to its bulk. As we stood gaping at it, unable to move or look away, it twisted lazily through the air and continued into the etherealness of space.

What you will find if you reach The End of the World:

The Testing Ground

The Testing Ground floats in the void at the End of the World, an enormous castle beyond a treacherous stream of jagged rocks. The castle is dim and empty, with torches set into brackets and candles flickering along the walls, void of all life, frozen in time. Like the void, the castle is endless. Guest rooms are provided for those who make it to the Testing Ground, filled with food, clean beds and lit fireplaces. The rooms contain bookshelves filled with forgotten tomes, some of which wail if opened, others written in languages that hurt to look upon.

It is not known whether the Testing Ground changes based on the visitor, but when Ash visited, it contained an ice-covered garden with crystallized, skeletal trees and a fountain in the middle spouting frozen water. Above the garden, a stone bridge crosses the void to a huge, jagged mountain, the top of which was the site of Ash's first trial.

The Guardian

The Guardian at the End of the World is an eight-foot-tall, robed figure, its face hidden in the darkness of a cowl. Its pale, bony hand clutches a gleaming staff of twisted black wood. It has a voice that echoes through bone and into the heads of all who listen.

The Guardian is the keeper of the Testing Grounds, and master of the Gauntlet. It is the being that tests Ash and deems him worthy of receiving a soul.

**That brings us to the end of your tour
of the realms of the Nevernever.
We hope you enjoyed the journey—and that you will
return again—to the worlds between the pages of
THE IRON FEY series.**

THE IRON QUOTES

How well do you know the characters of the Iron Fey?
If you can name every speaker without peeking
at the key, Grimalkin *might* say, "Not bad, human.
Not bad." Give yourself bonus Grim points
if you can name the scene each quote
comes from.

QUOTES

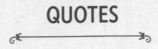

1. "And to think, I lost you that day in the forest and didn't even know what I was chasing."

   SAID BY: _____

   SCENE: _____

   _____

2. "Oh, we're playing nice now? Shall we have tea first? Brew up a nice pot of kiss-my-ass?"

   SAID BY: _____

   SCENE: _____

   _____

3. "Follow me. And do try to keep up."

   SAID BY: _____

   SCENE: _____

   _____

4. "It speaks, as if it knows me. As if being Oberon's throwback will protect it from my wrath."

   SAID BY: _____

   SCENE: _____

   _____

5. "Meghan Chase. Welcome. I've been expecting you."

   SAID BY: _____

   SCENE: _____

   _____

6. "I'm not stupid. I know the daughter of the Erlking when I see her. So, the question is, what do I get out of this?"

   SAID BY: _____

   SCENE: _____

   _____

7. *"THOUGHT YOU GOT RID OF ME, DID YOU?"*

   SAID BY: _____

   SCENE: _____

   _____

8. "Oh, I don't think so, little brother. When Mab finds out, you'll *both* be decorating the courtyard."

   SAID BY: _____

   SCENE: _____

   _____

9. "Wow, icy reception here. And to think I came back from the dead for this."

   SAID BY: _____

   SCENE: _____

   _____

10. "Yes, I know, darling. But if you don't leave, I'll have to turn you into a harp. Go on, now. Shoo, shoo."

SAID BY: _____

SCENE: _____

_____

11. "Summer and Winter share many things, but love is not one of them."

SAID BY: _____

SCENE: _____

_____

12. "Come off it, prince. You really think I would hurt her? I'm the one who doesn't want her running off on a suicide mission."

SAID BY: _____

SCENE: _____

_____

13. "I will be here. You cannot win without me, Meghan Chase. Until we are one, you are destined to lose this war."

SAID BY: _____

SCENE: _____

_____

_____

14. "I have no idea why two-legs wish to stand around and talk so much."

SAID BY: _____

SCENE: _____

_____

15. "There is no pass or fail. There is only endure. Survive."

SAID BY: _____

SCENE: _____

_____

16. "Nothing like a little attempted murder to feel close to someone, right?"

SAID BY: _____

SCENE: _____

_____

17. "I can't let you die because of me. I won't allow it."

SAID BY: _____

SCENE: _____

_____

18. "Why should individuals have to bend to the prejudices between the courts?"

SAID BY: _____

SCENE: _____

_____

19. "Don't remember! Don't remember! The rats scream, but I don't remember! Go away, go away."

SAID BY: _____

SCENE: _____

_____

20. "So, either you say, 'sure, I'd love to have you along,' or you have a big bird dropping things on your head the whole trip."

SAID BY: _____

SCENE: _____

_____

21. "I waited for this day for so long—please don't walk out and leave me behind. Not again."

SAID BY: _____

SCENE: _____

_____

22. "When I said I'd follow you to hell and back, I wasn't trying to be literal, princess."

SAID BY: _____

SCENE: _____

_____

23. "Give me your solemn vow, or be damned to the mortal world forever. Make your choice."

SAID BY: _____

SCENE: _____

_____

24. "You're going away again, aren't you? You didn't come back to stay with me."

SAID BY: _____

SCENE: _____

_____

25. "Her desires are mine. Her wishes are mine. Should even the world stand against her, my blade will be at her side."

SAID BY: _____

SCENE: _____

_____

QUOTES KEY

1. *The Iron King:* Ash to Meghan, during their first Elysium.

2. *The Iron King:* Puck to Meghan regarding Ash, after their escape from Ironhorse.

3. *The Iron King:* Grimalkin to Meghan, when they first strike the bargain for him to take her to Puck.

4. *The Iron King:* Titania, just before attempting to turn Meghan into a hart.

5. *The Iron King:* Machina to Meghan, when she enters his throne room on the Iron tower.

6. *The Iron King:* Shard to Grim, as he and Meghan bargain to use the trod in Blue Chaos.

7. *The Iron King:* Ironhorse to Meghan and Ash, upon catching them infiltrating the Iron Kingdom.

8. *The Iron Daughter:* Rowan to Ash, upon discovering him trying to help Meghan escape from Winter.

9. *The Iron Daughter:* Puck to Meghan and Ash after he returns, recovered from his injuries in *The Iron King*, to help them fight off the attacking wiremen.

10. *The Iron Daughter:* Leanansidhe to "Charles," Meghan's father, after Meghan first sees him in the Between.

11. *The Iron Daughter:* Oberon to Meghan, just before Mab banishes Ash from Winter.

12. *The Iron Queen:* Glitch to Ash, just before he shows Meghan the extent of the false king's army via glider.

13. *The Iron Queen:* Machina, in Meghan's dream, the first night in the Iron Realm as she, Grim, Puck and Ash go in search of the false king.

14. *The Iron Knight:* The Big Bad Wolf to Ash, Puck and Ariella, after Ash recovers from the hobyah venom.

15. *The Iron Knight:* The Guardian to Ash, before he begins the second trial.

16. *The Iron Knight:* Puck to Ash, after they escape the Forgotten.

17. *The Iron Queen:* Meghan to Ash, as she releases him from his vow.

18. *The Iron Knight:* Keirran, Meghan and Ash's future son, to Ash, during his trial vision of being human.

19. *The Iron Queen:* Paul, Meghan's human father-figure, as he begins to regain his memories in the cabin.

20. *The Iron Queen:* Puck to Ash, as they set off together to begin Ash's journey to earn a soul.

21. *The Iron Knight:* Ariella to Ash, offering to show the way to the End of the World.

22. *The Iron Queen:* Puck to Meghan by the magma lake, after they escape the false king's attack on Machina's old tower.

23. *The Iron Daughter:* Mab, giving Ash his final ultimatum.

24. *The Iron Daughter:* Ethan to Meghan, after she and Puck stop the bugged Ash from attacking her home.

25. *The Iron Queen:* Ash, making the knight's vow to Meghan.

Q&A WITH JULIE KAGAWA

Thank you, Julie, for taking your life into your hands and entering the Nevernever to answer a few questions.

Q: When you first began writing *The Iron King*, what were your hopes for the story? How do you feel about what The Iron Fey has become?

A: Honestly, I am utterly thrilled and delighted. When I first started writing *The Iron King*, I was one of those hopeful writers just looking to be published. I never dreamed it would grow the way it did, but I'm so grateful for the readers and fans who made this series what it is today.

Q: Did you plan out the whole Iron Fey series before you started writing it, or did it develop organically as you wrote each book?

A: I knew the basic plotlines for all the books, and with the original trilogy (*King, Daughter* and *Queen*), I knew how I wanted it to end. Within the individual books, I have "high points" that I know have to happen, but the story usually develops as I go along.

Q: You've written Iron Fey stories from Meghan's, Ash's and Puck's points of view. How do you change perspective and get into a new character's head?

A: I think the key is knowing your characters, and making sure each one is very different from the others. Voice, personality, motives, desires—they should all have their own unique look on life, and once you really know them, it's fairly easy to switch to their voice.

Q: Grimalkin is another fan favorite. How do you channel Grim onto the page?

A: LOL, Grimalkin is based on every cat I've ever known, and his voice is actually pretty easy to write. (Don't tell him that, though; I'd never hear the end of it.) [I heard that. And you won't.] He is bored, blunt, proud, independent and says exactly what he means in any situation. He is not afraid to tell the others they are being foolish, and doesn't have anything to hide. In his own words: he is a cat. 'Nuff said.

Q: You often create drawings of your Iron Fey characters. What is your background as an artist?

A: I've always enjoyed sketching, doodling and painting. (I often doodled in math class, when I wasn't reading novels behind my textbooks. My teachers despaired.) I haven't taken any formal art classes, though. I just enjoy painting and drawing. I suppose it's like writing in a way; you have to practice to get better.

Q: You're an avid gamer. How has gaming influenced your career as a writer?

A: I'm a firm believer that video games are just another medium of storytelling, and the truly good games are just as compelling as a book. Most of my inspiration comes from video games and anime, especially when it comes to character and setting. The ending of some games (Dragon Age, Final Fantasy X) made me sob my eyes out, I was so attached to the characters and their stories. And some have been so inspiring and uplifting that all I wanted to do was write a story as magnificent as that. If that's not an argument against "All video games do is rot your brain," I don't know what is.

Q: Tell us a little about you personally. What do you do— besides art and gaming!—when you aren't writing?

A: I enjoy reading, painting, playing in my garden, playing with my animals (dogs, cats and chickens), watching television with my hubby and martial arts. My husband and I take both kung fu and Kali, which I lovingly refer to as "Hit People with Sticks" class.

Q: What does the future hold for The Iron Fey?

A: Well, the first book of the new Iron Fey trilogy will be out this fall. It's called *The Lost Prince,* and it stars Meghan's brother, Ethan Chase, when he is older. There will also be cameos from several familiar faces, so be on the lookout for that!

Turn the page for an exclusive excerpt
from Julie Kagawa's next Iron Fey novel

Book 1 of Call of the Forgotten, a new trilogy
starring Meghan's younger brother, Ethan Chase!

The demonstration started with a couple of the beginner students doing a pattern known as Heaven Six, and the clacks of their rattan sticks echoed noisily throughout the room. I saw Kenzie take a few pictures as they circled the mats. Then the more advanced students demonstrated a few disarms, takedowns and freestyle sparring. Guro circled with them, explaining what they were doing, how we practiced and how it could be applied to real life.

Then it was my turn.

"Of course," Guro said as I stepped onto the mats, holding the swords at my sides, "the rattan—the kali sticks—are proxies for real blades. We practice with sticks, but everything we do can be transferred to blades, knives or empty hands. As Ethan will demonstrate. This is an advanced technique," he cautioned, as I stepped across him, standing a few yards away. "Do not try this at home."

I bowed to him and the audience. He raised a rattan stick, twirled it once and suddenly tossed it at me. I responded instantly, whipping the blades through the air, cutting it into three parts. The audience gasped, sitting straighter in their chairs, and I smiled.

Yes, these are real swords.

Guro nodded and stepped away. I half closed my eyes and brought my swords into position, one held vertically over one shoulder, the other tucked against my ribs. Balanced on the balls of my feet, I let my mind drift, forgetting the audience and the onlookers and my fellow students, watching along the wall. I breathed out slowly and let my mind go blank.

Music began, drumming a rhythm over the loudspeakers, and I started to move.

I started slowly at first, both weapons whirling around me, sliding from one motion to the next. *Don't think about what you're doing, just move, flow.* I danced around the floor, throwing a few flips and kicks into the pattern because I could, keeping time with the music. As the drums picked up, pounding out a frantic rhythm, I moved faster, faster, whipping the blades around my body, until I could feel the wind from their passing, hear the vicious hum as they sliced through the air around me.

Someone whooped out in the audience, but I barely heard them. The people watching didn't matter. Nothing mattered except the blades in my hands and the flowing motion of the dance. The swords flashed silver in the dim light, fluid and flexible, almost liquid. There was no block or strike, dodge or parry—the dance was all of these things, and none, all at once. I pushed myself harder than I ever had before, until I couldn't tell where the swords ended and my arms began, until I was just a weapon in the center of the floor, and no one could touch me.

With a final flourish, I spun around, ending the demonstration on one knee, the blades back in their ready position. For a heartbeat after I finished, there was absolute silence. Then, like a dam breaking, a roar of applause swept over me, laced with whistles and scraping chairs as people surged to their feet. I rose and bowed to the audience, then to my master, who gave me a proud nod. He understood. This wasn't just a demonstration for me; it was something I'd worked for, trained for and finally pulled off—without getting into trouble or hurting anyone in the process. I had actually done something right for a change.

I looked up and met Kenzie's eyes on the other side of the mats. She was grinning and clapping frantically, her notebook lying on the floor beside her, and I smiled back.

"That was awesome," she said, weaving around the edge of the mat when I stepped off the floor, breathing hard. "I had no idea you could do...that. Congratulations, you're a certified badass."

I felt a warm glow of...something, deep inside. "Thanks," I muttered, carefully sliding the blades back into their sheaths before laying them gently atop Guro's bag. It was hard to give them up; I wanted to keep holding them, feeling their perfect weight as they danced through the air. I'd seen Guro practice with his own blades, and he looked so natural with them, like they were extensions of his arms. I wondered if I'd looked the same out there on the mat, the shining edges coming so close to my body but never touching it. I wondered if Guro would ever let me train with them again.

Our instructor had called the last student to demonstrate knife techniques with him, and he had the audience's full attention now. Meanwhile I caught several appreciative gazes directed at Kenzie from my fellow kali students, and felt myself bristle.

"Come on," I told her, stepping away from the others before Chris could jump in and introduce himself. "I need a soda. Want one?"

She nodded eagerly. Together, we slipped through the crowd, out the doors and into the hallway, leaving the noise and commotion behind.

I fed two dollars into the vending machine at the end of the hall, choosing a Pepsi for myself, then a Mountain Dew at Kenzie's request. She smiled her thanks as I tossed it to her, and we leaned against the corridor wall, basking in the silence.

"So," Kenzie ventured after several heartbeats. She gave me a sideways look. "Care to answer a few questions now?"

I knocked the back of my head against the wall. "Sure," I muttered, closing my eyes. The girl wouldn't let me be until we got this thing over with. "Let's have at it. Though I promise, you're going to be disappointed by how dull my life really is."

"I somehow doubt that." Kenzie's voice had changed. It was uncertain now, almost nervous. I frowned, listening to the flipping of notebook paper, then a quiet breath, as if she was steeling herself for something. "First question, then. How long have you been taking kali?"

"Since I was twelve," I said without moving. "That's... what...nearly five years now." Geez, had it really been that long? I remembered my first class as a shy, quiet kid, holding the rattan stick like it was a poisonous snake, and Guro's piercing eyes, appraising me.

"Okay. Cool. Second question." Kenzie hesitated, then said in a calm, clear voice, "What, exactly, is your take on faeries?"

My eyes flew open, and I jerked my head up, banging it against the wall again. My half-empty soda can dropped from my fingers and clanked to the floor, fizzing everywhere. Kenzie blinked and stepped back as I gaped at her, hardly believing what I'd just heard. "What?" I choked out, before I thought better of it, before the defensive walls came slamming down.

"You heard me." Kenzie regarded me intently, watching my reaction. "Faeries. What do you know about them? What's your interest in the fey?"

My mind spun. Faeries. Fey. She knew. How she knew, I had no idea. But she couldn't continue this line of questioning.

This had to end, now. Todd was already in trouble, because of Them. He might really be gone. The last thing I wanted was for Mackenzie St. James to vanish off the face of the earth because of me. And if I had to be nasty and cruel, so be it. It was better than the alternative.

Drawing myself up, I sneered at her, my voice suddenly ugly, hateful. "Wow, whatever you smoked last night, it must've been good." I curled my lip in a smirk. "Are you even listening to yourself? What kind of screwed-up question is that?"

Kenzie's eyes hardened. Flipping several pages, she held the notebook out to me, where the words *glamour, Unseelie* and *Seelie Courts* were underlined in red. I remembered her standing behind the bleachers when I faced that creepy transparent faery. My stomach went cold.

"I'm a reporter," Kenzie said, as I tried wrapping my brain around this. "I heard you talking to someone the day Todd disappeared. It wasn't hard to find the information." She flipped the notebook shut and stared me down, defiant. "Changelings, Fair Folk, All-Hallow's Eve, Summer and Winter Courts, the Good Neighbors. I learned a lot. And when I called Todd's house this afternoon, he still wasn't there." She pushed her hair back and gave me a worried look. "What's going on, Ethan? Are you and Todd in some sort of pagan cult? You don't actually believe in faeries, do you?"

I forced myself to stay calm. At least Kenzie was reacting like a normal person should, with disbelief and concern. Of course she didn't believe in faeries. Maybe I could scare her away from me for good. "Yes," I smirked, crossing my arms. "That's exactly right. I'm in a cult, and we sacrifice goats under the full moon and drink the blood of virgins and babies every month." She wrinkled her nose, and I took a threatening step forward. "It's a lot of fun, especially when we bring out the crack and Ouija boards. Wanna join?"

"Very funny, tough guy." I'd forgotten Kenzie didn't scare easily. She glared back, stubborn and unmovable as a wall. "What's really going on? Are you in some kind of trouble?"

"What if I am?" I challenged. "What are you going to do about it? You think you can save me? You think you can publish one of your little stories and everything will be fine? Wake up, Miss Nosey Reporter. The world's not like that."

"Quit being a jerkoff, Ethan," Kenzie snapped, narrowing her eyes. "You're not really like this, and you're not as bad as you think you are. I'm only trying to help."

"No one can help me." Suddenly, I was tired. I was tired of fighting, tired of forcing myself to be someone I wasn't. I didn't want to hurt her, but if she continued down this path, she would only rush headlong into a world that would do its best to tear her apart. And I couldn't let that happen. Not again.

"Look." I sighed, slumping against the wall. "I can't explain it. Just…leave me alone, okay? Please. You have no idea what you're getting into."

"Ethan—"

"Stop asking questions," I whispered, drawing away. Her eyes followed me, confused and sad, and I hardened my voice. "Stop asking questions, and stay the hell away from me. Or you're only going to get hurt."

"Advice you should have followed yourself, Ethan Chase," a voice hissed out of the darkness.

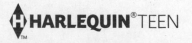

THE GODDESS TEST NOVELS

Available wherever books are sold!

A modern saga inspired by the Persephone myth.

Kate Winters's life hasn't been easy. She's battling with the upcoming death of her mother, and only a mysterious stranger called Henry is giving her hope. But he must be crazy, right? Because there is no way the god of the Underworld—Hades himself—is going to choose Kate to take the seven tests that might make her an immortal...and his wife. And even if she passes the tests, is there any hope for happiness with a war brewing between the gods?

Also available:
The Goddess Hunt, a digital-only novella.

The Clann

Available Now

Coming October 2012!

The powerful magic users of the Clann have always feared and mistrusted vampires. But when Clann golden boy Tristan Coleman falls for Savannah Colbert—the banished half Clann, half vampire girl who is just coming into her powers—a fuse is lit that may explode into war. Forbidden love, dangerous secrets and bloodlust combine in a deadly hurricane that some will not survive.

The Spellbound Novels

In this contemporary series of spells and magic, curses and love, new-girl Emma Connor faces snobs and bullies at her elite Manhattan prep school. When the hottest boy in school inexplicably becomes her protector, Emma finds her ordinary world changing and a new life opening to her, filled with surprising friendships, deadly enemies and a witchy heritage she never suspected.

AVAILABLE WHEREVER BOOKS ARE SOLD!